MURDER BY SUICIDE

A Jack Dantzler Mystery

TOM WALLACE

Printed in the United States of America

ISBN: 978-1-942212-82-9

Hydra Publications
Goshen, Kentucky 40026
www.hydrapublications.com

ALSO BY TOM WALLACE

Jack Dantzler Mysteries

The Poker Game

The Fire of Heaven

The List

Gnosis

The Devil's Racket

What Matters Blood

Heirs of Cain.

This book is dedicated to Dennis Randall Slinker,
who graciously allows me to do in fiction
what I can't do in real life—beat him at tennis.

CHAPTER ONE

For a fraction of a second, as the yellow ball headed in his direction, Jack Dantzler gave thought to showing mercy. To displaying a kind and generous spirit. To being a nice guy. Why not? he wondered. After all, his opponent was a long-time friend, one he had beaten countless times over the years, one whose skill and talent levels were not even close to being in his class. A guy who had never once won a game against him, much less a set. But that could all change if Dantzler chose to let it happen. Now, leading the set five-love but down 30-40 in this game, if Dantzler purposely missed the return shot, Randall Dennis could finally lay claim to winning a game.

What could possibly be wrong with giving Dennis his moment of glory?

Nothing.

Yet Dantzler couldn't do it. Couldn't locate that inner source of mercy. Couldn't be a nice guy. And he knew why, too. Lions never yield to opponents, regardless of the circumstances. Mercy is alien to a lion. You don't become king by giving in.

Dennis's shot was actually a fairly decent one, especially for a club player. He had scurried to his right, arriving just as the ball rose to waist level. Seeing that Dantzler had been pulled to his extreme left,

Dennis knew that a clean, well-struck shot to the far right corner could be a winner. This was, he felt, his moment.

Drawing his racket back, Dennis swung with all his might, making what had to be the cleanest connection he'd ever made. He could feel his own power, sense the energy and force he'd put into that fuzzy yellow ball. He swung so hard his entire body lifted off the court. There was simply no way an opponent could successfully handle such a shot.

But this wasn't *any* opponent—this was Jack Dantzler.

Just maybe the finest tennis player Lexington had ever produced.

Dennis had hustled hard to get into position to hit his shot. Really busted his ass. It took every bit of effort he could muster, and yet he'd barely gotten there in time. But he had. He not only got there, he managed to get off the best shot in his lifetime of playing tennis.

He was going to win a game against Dantzler. This would mean an end to a lifetime of being bageled. A long-held dream was about to finally come true.

Looking across the net he saw Dantzler move effortlessly—glide, really—to his right. He marveled that Dantzler was already in place, racket drawn back and ready to hit a full two seconds before the ball arrived. *How the hell did he move that fast?* Dennis asked himself. *Isn't this bastard ever gonna slow down?*

At that moment, even before Dantzler hit the ball, Dennis understood that his goose was cooked. *Again.* He was about to be an actor in a scene that had played out countless times in the past. Once again he would be relegated to the role of sidekick playing second fiddle to the star. Tonto to the Lone Ranger. Robin to Batman.

And Dennis knew how it was going to play out long before it actually happened.

Dantzler's shot would be spectacular, the ball would land out of reach, the score would now be 40-all—deuce—and Dantzler would go on to win the game, thus taking the set six-love.

Dennis would be served yet another bagel.

This was the rerun from hell.

In certain ways this movie never changes.

Ten minutes later, when the final shot sailed past Dennis to end the set at six-love, the two men met at the net and shook hands.

"One of these days, Jack, you are going to lose a step or two," Dennis proclaimed, "and when that happens I'll take a game from you. It's just a matter of time."

"Aren't you forgetting a rather important fact?" Dantzler asked.

"What?"

"You're a couple years older than I am. Time's running out on you."

"Doesn't matter, Jack. See, I can't lose a step, because I was never fast or quick to begin with. On the other hand, if you lose a step it will make a huge difference in your game. And when that happens—and it will—then *voila!* I claim victory. A small victory, true, but a victory nonetheless."

"As I've told you a hundred times in the past, Randall, the Messiah will show up before that happens."

"Well, when he does I hope he beats you like an ugly stepchild."

Dantzler laughed, said, "That ain't gonna happen, Randall, unless he's a helluva lot better tennis player than you are."

"Can't you accept victory with quiet dignity, Jack?"

"Against you? Never. That would take all the fun out of it." Dantzler put his racket in his equipment bag, picked it up, and slug it over his shoulder. "But not to worry, Randall. You know I love you."

"Yeah, right. The only love you show me is in those scores you put up match after match."

Dantzler said, "Have time for a drink upstairs?"

"Love to, but I have a couple of errands to run for the wife. Maybe next time."

After showering and getting dressed Dantzler headed up to the second floor concession area. Arriving, he saw Sean Montgomery purchase a bottle of water and make his way toward a corner table. Sean was an ex-cop who left the force, went back to college, earned a law degree, and was now a defense attorney. He was also one of Dantzler's closest and most-trusted friends. Sean, Dantzler and David Bloom, the psychiatrist and Dantzler's college teammate, were owners of the Lexington Tennis Center.

Dantzler went to the counter, ordered a Diet Pepsi, and then joined Sean at the table.

"What was it? Bagel and bagel?" Sean asked, after taking a sip from the bottle.

"And bagel."

"Damn, Jack, three six-love sets? Can't you find it in your heart to give the poor guy a break? Trust me, your reputation will not be shattered if Randall Dennis takes a game against you. Hell, everybody will know you let him win."

"And where's the fun in that, Sean? If he doesn't want to keep getting his ass kicked he should stop begging me to play. Way I see it, he's a glutton for punishment."

"He's a dreamer. Why not allow him to see his dream come true?"

"Yielding is simply not in my DNA."

"To borrow an often-used word by our colleague, the esteemed Hebrew Dr. David Bloom, you are a first-class *putz*."

"You're Scottish, Sean. Do you even know the meaning of that word?"

"Yeah, means you're a dick." Sean took another drink of water. "The rumor mill has it that Rich is seriously considering calling it quits."

Captain Richard Bird was the long-time head of the Homicide Unit.

"Rumor mill? You mean Rawlinson, don't you?" Dantzler answered, referring to Bruce Rawlinson, the veteran desk sergeant, dedicated ball-breaker, and notorious spreader of in-house gossip. "If I told that guy where Jimmy Hoffa was buried, next thing you know half the people in this city would be heading in that direction, each one carrying a shovel. Rawlinson is some piece of work, that's for sure."

"But is he wrong about Rich?"

Dantzler took a drink of Diet Pepsi and shook his head. "Can't say for sure either way, but I do get the feeling that Rich is giving it serious thought."

"Why now? He's still a relatively young guy. No health issues, I hope."

"He's been at it a long time. I think he's kind of burned out. Plus, the timing is favorable. His oldest daughter has already graduated college, and his youngest is now a senior at Duke. Those two financial concerns have pretty much been taken care of. Truth is, I'm not sure he wouldn't have called it quits years ago had it not been for money worries. Let's face it. Rich is a superb administrator but he's never really had the stomach to be a cop. Especially when it comes to homicide."

"Shit, Jack, if he does hang it up, that means you move to the top of the ladder."

"Don't hold your breath, Sean. Randall will win a game against me before I take Rich's job."

"You know you're next in line. *Everybody* knows it. It's a foregone conclusion."

"Nothing I've ever concluded."

"If not you, then who?"

"Eric."

"I agree Eric is a terrific cop, but is he ready to run the department?"

"Damn right he is. In fact, he'd be much better at it than I could ever hope to be."

"You are the best homicide detective this city has ever had, Jack. And that's not just my opinion. Everyone recognizes you as the ace of aces."

"I'm too much of a lone wolf, Sean. You know that. I don't always play well with others, heed other voices or opinions. Too often I go my own way when I probably should be more of a team player. There are some who say that I have a tendency toward arrogance. Those aren't good qualities for a person charged with the task of running a team."

"You would be great at the job and you'll never convince me otherwise."

"I wouldn't take the job even if they begged me."

"Why not?"

"Two reasons. First, I don't want it. I simply have no interest in taking over that position. Second, I'm also thinking about handing in my badge at the end of the year."

"You're kidding, right?"

"Nope. I'm dead serious."

Sean leaned back and studied Dantzler. After a minute of silence, he said, "What, exactly, brought this on?"

Dantzler shrugged and said, "I just need to make a change, that's all. I've been doing this a longtime, too. I got my gold shield in my early twenties. That's a longtime ago. I would like to explore other options, see what new trails I might follow. It would be a welcomed change to follow one that didn't invariably lead to a dead body."

"What would you do? Give tennis lessons all day? Join McEnroe and Agassi on the Seniors tennis circuit? You'd be bored with any of that within a month."

"Maybe I'll get my P.I. license, become a private investigator. Hey, that way I could do some work for you."

"Damn, Jack, I'm totally blown away hearing this shit."

Dantzler's cell phone buzzed. He picked it off the table and answered. "Jack Dantzler." He listened intently, his expression instantly shifting from a smile to a frown. "Where did this happen? Jacobson Park? And you have a positive ID on the victim? Who's there? Eric and Arnie are on their way? Good. Tell them I'll be there in thirty minutes. No, don't worry about Jake. He's out of town." He paused for a second, and then said, "You're certain about the victim's identity? And it appears to be a suicide? Okay, I'm on my way."

"Sounds serious," Sean said, after Dantzler ended the call and stood.

"Possible suicide, Jacobson Park.

"I got all that. Who's the victim?"

"Dale Larraby."

CHAPTER TWO

"Nice ride," Sean commented. "When did you get it?"

"Yesterday."

"Gotta love that new car smell."

He and Sean were in Dantzler's first new vehicle in more than a dozen years, a maroon Mecedes SUV. They had just left New Circle and were now on Richmond Road. Sean had asked if he could ride along and Dantzler agreed.

"The trusty old Forester served me well for almost thirteen years, but it was time for a change," Dantzler noted. "But you know what? Whether you are in a Subaru or a Mercedes, on Richmond Road at this time of day you're not going anywhere very fast."

Sean glanced at his watch. "It's a little past five. Workers going home, locals looking for a restaurant or a bar, and folks from neighboring counties flooding into the big city. Worst time of day for traffic. And on a Friday to boot."

It was a beautiful May afternoon, the temperature was in the mid-seventies, there was a gentle breeze, and the humidity was low. The sun was drifting toward the western horizon, having broken free from the shackles of its eastern counterpart. Darkness was closing in, and forecasters were calling for possible thunderstorms, but by any standard this was one of those days that made you appreciate life.

And yet, Dale Larraby apparently chose to end his life.

Not such a good day for him.

Dantzler carefully maneuvered the Mercedes into a left lane, said, "How well did you know Larraby?"

"Not well at all," Sean answered. "Hell, did anybody really know him?"

"Good question."

"We briefly worked together in Missing Persons. But I was only in that unit for a little over a year before being bumped up to Homicide. I don't recall that he and I ever worked a case together. I do know he wasn't happy when I was promoted to Homicide before he was. He made that known to everyone at the time."

"Dale Larraby was never happy," Dantzler said.

"Yeah, but suicide. Damn . . . how unhappy do you have to be to make that decision?"

"He's not the first cop to check himself out. Won't be the last, either."

"Think you could ever do it, Jack?"

Dantzler shrugged but didn't answer.

Sean continued, "Thing is, suicide seems to have several different fathers. Different reasons, is what I really mean by that. Depression, anger, hopelessness, terminal illness, fear, madness. Some will even argue that a person commits suicide only after experiencing a moment of clarity, and that such an individual is acting bravely. I hate to admit this, but my feeling is that everyone is capable of taking his or her own life, given a certain set of circumstances. If I had one of those crappy diseases like Alzheimer's or ALS, I would like to think I had the courage to save others from the burden of taking care of me for God only knows how many years."

"Maybe that was Larraby's situation."

"Maybe. Hope that was the case."

"Camus said the only serious philosophical problem revolved around the issue of suicide. He believed the question of whether life is or is not worth living is the fundamental question of philosophy. Everything else comes after that. For him, suicide is a confession. What the person is saying by committing suicide is that the burden of living has become too much for him to bear. Therefore, his act is his confession. Camus also argues that the act of suicide is prepared within the silence of the heart, same as a great work of art."

"And you believe that dreck? I know Camus is one of your heroes, Jack, but, hey, come on. I don't see how suicide and art could possibly belong in the same sentence."

"I didn't say I believed it, Sean. I'm just expressing Camus's thoughts on the subject."

"Camus also said we should believe that Sisyphus is happy. Really? Are you kidding me or what? Here's this guy who has been condemned by the gods to roll a huge boulder up a mountain, and then once he gets it to the top, the damn boulder rolls back down to the bottom, thus forcing him to begin the process over again. And he has to do this through all eternity. I don't give a shit what Camus wants us to believe. Sisyphus is anything but a happy man."

"Actually, Camus said we should *imagine* that Sisyphus is happy."

"Well, I imagine that he is one miserable bastard."

"You're the defense attorney, Sean. Think maybe you could work your magic and get Sisyphus's conviction overturned."

"Nah, I don't mess with the gods."

"Wise thinking on your part."

Jacobson Park, an area comprised of more than two-hundred acres, was located approximately a dozen miles from downtown Lexington. It ranked as one of the best recreation parks in the region, a place where families or individuals could come and take part in any number of activities. There was a marina where water lovers could take paddle boat rides on the lake, fish, or feed the many ducks that waddled over. For the land locked there were volleyball courts, a large playground for the youngsters, picnic tables for family outings, walking and biking trails, and a large open field often used by those tossing Frisbees to their friends or their dogs, or those hoping to send kites skyward. All in all, a wonderful place for folks seeking to have fun with loved ones, enjoy nature, or simply lie in the grass on a blanket and let their thoughts drift off in a deeper direction.

On a gorgeous afternoon like this one Dantzler fully expected Jacobson Park to be packed with visitors. And he was right. Pulling off Athens-Boonesboro Road into the main entrance, after being waved through by a uniformed patrolman, he eased to the left and wound around a sharp curve before spotting what had to be a couple hundred people congregated near the parking area. Men and women of all ages, some accompanied by children, many of whom—the older ones in particular—were desperate to get a closer look inside the vehicle that Dantzler assumed was where Dale Larraby had apparently taken his own life. But that wasn't going to happen. The curious were out of luck today. A wide area around the car had been cordoned off by yellow crime scene tape, and a trio of patrolmen was stationed like sentries to keep the nosey from getting close enough to possibly screw up any potential evidence.

The road leading to Larraby's car was blocked by a fleet of official vehicles, including five patrol cars, three unmarked sedans, a fire truck, and the coroner's van. Dantzler did his best to navigate around and through the blockade but quickly decided that it wasn't worth the effort. Try as he might, he couldn't find enough room between vehicles to allow progress. Plus, he had no desire to accidently put a ding in his new ride. So he pulled off to the side and cut the engine. Then he and Sean exited the car and began the trek down to where all the action was, a distance about fifty yards away.

Dantzler nodded to one of the patrolmen and ducked under the yellow tape. But when Sean tried to follow, the patrolman held up his hand, stepped directly in front of Sean, and blocked his path. He didn't recognize Sean, and Sean flashed no official credentials. The officer was just doing his job.

"It's okay, officer," Dantzler said. "He's with me."

"Yes, sir," the officer said, as he lifted the tape and allowed Sean to duck under it.

Dantzler spied Eric Gamble off to his left talking with another uniformed officer who was also black. Her name, Dantzler recalled, was Victoria Jefferson. She was a sergeant who had earned the reputation as a superb cop, one who was destined for greater things. Seeing Eric and Jefferson standing side by side triggered a memory in Dantzler's brain but one he couldn't seem to locate at the moment.

Dantzler cast aside his lost memory and turned his attention to Larraby's vehicle—a white Toyota Avalon that looked to be several years old. The driver's side door was open but Dantzler couldn't see inside the car. That's because Arnie Edwards, the medical examiner, was closely examining the body. Arnie's backside was blocking Dantzler's view.

Moving around the car with Sean following close behind, Dantzler peered in through the window on the passenger's side. The deceased was definitely Dale Larraby. There was no mistaking that, despite the extensive damage caused by what had obviously resulted from a gunshot. Although his years of experience as a homicide investigator had taught him to refrain from making snap judgments, Dantzler was virtually one-hundred percent certain that what he now observed was a classic case of suicide and not homicide. He could be wrong but he doubted that he was. Everything he was looking at pointed clearly toward that conclusion.

Larraby was seated upright behind the steering wheel, his head tilted back against the blood-soaked cushion. He was dressed in cut-off Levis, a tank top, and brown sandals. His eyes were closed, not unlike someone who had fallen asleep. And in a sense he was sleeping, and would be forever. Dantzler also knew how Larraby chose to end his life. He didn't put the gun against his temple and pull the trigger. Nor did he put the barrel in his mouth, as do so many who opt to kill themselves with a pistol. No, it hadn't happened in either of those more traditional ways. Dale Larraby put the gun under his chin and squeezed the trigger. Dantzler knew this because a straight line could be drawn from the bottom of Larraby's chin, to the missing back of his head, to the massive amount of blood and brain tissue on the ceiling.

The gun, a Glock G21, same as the one Dantzler carried, was in Larraby's lap still clutched in his right hand. On the passenger's side floorboard Dantzler noticed an empty bottle of Jack Daniels. He looked around inside the vehicle for a few more seconds before deciding that there wasn't much else to see.

When Dantzler stepped away, Sean looked inside, and said, "Damn, what a mess." Then Sean crossed himself, which reminded Dantzler that his friend was a Catholic.

"Find anything surprising, Arnie?" Dantzler asked the medical examiner.

"Not really. Of course, I won't have an official assessment until later on, but everything I see thus far indicates suicide. That empty whiskey bottle tells me he did some heavy drinking before he pulled the trigger. I'll venture a wild guess that we'll find that his blood-alcohol level was extremely high. Probably needed the alcohol to work up the nerve to do it, or to break down the fear standing in his way. Obviously, it worked, as you can plainly see."

"Who was first on the scene?"

"Sergeant Jefferson. Eric's cousin."

That was the memory Dantzler couldn't locate when he saw Eric talking with Jefferson. "Thanks, Arnie. And let me know if you find anything interesting."

"Will do."

Dantzler looked up and saw Richard Bird heading in his direction. The captain passed without speaking, went around to the passenger's side of the Avalon, and looked inside at Larraby's body. But only for a brief moment. Dantzler had been right when he told Sean that Bird had no stomach for the ugliness that went hand in hand with violent, bloody death.

"Damn, I know Larraby had some issues, but to check himself out like this," Bird said to Dantzler and Sean. "It's . . . it's just hard to fathom." Only then did Bird seem to register Sean's presence. "Hello, Sean."

"Captain."

"What the hell are you doing here? Surely you have better things to do than look at a dead body."

"I just happened to be with Jack. I asked if I could tag along, he said yes."

"You looking to get back in Homicide? If you are there's a place for you. All you have to do is say yes."

"Thanks, Captain. But I'll stay put."

"Can't say that I blame you. I'm sure the living pay better than the dead."

"*Some* living do," Sean said, laughing. "And some don't."

While Bird and Sean continued chatting Dantzler wandered over to where Victoria Jefferson was standing. Seconds later they were joined by Eric. Seeing them side by side, Dantzler could easily detect a strong family resemblance.

"You're Victoria, right?" Dantzler asked her.

"Yes, sir. But everyone calls me Vee."

"Break it down for me, Vee," Dantzler said.

"I was at the corner of Richmond Road and Man 'o War when the call came," Vee quickly answered. "Shots fired at Jacobson Park. This was . . ."

"Shots, or shot?"

"I'm pretty sure the dispatcher said shots. But you might want to listen to the tape to make sure I'm being accurate."

Dantzler liked that answer. It told him she would rather get it right than forward information that may not be correct. What this also told Dantzler was that the positive reports concerning Victoria Jefferson's abilities had not been overstated. She was, Dantzler conceded, a star on the rise.

"What time did you get the call?" Dantzler asked.

"Three forty-eight. I lit it up and was on the scene at three fifty-four."

"When did you show up, Eric?" Dantzler said.

"Four-twenty. Arnie arrived about five minutes later."

Dantzler turned back to Vee and said, "What did you do next?"

"Checked the victim, ascertained that he was deceased. Then I began to secure the scene and waited for you guys to show up."

"Tell him about that guy over there, Vee," Eric said, as he pointed at a man located about twenty feet off to their right. The man was standing with a woman and two boys, both of whom appeared to be about ten-years-old. The man, a Caucasian, was tall, broad shouldered, dressed in Cargo shorts, a Polo shirt, and boat shoes. He had closely cropped hair, and his eyes were hidden behind sunglasses. He stood ramrod straight and appeared to be in excellent physical shape.

"What about him?" Dantzler asked Vee.

"He had pretty much secured the crime scene for us," she answered.

"How so?"

"He kept everybody's ass away from the vehicle. You know how it goes at a scene like this. No matter how gory or bloody or tragic it is there are always those who feel compelled to check things out. That's especially true of young kids, who are naturally curious anyway. Something this gruesome draws them like flies to a pile of steaming horse-shit. But he made sure no one got close to the car."

"What's the guy's name?"

Vee checked her notes. "Joe Conrad. The lady is his wife, and one of the boys is their son. The other kid is their son's friend."

"Okay, Eric, here's what I want you to do." Dantzler then turned to Vee. "You game for some real detective work?"

"Sure, anything you need."

"Good. Eric, call the station and get a location for Larraby's residence. Then you and Vee go there and really give the place a thorough search. If the door's locked and you can't find someone to let you in, then bust it down. See if you can find something—*anything*—that might help us figure out why he opted to kill himself. Once you guys have done that, talk with his neighbors. See if they can shed any light on his recent behavior."

After Eric and Vee left, Dantzler walked over and introduced himself to Joe Conrad. "Mind if I ask you a few questions?" Dantzler said, after the two men shook hands. "I realize you've already spoken to one officer, but I'm the lead investigator, so I'd like to hear your version for myself."

"Understood."

"Take me back to the beginning. Where were you when this happened?"

"My wife and I and the two boys were up in that open field trying our best to get kites in the air. We weren't having much luck, to tell you the truth. It seems that flying kites is not my specialty." He chuckled. "We'd been at it for close to an hour. Anyway, I was in the process of demonstrating my kiting incompetence when I heard the shot."

"Shot, or shots?"

"One. A single shot. I recognized immediately that it was a gunshot, and that it came from a handgun and not a long rifle."

Dantzler glanced at the large open field where people flew their kites. "That's fifty to seventy-five yards away," he pointed out. "How could you possibly distinguish between a pistol and a rifle?"

"Two tours in Iraq. I was an Army Ranger. I know weapons. I also knew for certain where the shot came from. That it had come from this parking area."

"What did you do next?"

"I turned and headed this way."

"Did you happen to notice the time?"

"Fifteen-hundred thirty-four hours. Three thirty-four in civilian terms."

"Approximately how much time elapsed between when you heard the shot and when you turned around?"

"A second. Two at the most."

"Did you see anyone around the vehicle? Coming, going, moving suspiciously?"

"Not a soul. And believe me I would have if anyone had been close by. No one could have gotten away that quickly. I approached the vehicle—cautiously at first—but once I looked inside the car I realized there was no need for caution. The man was deceased. I didn't even bother checking for a pulse. I've seen enough dead people to know when life has departed."

Dantzler said, "I understand we have you to thank for helping keep the gawkers at bay. Not many people would have done that."

"Detective, not many people have seen the kind of ugly shit that you and I have had to look at. And, thank God, they haven't."

"And, hopefully, never will."

"Amen to that, Detective," Joe Conrad said, before heading back to join his wife and the two young boys. It had been an afternoon none of them expected when they left the house a few short hours ago. And one they—the boys in particular—would never forget.

Dantzler was standing alone, lost in thought, when he heard Arnie Edwards call his name. "What do you need, Arnie?" he responded.

"Can I take the body?"

"You need anything else from me?"

"Not a thing."

"Then he's all yours. Just let me know if you find anything that might be of interest."

"Don't hold your breath, Detective. I don't think we're dealing with a mystery here."

Not true, Arnie, Dantzler said to himself. Suicide can be wrapped in a blanket of mystery thicker than one wrapped around a homicide. Dale Larraby had chosen to end his life in a horrible, painful manner. Why? And why today? Why not yesterday, tomorrow, or next week? What made him choose this particular moment? What was the deciding factor that ultimately pushed him over the edge?

Those were questions that in all likelihood might never be answered. A mystery perhaps destined to go unsolved.

To Dantzler's way of thinking, suicide was simply another form of murder. The life of a human being was ended prematurely. Violently. In this case the victim was also the murderer. And vice versa. It was a freaky formula that hardly made sense. Yet, hundreds of individuals commit suicide every day. And contra Camus, they can't all be the end result of a work of art.

But they all can be a mystery.

CHAPTER THREE

Dantzler waited until Sean ended a conversation with one of the female officers he knew before heading back to his vehicle. Once they were inside and buckled up Dantzler performed a quick U-turn and drove up to the main entrance. After checking in both directions he pulled out onto the highway and took off for downtown.

Neither man was in much of a mood for conversation. Dantzler stared straight ahead at the road, while Sean took out his cell phone and began typing a text. A few drops of rain hit the windshield, but not enough to cause Dantzler to use his wipers for the first time since purchasing the car. Just for the hell of it, necessary or not, he turned them on and let them make a couple of swipes. He wanted to make sure the damn things worked. For the money he'd spent on this ride, they'd better work.

Dantzler's thoughts were on Dale Larraby, a fact that would come as a surprise to virtually everyone acquainted with the two men. Most would likely doubt that Dantzler gave Larraby's death a second thought. After all, it was no secret that there was no love lost between them. They had clashed on many occasions, several of which almost ended with the two men coming to blows. Simply stated, Larraby hated Dantzler, and Dantzler despised Larraby.

Reflecting back on it now, Dantzler realized that almost all arguments and confrontations were instigated by Larraby. The man challenged every idea, plan, or notion Dantzler put forth. If Dantzler wanted to go with Plan A, Larraby countered by saying Plan B was the better option. If Dantzler had wanted a hamburger, Larraby would have chosen a hot dog.

They were oil and water, wine and vinegar. Complete opposites in every regard.

Dantzler understood that a big reason for Larraby's feelings toward him stemmed from old-fashioned jealousy. Larraby had been on the force for seven years before Dantzler signed on, yet it was Dantzler who quickly rose through the ranks, becoming the youngest Lexington cop to earn a gold shield and join the Homicide Unit. While Dantzler's star was ascending, Larraby moved more slowly up the ladder, spending the majority of his career in the Missing Persons Unit. He did eventually land a spot in Homicide about ten years ago, but only because there had been a series of murders that forced Captain Richard Bird to promote Larraby. It was not a promotion that met with universal praise. No one shed a tear when Larraby retired five years ago.

Sean seemed to know what Dantzler was thinking. Breaking almost ten minutes of silence, he said, "Given your disparate personalities, Jack, it was inevitable that you and Larraby were never going to get along. You guys were bound to butt heads. And you did, all the time. The two of you clashed more than an unhappy married couple. And it's no secret why. Larraby was extremely jealous and envious of you. Everybody knew that. He always referred to you as the 'Golden Boy.' As he saw things, you got all the breaks, all the glory, while he kept getting overlooked and underappreciated. Of course, everyone also knows that's a joke. What was the classic line about Larraby when he was with Homicide?"

"That he couldn't find a Jew in Tel Aviv, much less a murderer," Dantzler answered.

"He was a lousy cop, Jack. That's the bottom line. He never excelled. Never. Though I didn't spend much time with him when I worked Missing Persons, I knew I was looking at a mediocre police officer at best. You were his complete opposite in every way. You are intelligent and you are unbelievably talented. He was never in your league, and regardless of how hard he might've tried, or how much effort he might've expended, he wasn't ever going to be a match for you. Rather than accept his limitations and strive to get better, which a wiser man would have done, he made you his enemy. His scapegoat for lacking your talent."

"Sean, I'm going to let you in on a little secret—my so-called *talent* is vastly overrated. If I do have a true talent, it's tenacity. I don't stop digging and plugging away until I find the answers I'm looking for. I keep my head down until I hit the finish line. Larraby didn't do that. He was lazy and not committed to succeeding. I can tolerate many things, but not laziness. We are public servants, and the public deserves our best effort. Always. Larraby either never understood that or he simply didn't care. And that's why he was such a shitty cop."

"And yet here you are thinking about him."

"Well, he *was* a cop, even if he wasn't a good one. He did wear the uniform. I suppose that has to count for something. Plus, he did have a kid."

"Damn, I forgot all about that. Yeah, a girl. With Carole, right?"

"Yes."

"They've been divorced forever. If I'm not mistaken, Carole has been married and divorced again since splitting from Larraby."

"Married another cop."

"Who?"

"Mike Perkins."

"'Iron' Mike?"

"None other."

"Didn't he work with Larraby in Missing Persons?"

"He did."

"Poor Carole. Talk about doubling down on your mistakes," Sean said, adding, "have you seen Mike lately?"

"Not for years."

"You ever see the movie *A Bronx Tale?*"

"Sure. De Niro directed it."

"Remember that line *the saddest thing in life is wasted potential?* Well, those words could've been written for Mike Perkins. And let me tell you, Jack. If you saw him on the street you wouldn't recognize him. I was leaving McCarthy's a couple of days ago when I happened to bump into him. If he hadn't spoken to me I would never have said anything to him. God, it was so sad. *He* was so sad."

"I'd heard some rumors about him, but you know how that goes. Maybe true, maybe not."

"You remember how he looked when he first joined the force?"

"Sure. I also recall everyone thinking he'd make a great cop. Then all that shit started to happen."

"The guy was ripped when he became a cop," Sean noted. "Looked like a fuckin' Greek god. Men work for years and never get a body like his. He didn't need to do all that other stuff. All the steroids and everything else he was using. In a few months he went from looking like a Greek god to looking like Mount Olympus. His neck was bigger than a regular man's waist. It finally became so obvious that he was on *something* that the department had no choice but to have him tested. That's when they discovered that he was using more than steroids."

"PCP, if I remember correctly."

"Crack, meth, cocaine, heroin . . . he wasn't leaving anything out. They said his apartment looked like a junkie's pharmacy. No way a guy in that condition could remain on the force. So, he got booted. All that potential down the drain."

"Did Carole marry him before or after all that happened?" Dantzler asked.

Sean shrugged, said, "I don't know. But what I can tell you is that Mike looked like death warmed over when I saw him. He weighed maybe one-twenty, he had several missing teeth, and he was dirty and ratty looking. He certainly didn't resemble a Greek god anymore. The Mike Perkins I ran into looked like your classic homeless person. A typical bum."

As Dantzler pulled the Mercedes into the Tennis Center parking lot his cell phone buzzed. The call was from Eric. "Hey, Eric. Find anything of interest?"

"Nothing that raised the hair on the back of my neck. We did gather up some personal items you need to look at. I'll bring them to the office when I drop Vee off. She's still interviewing neighbors. The few I spoke with all seemed shocked by what happened. None saw any signs that Larraby was falling off the deep end."

"Did you by any chance run across an address for his ex-wife? Could be either Carole Larraby or Carole Perkins."

Dantzler could hear Eric shuffling through some papers. After a few seconds, Eric said, "Yeah, Carole Perkins. Got her address right here. Found it in his will. Seems he left everything to her."

"Really? That's interesting. Give me her address." Dantzler wrote it down, then said, "See you in the office tomorrow."

"Tomorrow's Saturday," Eric reminded Dantzler.

"Yes, it is, isn't it? Okay, unless you come up with something earth shattering, I'll see you Monday."

Sean opened the car door and started to get out. Turning, he said, "You going to visit Carole?"

"She's probably already heard the news by now, but I need to pay my respects. Professional courtesy and all. Plus, I'd like to know when she last spoke with Larraby, and what his frame of mind was at the time."

"What were you referring to when you said 'that's interesting' to Eric?" Sean asked.

"Eric found Larraby's will. Carole was his sole beneficiary."

"Well, I have to agree with you. That *is* interesting."

_-^-_

Carole Perkins lived in a modest one-story brick house located in the Chevy Chase area not far from the University of Kentucky campus. Flanking her house were two much larger homes, not unlike many others in this area. Chevy Chase had become a trendy neighborhood where houses of any size didn't come cheap. Most were older structures built back in the old days when the term pre-fab probably hadn't yet been coined. These homes were built to last.

Dantzler found her house and pulled into the driveway. The digital clock on his new dashboard said it was a little past nine. He realized it was late for a visit, and he gave serious consideration to taking a pass and grabbing dinner before heading home. But his internal debate was a brief one. Like it or not, regardless of the time, he needed to pay his respects.

Even for a man he despised.

Carole Perkins hadn't changed much since the last time Dantzler saw her, which must have been at least a dozen years ago. She was of medium height, had short dark hair that was liberally sprinkled with gray, and wide blue eyes set far apart. Her tanned skin told Dantzler she spent a good deal of time in the outdoors. So did her outfit—a black skirt, sleeveless teal shirt, and tennis shoes. A classic golfer's attire. All that was missing was a viser on her head and a putter in her hands.

Seeing her for the first time in years reminded Dantzler that she was a lady who rarely smiled. But after marriages to Dale Larraby and Mike Perkins, who could blame her for that? Neither man was noted for instilling joy or mirth.

Despite her obvious surprise at his showing up she graciously invited him to come in. After leading him to the living room and motioning for him to take a seat on the sofa, she asked if he wanted something to drink. Dantzler was thirsty—and hungry—but he declined her offer. Excusing herself, she went into the kitchen for a few minutes before returning with a glass of orange juice in her hand. Dantzler doubted that orange juice was the only liquid in the glass.

Taking a seat next to Dantzler, she said, "Given your history with Dale, you were probably the last person I expected to see tonight."

"You have heard the news, then?"

"Yes. Bruce Rawlinson phoned to inform me."

That damn Rawlinson. "I am sorry, Carole. I don't know about your relationship with him, but I do know you guys had a daughter together. This has to be tough for her."

"Much more difficult for her than it is for me, that's for sure. But having said that, Dale really hadn't been much of a presence in her life for many years. Not since she was a young girl."

"How long were you and Dale married?"

"Seven years. And we've been divorced for seventeen."

"When was the last time you saw or spoke to him?" Dantzler said.

"Funny you should ask that. I hadn't seen him or even talked to him in five or six years. Then, out of the blue, four days ago he called. Shocked the hell out of me."

"What was the reason for his call?"

"He wanted to know how I was doing. How Becky was doing. Strange, him inquiring about us after staying away for so many years. I told him we were both doing well, which is true. We are. I'm a real estate agent, and Becky is a paralegal at a firm downtown. He seemed genuinely pleased to hear that."

"Did he sound depressed?"

"Dale almost always *was* depressed, but I can't say he sounded more down or depressed than usual. Still, to take his own life like that, he . . ." Carole closed her eyes and swiped at a tear trickling down her cheek. "You know he admired you, Detective Dantzler. Said you were the best cop he ever saw."

"Admired? I think you've got it wrong, Carole. He hated me. We never got along."

"Why do you think that is? I'll tell you why. Because you never fail. He may not have liked you personally, but on a professional level he most certainly did. He told me that many times."

"That comes as a surprise."

"You know, Detective, when Dale and I first got married he was a terrific guy. Kind, funny, considerate, caring . . . the complete opposite of what he eventually became. I would never have married *that* Dale Larraby. Not in a million years. But . . . after five years of marriage, he suddenly changed. He became this whole other person, this stranger. Dark, sullen, moody, distant. Just not a pleasant man to be around. I stuck it out for a couple of years, then I said no more. Life is too short for that kind of misery. So I took Becky, moved out, and filed for divorce."

"Why do you think he changed?"

"I don't know. But he did, and it was almost overnight."

"Was he with Missing Persons back then?"

"Yes."

"Did he physically abuse you?"

"Never. I mean, I never would have allowed that. Hit me once and I'm outta here. No, he yelled, screamed, and cursed quite a bit, but he didn't lay a finger on me."

"Alcohol, drugs, possibly?" Dantzler asked.

"Dale was never much of a drinker. Oh, he'd have a few beers with the guys from time to time, but nothing heavy. Drugs? I don't think so." She took a long sip of orange juice. "Which leads us right into my second marriage, doesn't it?"

"'Iron' Mike."

"How many times do you think I've ask myself how I allowed that to happen?" Carole said, shaking her head. "God, what a disaster. Mike also changed overnight, but in his case we all know the reason why. He went steroid and drug crazy. Also, I found out that he had fallen in love with another woman. He admitted that to me. With all that going on, his behavior became so erratic, so strange and dangerous that I had no choice but to leave. Which I did after a year of marriage. Had I stayed with him he might easily have killed me or Becky."

"Have you seen Mike lately?"

"Not for years."

"Sean Montgomery recently bumped into Mike downtown and barely recognized him. Said he was pitifully thin, unhealthy looking, and dressed like a homeless person."

"What a shame. And he was such a handsome man before all that happened. Handsome and sexy."

"One last thing, Carole. When you spoke with Dale, did he mention anything about his will?"

"No. Why would he?"

"Eric Gamble found a copy at Dale's condo. I haven't read it yet, but Eric said you are the sole beneficiary."

"You're joking, right?"

"No. Like I said, I've not studied it, so I don't know the particulars. When I do read it I'll fill you in. Who was Dale's attorney?"

"I can't answer that. When we were married it was Lawrence Brady. Whether or not he still is, I don't know."

"I'll check with Brady. If he's no longer Dale's attorney he can probably point me in the right direction." Dantzler stood and stretched. "Thanks for taking time to speak with me, Carole. And I'm truly sorry about all this. I hope Becky comes through it okay."

"She will. Becky's like me—she's tough."

"Good for her. And I'll get you a copy of Dale's will early next week."

"Thank you, Detective Dantzler." She gently touched his arm. "I can understand why Dale admired you, even if it was secretly."

Maybe the best-kept secret in the world, Dantzler thought to himself as he strolled toward his shiny new Mercedes.

.-^-.

Dantzler stopped at the first Wendy's he saw, ordered a double cheeseburger with mustard and onions, large fries and a Diet Coke, and then drove home. He lived in a small ranch-style house on Lakeshore Drive, which he purchased in the early nineteen-nineties after years as an apartment dweller. It was an average house with three bedrooms, two full baths, den, living room, basement, and a screened-in back porch. While it was modest when compared to some of the more opulent mansions located less than a mile away, this place suited him just fine. What made it so special for him was the lake that bumped up against his backyard. He spent many nights sitting on his porch listening as the crickets and frogs sang to their heart's content. Together they formed a chorus whose music he could listen to for hours.

In those moments life truly was sublime. Like now, sitting on the deck with a glass of Pernod and orange juice in hand, watching the moon's reflection dance on the black water, listening to the night creatures sing in the dark.

Unfortunately, those quiet moments seldom lasted very long.

Death invariably intruded, bringing with it darkness, pain, suffering, and ugliness. Right now, somewhere in this city, the next murder plan was being hatched. Or maybe there was no plan. Maybe an argument would end when one man pulled a gun and shot another man. Either scenario resulted in some unsuspecting citizen's life being snuffed out. It wasn't a matter of if; it was a matter of when. Dantzler knew this with absolute certainty. Knew it because some people have evil buried somewhere deep in their DNA. And those who do are hell-bent on fulfilling their twisted destiny.

Dantzler had once heard someone say that human beings are risen apes, not fallen angels. He believed that assessment to be accurate. In his line of work it was proved true on a regular basis.

He grabbed his phone off the chair next to him and dialed Sean's number. Odds were good that Sean was home at this hour, and even bigger odds that he wasn't alone. Sean had more lady friends than George Clooney did when he was still single.

"What?" Sean answered after a couple of rings. "This better be important, 'cause I'm kinda tied up at the moment."

"Physically or metaphorically?"

"Both, probably."

Dantzler chuckled. "One question, Sean, and then you can get back to business."

"Ask away."

"Do you know Lawrence Brady?"

Now it was Sean who chuckled. "You mean, 'Shady' Brady? Yeah, I know Brady, but not very well. Why are you asking about him?"

"Back in the day he was Larraby's attorney. I want to know if he still is."

"You interrupted me to inquire about that?" Sean said. "I mean, you could have waited until Monday to get the answer to that question."

"But I figured you'd be busy and I wanted to annoy you."

"Well, you succeeded. Goodbye, Jack."

"Wait. One more question. Why . . ."

"Is he called 'Shady'? Why do you think? He ain't exactly got a sterling reputation."

"Meaning?"

"Meaning call me tomorrow afternoon. Or Monday morning. Then I'll tell you what I know, which ain't much. But I can give you the names of a few barristers who will gladly provide you with much more skinny on Brady than I can. Now, for the second and final time, good-night. I have important business to take care of."

Dantzler was laughing out loud when he closed his phone.

CHAPTER FOUR

A s the rain peppered the balcony of her condo overlooking
the Ohio River Julie Bradley sat on the sofa, a glass of wine
in her hand and a worried look on her face. A half-empty
bottle of Merlot, two empty wine glasses and her cell phone rested on
the ottoman in front of the sofa. Checking her watch, she noted that
her two guests were already twenty minutes late. It was unlike them to
be tardy.

The expected duo was Darvis Bernstein and his wife, Nancy Sloan,
publisher and editor, respectively, of Five Points Publishing, located in
Chicago. They were on their way to Julie's for the purpose of
discussing—and deciding on—her next book project. Julie was eager to
get the conversation underway. Eager to make her pitch.

She was confident that they would green light the book—how
could they refuse, given that Julie's two previous books made millions
and practically saved their company?—but still, she was nervous. She
set the odds at seventy-thirty that they would give a thumbs-up. But
what if they surprised her and said no deal? Publishing a book, any
book, is always a dicey proposition. Most books, in fact, lose money.
Her two hadn't. Both had been big sellers, both had been optioned by

Hollywood producers, and one had been made into a successful Lifetime Channel movie. History was certainly in her corner.

Still . . .

Darvis might say no this time around. What if he did? Julie asked herself. Should she simply accept the rejection and let the project die? Not put up an argument? No way. She was not a quitter. If Darvis turned her down she would move on and search for a new publisher. Loyalty is a fine quality, but it cuts both ways. If he says no, she thought, I'll walk out the door. Yes, it would hurt—rejection is never easy to accept—and saying farewell to two people she genuinely adored would add to her hurt feelings. But . . . business is business.

With her resume Julie had no doubt that once word got out that she was no longer with Five Points other publishers would be burning up her phone in a matter of hours. She was currently a hot commodity, and publishers are forever seeking writers whose names can be found on the best-seller list. In any business making money tends to guarantee job security.

Julie had become an author by accident. A native of Clarksville, Indiana, she graduated high school near the top of her class. Next, she attended Western Kentucky University in Bowling Green, graduating with a degree in journalism. Several job offers came her way, including two from highly respected big city daily newspapers. However, she spurned those offers, choosing instead to work for a twice-weekly paper located in a small southern Indiana community. She went with the smaller paper over the larger ones primarily for one reason—Stan Johnson.

A gruff cigar-chomping man with the personality of an angry bear and a heart of gold, Johnson was regarded as something of a genius in the newspaper world. He was old school, an unrepentant liberal, a lover of proper English who regarded Strunk and White's book as divinely inspired, and the single most intelligent human being Julie had ever encountered. During his more-than-forty-year career he had mentored dozens of young reporters, all of whom moved on to bigger and better things. He only hired those with true talent, knowing none of them would be with him two or three years down the road. He not only expected them to move on, he encouraged them to do so. Genuine talent should be free to seek its own level.

Julie stayed at the paper longer than most—almost five years. And she loved every minute of it. While at the paper she covered everything from city hall to school board meetings to the local beauty pageant. During the school year she reported on the girls' soccer and basketball teams. Occasionally, once Stan trusted her judgment and her talent, he allowed her to write editorials. But without question the police beat was her favorite job at the paper. And it was because of this assignment that she remained at the paper for a longer stint than any of her predecessors.

During her third year at the paper Julie found herself living in the middle of a small town that was suddenly at the center of a sensational murder mystery. On a cold December night, a week before Christmas, one of the town's wealthiest citizens was brutally murdered. Suspicion was instantly cast in the direction of his much-younger wife, a former Miss USA winner he had married only two years previously. Those suspicions gained even more traction when it was learned that she would inherit his entire fortune, and that he had recently taken out a two-million dollar life insurance policy in which she was the sole beneficiary. This did not go over very well with the dead man's two adult children from his first marriage. They immediately challenged the validity of the will, arguing that under no circumstances would their father cut them out completely. They further contended that any changes to the will had been made under duress, and that it was their gold-digging stepmother who had their father killed.

But there was a problem with that theory—the wife had been in Key West at the time of the murder. Her alibi was simple: How could I possibly shoot a man living in Indiana while I'm vacationing in Florida, ninety miles from Cuba?

Turns out, she couldn't. But what she could do was get someone else to pull the trigger, which is exactly what she did. Her alibi was solid but her story was a lie. And when everything came to light, what most people had suspected from the very beginning turned out to be true. Almost. The consensus among most of the town's citizenry was that the younger woman eliminated her husband so she could be with a different man. That scenario was half true. The killer was indeed her lover, but in this relationship her paramour happened to be a woman. That was the wrinkle no one saw coming.

Julie covered the story from crime scene to the courtroom, a time span of almost a full year. When the trial concluded—both women were found guilty and sentenced to life in prison with no possibility for parole—Julie sensed that there was more to the story than had been revealed. She just *knew* in her gut that a book was begging to be written. And who better than her to write it? No one, that's who.

On her own time—and her own dime—she managed to finagle a series of interviews with the two women. Miss USA was less forthcoming than her lover, but over the course of a dozen interviews recorded on thirty-three cassette tapes, Julie had more than enough material for a book about the crime. Not wanting to write the book on spec, meaning write it before acquiring a publisher, she began her search for a legitimate publishing house. It didn't take her long to find one. Less than two weeks after sending a proposal and an outline to seven publishers, the call she was praying for finally came. Darvis Bernstein said he loved what he read, and that Five Points would be proud to publish the book. He even offered her a modest advance, which, according to him, he rarely did.

The book, titled *Long-Distance Bullet: The Rise and Fall of Miss USA*, was an instant best-seller on the True Crimes list. Within two weeks of the book's release it was ranked number ten. The next week it was number one. Julie did signings and readings in bookstores all across the country. With her long brown hair, bright green eyes, and expressive face, she was a natural for TV, and she did indeed give interviews on a half-dozen programs. Thanks to the book's success, at age twenty-nine she was having her first brush with celebrity.

It was also the book that became the Lifetime Channel movie. With money from the book and the TV movie, Julie left Stan Johnson (but not before donating five percent of the money she earned to the newspaper editor who trained and nurtured her) and went in search of material for another true crime book. Three years later, *Basher: A Pro Football Standout's Journey from Glory to Murder*, hit the bookstores. Like her first book, Julie's follow-up effort was also very successful, once again rising to the top spot on the best-seller list. A big-name Hollywood producer/director optioned the book, and currently had it in development.

Again, more cash for Julie's bank account. Enough, in fact, to purchase a nice condo on Mount Adams in Cincinnati.

CHAPTER FIVE

"I have to tell you, Julie, what you've given us thus far doesn't excite me all that much," Darvis Bernstein said. He and Nancy showed up thirty minutes ago, saying their late arrival was due to a heavy thunderstorm just outside of Chicago that slowed traffic to a standstill. "And unless I'm badly mistaken, you appear to be having doubts of your own."

Julie looked at Nancy, hoping to find an ally for her cause. She didn't. Nancy's expression remained as unreadable as a foreign language. "You're dead wrong, Darvis," Julie finally said. "While I will admit that more information is needed, which I will get, I do not have any doubts whatsoever."

"Well, I do." Darvis turned to his wife. "Your thoughts, Nancy?"

"At this stage I'm an agnostic," Nancy replied. Then, looking at Julie, she said, "Are you positive you can get more information?"

"Absolutely."

Nancy put a hand on her husband's knee, then said, "My recommendation would be to give Julie a certain time frame—say one or two weeks—to gather enough information to satisfy your concerns. I say we owe her that much."

Darvis stood, picked up his glass of wine, walked to the window, and looked out at the pouring rain. Julie could see the wheels churning in his head. She knew an internal debate was raging. And she also knew exactly what the opposing sides were saying: *My instinct is to say no, but if I do, she will approach other publishers, and given her past record, one of them will gobble her up in a heartbeat.* Julie couldn't be sure which side would emerge victorious, and Darvis was certainly a hard man to read, but she held firm to the belief that her side would prevail.

Darvis turned away from the window, ambled back to the sofa, and took his seat next to Nancy. "Okay, Julie, tell us again what you do know," he said. "Start with the basics. What's the story about?"

"The murder of a young woman fifteen years ago."

"In Lexington, Kentucky? Right?"

"Correct."

"Solved or unsolved?"

"Neither. According to my source, law enforcement isn't even aware that she was murdered."

"How can that be?" Darvis asked. "And if it is true, that doesn't speak very highly of the Lexington police force."

"The woman was a prostitute who had very little family—only an older sister—so no big issue was made when she went missing. The sister did report it, and Missing Persons looked into it, but she was never located."

"And your informant is telling you that she wasn't found because she was dead?"

"Yes."

"Dead, the result of a homicide?"

"That's what he told me."

Darvis emptied his glass of wine, carefully set it on the ottoman, and said, "Now, for the two big questions: Who is your informant, and what was the murdered woman's name?"

"Danny Michaels and Gloria Nash," Julie quickly answered.

"Have you done any research on either of them?"

"Briefly."

"Why briefly? You're known for being quick, detailed, and thorough. Why haven't you really researched it?"

"I wanted to speak with you and Nancy first. Before I really start digging into it."

"Which translates into you wanting an advance, right?"

"A small one. Just enough to help cover a few basic expenses."

"What's your notion of small?"

"Ten thousand."

Darvis was silent for almost a minute. Finally, he said, "What's your arrangement with this informant?"

"You mean, money-wise?"

Darvis nodded.

"Nothing," Julie answered. "I don't pay informants. You know that."

"When are you expecting to meet with him?"

"I'm not sure."

"Jesus, Julie, you're not helping your cause here."

"He's supposed to call me within the next week. When he does I'll set a meeting."

"Why not put the ball in your court and phone him?"

"I tried but got no answer. My feeling is he used a burner phone."

"If that's the case you ought to have some concerns about him," Darvis said, shaking his head. "Could be a con artist looking to use you to make a few quick bucks."

"Or he could be the murderer," Nancy added.

"Look, guys, I'm a big girl," Julie said. "I understand there might be risks, and I won't take anything for granted. I'll make sure my ass is safe. And I'm no hero. If things do get scary I'm outta there."

"I'll give you five thousand for now," Darvis said, taking out his checkbook. "If this does turn into something worthwhile and you need more cash, I'll certainly consider it. But that is contingent on you giving me more than you already have."

"Thanks, Darvis. I appreciate the money. And your confidence in me."

Darvis finished writing the check, ripped it out of his checkbook, and handed it to Julie. "Hell, I don't know why I'm giving you money," he said, laughing. "You've got more of it than we do." He rose, then helped Nancy to her feet. "Come, love, it's onward to the hotel, where I will spend the night praying to the Big Weatherman upstairs to put a stop to this rain. If he doesn't, we will not be watching our beloved Cubs take on the hated Reds tomorrow afternoon."

"If the Big Weatherman upstairs hears a prayer coming from you I have no doubt he'll keel over from a heart attack," Nancy said. To Julie, she said, "Take care, my dear. Stay in touch, and most of all stay safe."

"Safe is my middle name," Julie said, as she led them to the door. When they were gone, she grinned and whispered "yes."

She was back in business.

CHAPTER SIX

When Dantzler walked into the War Room at eight Monday morning Eric and Jake Thomas were sitting on opposite sides of the long wooden table that bore multiple scars from having been around for decades. Jake was looking at several 8x10 photos, while Eric was studying the contents of a folder. A box filled with glazed doughnuts rested at the center of the table.

Dantzler eyed the sweets as he made his way to the water cooler. "Who brought those?" he asked.

"Rawlinson," Jake answered.

"Didn't know Bruce was so philanthropic." Dantzler picked up a doughnut, eyed it for a few seconds, then quickly put it back in the box. "How long have they been here?"

"An hour at least."

"Things sure have changed," Dantzler noted. "There was a time when they wouldn't have lasted ten minutes. Probably wouldn't have made it upstairs. They'd have been gobbled up in a matter of seconds. Not these days. Now, everybody is a health nut. Sugar is the devil's creation, fat should be banned from all food, and calories must be avoided at the expense of forfeiting your very soul to the food police. It's a different world, fellas."

"I notice you didn't take one," Eric pointed out. "You handled the darn thing like it was sprinkled with plutonium."

"Only because I already had a bialy." After filling a cup with water, Dantzler said, "How's your mom, Jake?"

"Great. The surgery went really well, much better than expected. The doc says if nothing unforeseen happens she should be released on Wednesday."

"That is good news. I'm sure your entire family is relieved."

"Mom's a tough old bird. I knew she would come through it okay."

Dantzler pointed at the photos in Jake's hand. "Larraby?"

Jake nodded, said, "Any idea why he might choose to go out this way?"

"No. And there's a good chance we never will."

"I didn't know the guy at all," Jake added. "Only met him once or twice. But regardless of his reason I think it's a selfish act on his part. He's gone, but those he left behind, family and friends, are bound to wonder what they could have done differently that might've changed the outcome. Innocent victims are always left to suffer. Suicide is never a solitary act."

"You are wise beyond your years, Jake," Dantzler said. Turning to Eric, he asked, "Is that what you brought from Larraby's house?"

Eric flipped the folder around and scooted it toward Dantzler. "Yeah. That's his will on top. Not much to it. Just a couple of pages."

Dantzler immediately went to the second page, to the bottom, and began reading. There, he saw that the will had been signed by Larraby and two witnesses, that it had been notarized, and that Lawrence A. Brady had been the attorney of record. Dantzler also noted that the will had been finalized on July 8, 2010. This bit of information told Dantzler that Brady had been Larraby's attorney at least up until seven years ago. But had their relationship continued? That's what Dantzler wanted to know.

Digging out his cell phone he typed a text and sent it to Sean. While waiting for Sean's response, Dantzler said to Eric, "Tell me about your cousin."

"Vee? What do you want to know?"

"The first thing that pops into your head."

"For starters, Vee is incredibly intelligent," Eric answered.

"Then how could she possibly be related to you?" Jake quipped.

Ignoring Jake, Eric continued, "Vee's IQ is off the charts. She has a master's in criminology and is thinking about going for her doctorate. She aces every test she takes. Why she wants to be a cop is a mystery to me. She's like you, Jack. With so much brainpower, why work this job when there are so many other things she could do? But she does. And she loves it."

"Think she would have an interest in working Homicide?"

"Are you kidding? Every police officer wants to work Homicide. Why? You thinking about bringing her up?"

"There's a good chance some things are going to change around here in the next few months. If that happens we're gonna need some new blood in the department. From what I've seen and heard about Vee, I think she would fit in well with us."

"You make that call you'll cause a mild uproar around here," Eric said. "You do know that, don't you? She's black, she's female, she's young, and she hasn't been on the job nearly as long as some of the others have. You'll piss off a lot guys."

"I couldn't care less, Eric. Hurt feelings are of no concern to me. All that matters is keeping this department strong and efficient. I wouldn't bring her up if I wasn't convinced that she could handle the job. I want only the best here. Same goes for Captain Bird. If I—we— think she fits the bill, then she gets the gold shield. Case closed."

"I can promise you that's she'll say yes if you do go in that direction."

"No decision has been made—this is still in the early discussion stage—so keep this conversation between us." Dantzler paused before continuing. "My biggest concern with bringing her up would be you, Eric. Not what a bunch of pissed-off officers might be feeling."

"Why me?"

"Could you work with Vee? Seriously? Ask yourself this question: Could you go into a dangerous, life-threatening situation and concentrate on what had to be done rather than worrying about her safety? About her getting wounded? Or worse? She's family, Eric. That could cloud your judgment, alter your decision making, either of which might get her or you killed."

"Vee can handle herself, trust me on that. As for me, I'll always do the right thing, regardless of who I'm working with. You know that."

"Just saying it's something you need to consider, that's all."

Dantzler's phone vibrated, letting him know he had a message. Sean had responded. The message read *Brady is still Larraby's attorney*. Closing his phone, Dantzler said, "Jake, get on your computer, see if you can get me an address and phone number for Lawrence Brady. He's an attorney here in town."

Jake fired up the laptop and had the information within a minute. "Lawrence A. Brady has an office on North Upper," Jake said. "Here's his office phone number."

Dantzler scribbled down the numbers on the top section of Larraby's will. Opening his phone, he called Brady's office. Brady's receptionist said he was in court and would be for most of the morning. When Dantzler asked if there was a good time for an afternoon meeting, she said Brady had nothing scheduled between two and three. Dantzler told her to pencil him in for two-thirty.

As Dantzler ended the call Arnie Edwards stepped into the War Room and dropped a big envelope on the table. "The results of Dale Larraby's autopsy," he announced. "Just as I suspected, there isn't much of a tale to tell. Suicide, pure and simple."

"You are one-hundred percent certain?" Dantzler said.

"Absolutely. Wouldn't say it if I wasn't."

"How much alcohol had he consumed?" Eric asked.

"The entire bottle. A fifth. If he'd waited a little while longer he might not have needed the gun. Alcohol poisoning would have done him in."

"Anything else we need to know?" Dantzler said.

"Not a thing," Arnie replied, waving them goodbye.

"You still going to meet with Lawrence Brady?" Eric said.

"Yeah."

"Why so much interest in a suicide?"

"I want to talk to Brady about Larraby's will. Sean Montgomery told me Brady is known as 'Shady' Brady, and that he doesn't have a glowing reputation within the legal community. When I spoke with Carole Perkins, she wasn't aware that Larraby had a will, or that she had been listed as his beneficiary. Brady might not be inclined to mention that little fact to her. I'll disabuse him of that inclination by letting him know that I have a copy of the will. I want to make sure Carole Perkins gets what's coming her way."

"I thought *all* lawyers were shady," Jake said.

"All of them except Sean," Dantzler answered. "And the jury is still out on him. Just don't tell him I said that."

CHAPTER SEVEN

Julie Bradley had not been completely honest during last evening's conversation with Darvis and Nancy. No, she hadn't exactly lied, but she had withheld. Thinking about it now, she wasn't sure why she did so. But she had, and even though things might have gone more smoothly had she been more forthcoming, she felt no qualms about having kept what she knew to herself.

During her pitch to Darvis and Nancy she purposefully omitted one crucial detail: that she did indeed have more information she could've shared with them. Information provided to her in the one phone conversation with her source.

Danny Michaels.

In their initial talk Danny had given her six names, telling her they were men she needed to interview. Getting to them won't be easy, he told her, and persuading them to talk will be even more of a challenge, because these were men trained to keep secrets. But according to Danny, those six men "will be at the heart of your book."

When she pressed Danny for more information he went silent. She pressed harder, but he remained mute. Finally, Julie told him if he didn't give her more she had no choice but to drop the project. This was a lie, of course, but he didn't know that. It was nothing more than a bluff, one she had used with great success in the past. She knew he would cave and he did. Guys like him always gave in. Okay, he told her, you'll get more when I get in touch with you next week. With that, he ended the call.

Julie thought about this as she sped down I-75 toward Lexington. How much should she trust Danny Michaels? she asked herself. Not much was her silent answer. Like all informers, he was surely working some kind of an angle. Most informers were little more than self-serving hustlers. But what was he looking for? He hadn't asked for money. Not yet anyway. And if he did, she wasn't about to give him any. So . . . what was his angle? Was it remotely possible that she was judging him too harshly? Was she wrong about him? Could it be that his heart was in the right place, that he wanted to see an unsolved crime get solved? That he was truly seeking delayed justice for a murdered woman? If that were the case, then he was a one-of-a-kind informant. Informants always want something, and it usually wasn't to improve their self-esteem. Could it be that Danny was different? Was it possible that he was a legitimate whistle-blower?

Julie decided that she didn't give a damn whether Danny phoned her again or not. He had already given her enough to start work on the book. She had researched those six names, and what she learned was that all six had at one time or another worked in Missing Persons for the Lexington Police Department. She also learned that none of the six men were still on active duty.

But that information, good as it was, left her asking a troubling question: How does Missing Persons tie in with a murder?

‸

Two men sat across from each other at a back table in McDonald's. A third man had been asked to join them, but he declined. The two men had known each other for decades, yet they weren't particularly good friends. Their shared past, more than their personalities, was what connected them. They were both in their mid-sixties, one was short and muscular, one was tall and badly overweight.

"We have a problem," the tall man said. "A big problem."

The shorter man shrugged, said, "Problems can be eliminated."

"You do know who I'm referring to, don't you?"

"I know."

"Seems he's suddenly developed a conscience."

"Shit happens."

"And?"

"And what?"

"How do we deal with this?"

"Fuck, man, I just told you. We eliminate the problem."

"How?"

"Let me think about it. I'll come up with something. I always do, don't I?"

"What about our absent friend?" the tall one asked. "Any idea what he might say?"

"What he always says: Do what needs to be done. And no fuck-ups."

The tall man shook his head, said, "God, I can't believe this is happening now. Not after all this time. Why can't the dead stay buried?"

"Worrying too much is a weakness," the short man said. "You do know that, don't you?"

"Maybe so, but if this gets out, you know what the outcome will be."

The short man stood and picked up his empty soft drink cup. "Trust me, nothing is going to get out," he said. "Know why I can say that with such confidence?"

"No. Why?"

"Because the dead can't speak."

CHAPTER EIGHT

Lawrence Brady barely glanced at the two pages before tossing them on his desk. A burly fellow in his late fifties, he wore an inexpensive blue suit, white shirt, and a striped tie. What remained of his hair was white, he had a bulbous nose lined with bluish veins, and a whiny voice that didn't match his beefy physique. To Dantzler, the man resembled a third-rate movie character actor. The town's chief villain. The only thing missing was a cigar in the corner of his mouth.

Peering over his glasses, Brady let his fingers dance across the paper on his desk like he was keeping beat with some music only he was hearing. "Yep, that's Dale's last will and testament, all right," he said. "Signed it right here in this office."

"Is that the most current one on record?"

"Far as I know it's the only one. I don't see any reason why there would be a more recent one somewhere. And if there is a second or later will, I had nothing to do with it."

"Were you still Larraby's attorney at the time of his death?"

"Sure was. Matter of fact, I spoke with him only three days before he killed himself. He sat in that very chair. Spent about half an hour with me."

"That was my next question," Dantzler said. "What was his reason for the meeting?"

"Nothing important. He just wanted to shoot the breeze for a while. Like I told you, he stayed for thirty minutes or so, and then he left."

"What was his demeanor?"

"How should I know that? I'm no psychiatrist, no mind reader. I can't get inside another person's head. He was just . . . hell, he was just same old Dale. That's about all I can tell you."

"What was 'same old Dale' like?" Dantzler asked.

"You worked with him. Hell, you knew him better than I did."

"Maybe so. But I want to hear what you have to say."

"Dale was a guy who didn't say much, and he seldom seemed particularly happy. If I had to choose one word to describe him, it would be glum."

"Did he appear to be more glum than usual during that last meeting?"

"No, he did not. And he gave no indication that he was planning to take his own life, if that's what you're wondering."

"What happens with the will now?"

"Not much, really. It's all pretty cut and dried. There's a legal process that has to be followed, probate and such, but when all that gets taken care of, Carole gets it all."

"Which is?"

"Well, the condo, which is paid off, and all the furniture and anything else inside the condo. Dale's car, if she wants it, although I can't imagine that she would, given that's where he blew his brains out. She gets money from his life insurance policy, his police pension, his Social Security, and whatever money he had in his savings account at Central Bank. In short, he set her up rather nicely. Not many men take such good care of an ex-wife."

"Did Larraby have any outside work that you know of?"

"Outside work? Such as?"

"Security, perhaps."

"Not that I'm aware of."

Dantzler removed a card from his shirt pocket and handed it to

Brady. Standing, he said, "If you think of anything else that could be important give me a call at either of those numbers."

"Can't think what that might be, but if I do, I will certainly get in touch with you." As the two men went into the reception area, Brady said, "You know, I've read about you for years, as a detective and as a tennis player. You're the closest thing to a celebrity this city has. Seems odd that we never met before today."

"Not really. I'd say we run in different circles."

"Yeah, you're probably right."

Dantzler shook Brady's hand, thanked him for taking time to meet, and then walked outside. It was now three-fifteen and the afternoon sun was bright and hot. There was no breeze to speak of, and the temperature had to be approaching ninety. Climbing into the Mercedes, he finished off the last drops from a water bottle he'd left in the holder. The water was warm but it hit the spot nonetheless. If you're thirsty enough water temperature is irrelevant.

He had just started the car when his cell phone buzzed. The caller was Sean Montgomery.

"What's up, Sean?"

"Not much. Where are you?"

"Just leaving Lawrence Brady's office."

"You feel the need to take a shower?"

"He wasn't that bad, Sean. Perspires more than normal, but other than that, he seemed okay. Maybe the scouting report on him isn't accurate."

"That would mean a whole lot of scouts are in the wrong."

"And that's not possible?"

"Not in this case. There are simply too many attorneys I know and trust who don't have a very high opinion of Lawrence Brady. Male and female attorneys. There's a reason why they call him 'Shady' Brady."

"Got a scoop for you, Sean: I don't give a crap. Unless something unexpected happens—and I doubt that it will—this was my one and only meeting with the guy. Therefore, I have no interest in that scouting report."

"Fair enough, Jack. Anyway, the reason I called was to ask if you wanted to meet at McCarthy's later this afternoon."

"That sounds good. But I might be later than usual. I'm going to give Charlie a call, see if he's at home. If he is I want to pay him a visit."

"To talk about what? Larraby?"

"Yeah."

"You're sure working that one harder than you should."

"Something about it troubles me, Sean. I've got an itch that needs to be scratched. Trouble is, I can't seem to locate the itch."

"It was a suicide, wasn't it?"

"That's the medical examiner's official ruling."

"You think he's wrong?"

"No, I don't. I'm convinced Dale Larraby took his own life."

"Then why the itch?"

"Wish I could answer that, Sean, but I can't. Not now, anyway."

"Maybe there is no answer."

"Maybe."

"Call me when you're leaving Charlie's and on your way to McCarthy's. A few pints of Guinness should serve as the perfect cure for that itch of yours."

Dantzler laughed, said, "Hope you're right, Sean. But I kinda doubt it. My itch tends to become a rash."

.-^-.

Less than a minute after Sean ended his call with Dantzler, Sean's cell phone buzzed. He picked up the phone, and when he saw who the call was from he gave serious thought to not answering. A call from this guy anytime was never good news. But Sean was a defense attorney—his attorney—and that carried with it certain obligations, even if they weren't pleasant or profitable.

"What can I do for you, Danny?" Sean asked. "Or, more specifically, what kind of trouble are you in this time?"

"I've been arrested, Mr. Montgomery. And this time I'm innocent. Swear on my mother's grave that I didn't do nothing."

Danny, you haven't been innocent since you were about eight years old. "Slow down, Danny," Sean ordered. "Give me the details, beginning with where you are."

"Jail. That's where you go when you get arrested," Danny said, sounding like a teacher addressing an ignoramus. "I'm in jail. And you gotta get me out of here. Fast. I won't last two days behind bars. I'm a little guy. There are giants in this place."

"What's the charge?"

"Possession and distribution of a controlled substance. Total bullshit. I don't have nothing to do with drugs. Never have, never will. You gotta get me out of here. Please."

"Let me look into it, Danny, see what I can find out. If I can get you released on bail, will you be able to come up with the money?"

Sean knew the answer to that question before asking it—no. Danny never had money for bail. That meant one thing: If the past truly is prologue, then Danny's bail money would come straight out of Sean's pocket.

"Well, I can try," Danny stuttered. "But . . . I might need some help from someone."

That would be me, Danny. "You sit tight, Danny," Sean said. "And you do remember rule number one, don't you?"

"Don't talk to nobody."

"That's right. You stay as silent as Harpo Marx."

"Who the hell is that?"

"Don't worry about it. I'll sniff around, see what the deal is. When I find out I'll come see you. Until I do, you keep that mouth of yours closed tight. Got it?"

"Got it. But please, Mr. Montgomery, get me out of this place."

"Just hang tight, Danny. I'll do what I can."

CHAPTER NINE

No Lexington police officer, past or present, was more beloved or more revered than Charlie Bolton. The man was a legend. Now in his early eighties and long retired, he still commanded respect—and even a certain awe—from those on the force now, or those who worked with him in the long ago past. When he paid a visit to the police station he was treated like royalty, which, in the eyes of virtually everyone, he was. If he entered a room where everyone was sitting, they all came to their feet. Protocol dictated that they stand. It's impolite to remain seated when a god walks into a room.

Charlie had mentored dozens of young police officers, including Dantzler. It was Charlie who first recognized Dantzler's gift for police work, the first to see a young cop whose talent and potential was unlimited. Charlie took Dantzler under his wing, not so much as a teacher, but rather as a guide whose mission was to help his pupil sharpen those incredible instincts that came naturally to him. Charlie was the one who went to then Police Commissioner Robert Vincent and persuaded him to bump Dantzler up to the Homicide Unit. No one, not even the top dog, could deny a request from Charlie Bolton.

At age twenty-three, Jack Dantzler was handed his gold shield.

Knowing Charlie spent as much time on the lake fishing as he did at home, Dantzler phoned to be sure he wouldn't make the trip for nothing. He was in luck; Charlie was sitting in his living room when Dantzler phoned.

"Not going to the lake until sometime next week," Charlie said. "Come pay an old man a visit. I'd love to see you."

"I'm on my way," Dantzler said.

Charlie lived in a nice three bedroom, two bathroom brick house in the Palomar Estates subdivision. He was standing on the porch when Dantzler pulled into the driveway and parked behind an old red pickup truck. When Dantzler got out of his car he could hear Charlie whistling.

"That's a fine piece of German machinery you're driving, lad," Charlie said. "Detectives must be getting bigger paychecks than I got when I was still on the force. I couldn't afford that baby under any circumstances, then or now. What did it set you back? Hundred grand?"

"Not even close."

"Well, it's a beauty."

"Stand here and admire it all you want, Charlie. I'm going inside where it's cool."

"Sounds like a grand idea."

The two men went into the house, through the den and into the kitchen. Dantzler took a seat at the table, while Charlie opened the refrigerator. "Want a cold beer?" he asked. "I have Anchor Steam and Bud Lite. Don't have any of that damn Guinness you love so much. Sorry."

"I'll pass on the beer."

"Suit yourself. I'm having one." Charlie opened the beer, took a long pull, then sat across from Dantzler. "Word is, you're really worked up about this Larraby thing."

"How did you hear about that so fast?"

Charlie grinned but didn't answer.

"Who's your Deep Throat in that place, Charlie? That damn Rawlinson?"

"Jack, when are you going to learn that I know everything that happens in the police department? I have more sources than Woodward and Bernstein ever had. Nothing gets past me." Charlie took another sip of beer. "Let's talk about Larraby. Why the bug up your ass concerning him? The fool took his own life. Let it be."

"Why? That's my question. Never in a million years would I have thought him capable of putting a gun under his chin and pulling the trigger. But he did. And I'd like to know why."

"What difference does it make, Jack? It's not a homicide, so there's no reason for you to let your nuts get all twisted into a painful knot. Drop it and move on. That's my advice."

Charlie finished his beer, stood, tossed the empty bottle into a trash can, and opened the refrigerator. "Sure you don't want a beer?" he said. "There's plenty in here. I'm having another one."

Dantzler shook his head. "You knew Larraby from the first day he became a cop. Did you see him as someone capable of blowing his brain out?"

"Jack, if there is one thing I learned during my years as a police officer it's that everyone is capable of doing just about anything at any given time. We all possess elements of both saint and sinner. More often than not, circumstances dictate which side claims the top spot. For whatever reason, for who knows what circumstances, at that precise moment in Larraby's life, the sinner in him seized control. Bang! Off came the top of his head. And to answer your question, no, I'm not surprised that he chose to go out that way.

"Dale Larraby was never what you'd call a happy or contented man," he continued. "There was that giant chip on his shoulder, which made him angry, hostile. The man was a terrible cop, and he was from the first day he put on a uniform. He never should have been a cop. Never. He only became one because his uncle was one of Bob Vincent's close pals. Larraby had been on the job two months when I went to see Bob. I told him Larraby was not cut out to be in law enforcement. Know what Bob did? Put me in charge of teaching Larraby the ropes. As if that were possible. The man was hopeless. Not because he couldn't do the job, but because he refused to put forth serious effort. How the man stayed on long enough to retire is a mystery that is beyond my ability to solve."

"Want to hear a mystery that I can't begin to solve?" Dantzler said.

"Sure."

"I spoke with his ex, Carole, the other day. She said Larraby admired me."

"That doesn't surprise me, Jack. You're a great detective. Anyone can see that, even your enemies. I'm certainly no shrink, but I would venture a guess that Larraby's admiration for you was wrapped inside an equal amount of envy."

"Don't sell yourself short, Charlie. You're as much a shrink as Bloom is."

Charlie said, "Speaking of Carole. How is she doing?"

"Seems to be doing really well. Both Carole and her daughter. I read Larraby's will—he left everything to Carole."

"Well, at least he did one good deed in his miserable life."

Dantzler stood. "I need to hit the road, grab a bite to eat. Thanks for the talk."

"Anytime. You know that. My door is always open for you."

"Good luck with the fishing next week."

"Better to wish the fish good luck. Me, I don't need it."

"You've become arrogant in your old age, Charlie."

"Better late than never, I say." Charlie pointed at the door. "Can you see yourself out, Jack? These old bones are tired and creaky."

"See you, Charlie. And stay in touch."

On the way to his car Dantzler's cell phone went off. He figured the call was from Sean but he was wrong. The caller was Bruce Rawlinson.

"What's going on, Bruce?" he asked, not sure he wanted to hear the answer.

"Ace, there's a lady here says she needs to speak with you," Rawlinson answered. "Says it's kind of important."

"Is Eric or Jake around?"

"Jake is, Eric isn't."

"Can't she speak with Jake?"

"She didn't want to. She's adamant about meeting with you."

"Okay. Put her in my office and tell her I'm on my way. It might be thirty minutes before I get there, so make sure she's comfortable. Get her something to drink. Something to eat if she's hungry. I'll be there as soon as I can."

"You got it, Ace."

Dantzler got in the Mercedes and started it up. Backing out of the driveway, he wondered who the woman was, and what was her reason for wanting to speak with him? He didn't have any answers, but he did have the strange feeling it had something to do with that itch he needed to scratch.

CHAPTER TEN

The woman waiting in Dantzler's office was small, thin, pale, and well into her senior citizen years. She wore a plain yellow dress, what looked like some type of orthopedic shoes, and no makeup. A gold cross hung suspended from her neck, she had a wedding band on her left hand, and her hair was whiter than freshly picked cotton. For a woman her age she had excellent bone structure. When young, Dantzler concluded, she had been a beautiful woman.

In her right hand she held a water bottle, which she placed on the floor next to a small brown purse when Dantzler arrived. Upon seeing him she sat up straighter but made no effort to get out of the chair.

Dantzler stood above her and extended his right hand. "I'm Detective Jack Dantzler," he said.

Shaking his hand, she introduced herself as Mary Farmer.

"I apologize for being late, Miss Farmer . . ."

"Please, call me Mary. Miss makes me sound so old, which, of course, I am. Seventy-seven, to be exact. But I have been blessed with good health, so for an old biddy I have no complaints."

As Mary spoke she continually knotted and unknotted her thin fingers. She was, Dantzler could tell, extremely nervous. He wondered if that was because of what she had come to tell him, or because she was sitting in a police station. Perhaps it was a little of both, he decided.

"Again, I do apologize, Mary," he repeated. "I was across town when I got word that you were here."

"No, no, I'm the one who should apologize, dropping in like this so late in the day. And without first making an appointment. That was very discourteous on my part."

"I see that you've got some water; did anyone offer to get you coffee, a soft drink, maybe a snack?"

"Yes, Officer Rawlinson was very kind and very helpful. He offered me something to eat but I declined. He's a very nice man."

"Bruce is a saint," Dantzler said, suppressing a chuckle. "Now, Mary, what was it you needed to speak to me about?"

She clasped her hands together, shifted in the chair, and let out a deep sigh. "I can't believe I'm so nervous," she finally managed to say. "I'm shaking like I just stepped out of an icy river. I'm usually not like this."

"No need to be nervous, Mary. You're among friends. Just relax and take your time. I'm not going anywhere."

Mary hesitated for a few moments and looked away. Dantzler could see the tears filling her eyes. She picked her purse up from the floor, opened it, and took out a tissue. After setting the purse back down she wiped the tears away.

"My brother, Father Declan Riley, passed away ten days ago," Mary said.

"I'm very sorry for you loss," Dantzler said, still uncertain why this woman was in his office. If it had something to do with a man named Declan Riley, then that was even more confusing. As far as he knew he had never met or heard of the man. "Losing a family member at any age is never easy."

"Declan was a wonderful man, kind, generous, loving. He served God and the Catholic Church for more than sixty years. Everyone loved and respected him, from the older folks down to the youngest children. And he loved them all . . . he had so much love to give."

She hesitated as a second wave of tears began to fall. Taking a new tissue, she wiped them away, looked at Dantzler, and offered a sad smile.

"Declan was my big hero," she continued in a halting voice. "Always had been, always will be. There were four kids in our family and Declan was the oldest. He was nine years older than me. I was the youngest. Our mother died when I was five. Declan practically raised me. I mean, he helped raise all of the younger ones, but I was the youngest so I needed more attention. Our father was a good man but he had a love affair with alcohol. There were times, long stretches of time, when he was in no condition to do much of anything. There were many days when he couldn't function at all. Had it not been for Declan, and help from the church, I don't know what might have become of us. I shudder to think about that. But thanks to Declan we stayed together as a family."

She shifted again in the chair and took a sip of water before going on with her story. After carefully putting the water bottle back on the floor, she said, "Two years ago Declan was diagnosed with lung cancer. I felt God had played a very cruel joke on my brother, allowing him to have cancer in the lungs. You see, Declan never smoked a cigarette in his life. Not one. I understand anyone can contract cancer anywhere in the body, but when it occurs in the lungs, that poor individual is almost always a heavy smoker. Declan wasn't, so that caused me to get a little angry with Our Heavenly Father."

Dantzler listened patiently, still perplexed, wondering why he was hearing this sad tale about a man he didn't know being told to him by a woman he'd never seen in his life. At some point, he felt, there had to be a punch line. Or at least he hoped there was.

Mary forged ahead, saying, "Declan had surgery, losing part of a lung. Then he had chemo and radiation. Dreadful things to go through, almost worse than the cancer itself, if you want my opinion. Thankfully, those treatments worked; he was declared cancer free. That lasted for almost a year. Then about six months ago he learned that the cancer had returned, and that it was in his pancreas and his liver. Nothing could be done; this time it was terminal."

That last memory caused another wave of tears to leak down her cheeks. Once again a new tissue was called into action.

"The end for Declan came pretty fast," Mary said. "Which I suppose was a blessing. At least he didn't suffer too long. Anyway, I was with him during his final moments, the only one in the room at the time. Of course, by then he was heavily doped up and very much out of it. Occasionally, he would mumble something but it was incoherent and made no sense. Who knows what thoughts go through a person's mind when the brain is shutting down? What old memories and pictures might come flooding past for the final time? I suppose only God can answer that question."

This time Mary smiled, and said, "In case you're wondering, I made my peace with God. I forgave him for allowing Declan to get lung cancer. It's not wise to hold a grudge against God, is it, Detective?"

"No, I wouldn't think so," Dantzler answered. *What the hell else could he say?*

"Declan was lying there, eyes closed, his breathing becoming more and more labored. I knew the end was near. I got on my cell phone and called other family members, telling them they needed to get back to the hospital pronto. And to bring a priest, although Declan had already been given his last rites. Anyway, I had just glanced at the clock—it was two-twenty a.m.—when it happened. It was the strangest thing I have ever witnessed in my life. Simply bizarre. Declan opened his eyes and looked straight at me. It was the same way he'd looked at me a million times in the past. Then in a voice as loud and as clear as if he were giving one of his sermons, he said something that at the time made no sense to me."

She paused, almost dramatically, prompting Dantzler to ask the question, "What did he say?"

"He said, 'Dale Larraby knows.'"

With that startling revelation Dantzler's interest in Mary's sad tale shot up about 50 notches. He wasn't sure why, or even if the information was worth added interest, but there it was. Alongside his sudden interest were a couple of questions: What was Larraby's connection to a priest, and was Larraby a Catholic?

"You're positive that's what your brother said?" Dantzler asked.

"Absolutely. Like I said, he spoke in a voice that was perfectly clear.

Those were the last words he uttered. His heart gave out about twenty minutes later."

She reached into her purse and took out a newspaper clipping. Turning it around so Dantzler could see it, she pointed at a particular article. Dantzler knew which one she was indicating—the article concerning Larraby's death.

Mary said, "I didn't think anything about it at the time, other than the strangeness of the moment. What with Declan snapping out of his coma just long enough to speak those three words. But when I read this article it got me thinking that maybe I should share this information with someone. My sister suggested that I tell you. What do you make of it, Detective Dantzler?"

That was a very good question, one Dantzler couldn't begin to answer. What he did know was that he was intrigued. "Do you think your brother knew Dale Larraby?" he said. "Did you know him?"

"No, I didn't know the man. Whether or not my brother did is impossible for me to say. But Declan was a priest, so perhaps he knew him in that capacity. I really don't know."

Dantzler reached deep into his memory bank trying to recall if Larraby was a Catholic but no answer popped up. He and Larraby weren't close, so an exchange of personal information never took place. That was never going to happen. Information outside of work-related stuff simply wasn't part of their relationship. Therefore, Dantzler had no idea what religion—if any—Larraby belonged to.

Dantzler's attention was brought back to the present when he heard Mary's voice, which seemed miles away, say, "I hope I didn't waste your time by bringing this news to you, Detective. I just felt that you ought to know about it."

"You didn't waste my time, Mary. Not in the least. I don't know what this means—and it may not mean anything—but you were right to share it with me. I appreciate it."

"That's a big load off my mind." Mary leaned over, picked up her purse and the water bottle, and stood. "I have kept you long enough, Detective. And I've given you all I know. So unless you have more questions, I'll take off."

Dantzler stood, said, "No more questions for now. However, I do need to get some contact information from you in case I need to speak with you again."

"I gave my phone number to that nice Officer Rawlinson. Do I need to write it down for you as well?"

Dantzler shook his head. "I'll get it from Bruce." He walked her out of the office and down the stairs. At the front door, he said, "Thanks for coming in, Mary. And again, I'm truly sorry about your brother."

She thanked him, turned, and quickly walked away as another round of tears began to collect in her sad eyes.

Trudging back up the stairs, head down, Dantzler was lost in thought. What to make of this? he wondered. Was it nothing more than a dying man's wild ramblings, or was it something more? A dying man's last confession, perhaps?

Larraby and a priest. A priest and Dale Larraby.

Talk about a pairing that baffled the mind.

CHAPTER ELEVEN

As Dantzler was listening to Mary Farmer's story Julie Bradley was checking into the Embassy Suites on Newtown Pike. It was a little past six in the afternoon when she arrived and she was beat. Sleep-deprived, more than anything. The past two nights she had barely slept at all. Too much energy, too many things on her mind to allow for slumber.

Although there was no shortage of excellent hotels to choose from, she went with Embassy Suites for two main reasons: the hotel was located just off the interstate, and it was an easy commute to downtown Lexington. Plus, she had stayed there in the past so she knew what she was getting for her money.

Prior to checking in she went to a McDonald's across the road, bought a Big Mac, large fries, and a Coke. Once in her room, she set the sack of food and her laptop on a table, then spent the next ten minutes unpacking two suitcases filled with clothes. When that chore was taken care of she fired up the computer, bit heartily into the Big Mac, gobbled up a handful of fries, and washed it all down with a big drink of Coke.

Ten minutes later, her stomach filled with greasy—and tasty—fast food, she punched a few keys and her computer screen popped to life.

Next, she clicked on the icon she'd named Danny's Notes. Staring at what she had written was a reminder that she didn't have very much. Bare bones stuff and little else. She desperately needed to hear from Danny Michaels, to learn more from him. But in her gut she didn't think that was going to happen. Danny wasn't going to call. Had she been played? she repeatedly asked herself. Was Danny nothing more than the con man Darvis warned her about? Was he really just a bullshit artist? Was he trying to work some weird angle?

No. Julie didn't believe any of that. She was convinced Danny Michaels had a story to tell, and the story would lead to something big. She felt this at the very core of her deepest soul. But . . . if that were true then why hadn't he followed up like he promised to do? Why had he suddenly dropped off the grid?

No way to answer that, she decided. And I can't sit around waiting for something that may never happen. I have to put my fate in my own hands.

A successful reporter, like a good military commander, always has more than a single battle plan ready to be put into action. Neither commander nor reporter can succeed without contingencies in place. Any plan can be thwarted or go astray, regardless of how well conceived it might be. No one can know with absolute certainty how any situation will unfold. Shit, especially unexpected shit, happens all the time. When it does, if you don't have a back-up plan you're doomed to failure.

Always thinking ahead, Julie had prepared for just such an emergency. While waiting to hear from Danny she had done plenty of digging on those six names he had provided. And to a certain extent her efforts had been rewarded—she did manage to come up with addresses for each man. And if those addresses were still current, all six men resided in Lexington. And if they did, that should make life a lot simpler for her.

Getting addresses was easy; getting phone numbers, however, wasn't so simple. Not in today's world. Modern technology has rendered many things obsolete, and at the top of the list was the phone book. Nowadays, everyone had a cell phone, and rarely are cell numbers listed in a phone book. Yellow pages still existed to a certain extent, but white pages were heading in the same direction as manual typewriters.

During her research she only managed to come up with a phone number for one of the men—Sean Montgomery. According to what she learned on-line he was an attorney actively practicing in Lexington. And like most professionals, he had his own website, which included his contact information. Phone number, business address, photos, etc.

None of the other five men on the list had a website, nor were any of them on Facebook, Twitter, or Instagram. No surprise there. Not many men in their age bracket were involved with social media.

Julie thought about calling Sean Montgomery first thing tomorrow morning. Doing so was really her best option; after all, his was the only number she had. But she was a creature of habit, and as such she had a particular way of doing things. Her plan: she would try to contact the men in alphabetical order:

Eddie Campbell

Dale Larraby

Sean Montgomery

James Newman

Mike Perkins

Alex Shannon

No phones, no problem, she said to herself as she studied the list of names. I have an address for each of you, and if that's all I've got, I'll have to make do. I've faced tougher challenges in the past, and I have always come out on top. This time will be no different. I've spent enough time in Lexington to know my way around, which means it shouldn't be all that difficult to find each man's place of residence. And if I do get lost, well, that's what the GPS is for.

A cold chill suddenly ran through Julie's body. She was excited, pumped. A new adventure was ready to begin, one she hoped would be even more rewarding than the previous two had been. As for Danny Michaels, if he called, great, if he didn't, then to hell with him. She didn't need his help.

She had no qualms about flying solo.

_^_

Dantzler was still sitting at his desk an hour after Mary Farmer had departed. He had a stack of long-neglected paperwork that needed to be completed and this seemed as good a time as any to get it done. It was tedious, boring work but it went with the job. Better to get it out of the way now rather than sit around and watch the stack of papers continue to pile up. Anyway, meeting Sean Montgomery at McCarthy's was out. Sean phoned earlier to say he had to meet with a client, and that he wasn't sure how long the meeting might last. The Guinness would have to wait.

Dantzler picked up a piece of paper from the stack, quickly read through it, scribbled his name at the bottom, and placed it in the Out basket on his desk. Now the damn thing was someone else's worry. Good riddance.

Had Dantzler been focused, getting through the paperwork would have been a snap. Fifteen minutes, twenty, tops. But he hadn't been focused. His thoughts kept drifting back to his talk with Mary Farmer. Or, more specifically, to her story's three-word punch line.

Dale Larraby knows.

What the hell did that mean? What did Larraby know?

"You're working late, Ace."

Dantzler heard the words, unsure at first if he was thinking them out loud or if someone had actually spoken to him. It wasn't until he looked up and saw Bruce Rawlinson standing in the doorway that he had his answer.

"Just trying to knock out some of this damn paperwork," Dantzler said. "What about you, Bruce? Why are you still here?"

"I've been downstairs shooting the breeze with a couple of guys." Bruce came in and sat in the chair across from Dantzler's desk. "How did your talk with Mrs. Farmer go?"

"It was interesting. And thanks for taking such good care of her. She said you are a kind man. I told her you're a saint."

"Well, Blessed Holy Mother, you have finally recognized the truth. Hallelujah."

"Don't get ahead of yourself, Bruce. I had my fingers crossed when I said it."

"Makes no difference, Ace. Truth is truth. Your damn fingers don't have anything to do with it."

"Since you're conversing with the Blessed Holy Mother, am I correct in assuming that you are Catholic?"

"Yeah, but not a very good one, sad to say. And that's another truth."

"Was Larraby a Catholic?"

"I never knew it if he was. I don't attend Mass on a regular basis, but when I have I've never seen him there. That doesn't mean he wasn't Catholic. He could have attended a different church. Why do you want to know if he was Catholic?"

Dantzler ignored the question, said, "Are you familiar with a priest named Declan Riley?"

"No. Should I be?"

"Probably not. Just inquiring."

"Who was he?"

"Mary Farmer's brother. He died a week or so ago. Apparently, he had some connection to Larraby."

"That would make sense if Larraby was Catholic."

Dantzler picked up his cell phone, scanned through a list of names, then punched in the proper digits. The call was answered after several rings.

"Detective Dantzler, what can I do for you?" Carole Perkins asked.

"One question, Carole. Was Dale Catholic by any chance?"

"Catholic? No. Dale was raised a Baptist, same as me. But I don't recall him ever attending church. He certainly didn't while we were together. Why do you ask?"

"A priest passed away recently, and the last words he ever said were 'Dale Larraby knows.' His name was Declan Riley. Does that ring a bell with you?"

"Never heard of a Declan Riley," Carole said. "And his dying words were 'Dale Larraby knows'? That's beyond spooky."

"It's definitely intriguing." Changing the subject, Dantzler said, "I spoke with Lawrence Brady about the will. He's going to get in touch with you and fill you in on how the legal process works. He doesn't anticipate any problems. However, if you do have questions about the will, or about him, give me a call. Seems Brady doesn't have a sterling reputation within the legal community. If he gives you grief in any way, let me know and I'll put you in touch with an attorney I trust."

"I will. And thanks for everything, Detective Dantzler."

When Dantzler ended the call and looked up, Bruce was staring at him. "Is that true what you told her, Ace?" he asked. "That a priest's last words were about Dale Larraby?"

Dantzler nodded.

"Shit, man, that's spooky," Bruce said, shaking his head.

"Spooky. That's the same word Mary used."

"What do you make of it, Ace?"

"I don't know, Bruce. But I intend to find out."

CHAPTER TWELVE

S ean Montgomery's meeting was with Danny Michaels at the Fayette County Detention Center on Old Frankfort Pike. Danny was sitting at a table in an open area when Sean showed up. Sean looked at Danny, shook his head, and sat down across from him.

"Danny, Danny, Danny . . . what have you gotten yourself into this time?"

Danny lowered his head and didn't respond. Sean thought he saw tears in Danny's eyes.

Danny Michaels was a wisp of a man, barely five-foot-two ("same as Charlie Manson" he proudly boasted to anyone questioning his size), had a head of curly brown hair, and maybe weighed one-twenty if fully clothed and the clothes were soaking wet. He was twenty-eight but looked younger. Despite never getting past the seventh grade he had learned and absorbed every lesson available on the streets. When it came to street-smarts, Danny had a Ph.D.

Sean liked Danny and made no bones about it. In a strange way he even admired the guy. Danny never knew his father, and his mother, a drug addict, was sixteen when Danny was born. She died from a heroin overdose three years later. An aunt took Danny in but that situation was doomed from the start. After that, Child Services got involved. That also proved to be a disaster. Eventually, Danny was lost to the streets, just one more poor soul discarded and forgotten by his fellow citizens. Yet somehow, almost miraculously, despite enormous odds he had survived.

Danny was a petty thief and a hustler. But he wasn't violent, and he never did drugs, not even pot. Nor did he partake of alcohol. That made him different from about ninety-nine percent of those people living in conditions similar to his. Another thing that made him different was his personality. With his quick wit and a killer smile he was a genuinely likeable dude.

"You gotta get me out of here, Mr. Montgomery," Danny pleaded, even before Sean had settled into his chair. Danny was a fidgety, nervous guy, never sitting still, always shifting and moving, almost as if he was wired to a hidden electrical circuit somewhere. Nodding his head but not pointing, he said, "Take a look at that brother over there."

Sean shifted in his seat, glanced at the man sitting several tables away, turned back toward Danny, and said, "Okay, I saw him. So what?"

"So what? He's got to be six-six and go three-hundred pounds, that's what. I'm just five-two—same as Charlie Manson—which makes me a dwarf compared to that monster. I saw him looking at me this morning. Looked at me hard, like he wanted to have me for lunch."

"That's not gonna happen, Danny."

"You can't say that. No way do you have a clue what goes on in this joint."

"Let's worry about him later, okay? Right now, here's what's gonna happen. I'm going to lay out for you what the D.A. has. Then I want to hear your side of the story. After that, I'll tell you how we're going to proceed. You good with that?"

"I'm good with anything so long as you get me out of here."

"Given what they've got you for, that may not happen."

"Please, don't say that. I can't survive in prison."

"According to the arrest report, you sold two bottles of Ritalin pills to a kid up in Woodland Park. Is that true?"

"Yes."

"What'd you get for them?"

"Thirty bucks."

"You've never done a drug in your life, Danny. What were you thinking?"

"That I was hungry and needed money for food."

"Where did you get the Ritalin?"

"From a friend of mine."

"She give them to you, or did you swipe them?"

"They were in her medicine cabinet, so I kinda took them."

"Ritalin is a CDS, a controlled dangerous substances. It's a Schedule II narcotic. That thirty-dollar sale could cost you anywhere from one-thousand to ten-thousand dollars in fines, and up to ten years in prison."

"Oh, God, I'll kill myself if that happens."

"No, you're not going to kill yourself, Danny. Don't even think that."

"Can't you talk with the D.A., let him know this is my first offense, and that I'm truly sorry for what I did? That it was a mistake, and that I won't let it happen again?"

"This isn't your first offense, Danny."

"With drugs, it is."

"Okay, Danny, here's where we stand. I have good news and bad news for you. The good news is this place is overcrowded right now, which means they are going to kick you loose in about an hour. The assistant district attorney is a friend of mine, and she has agreed to in-house arrest. You will have to wear an ankle bracelet but you'll be at home. Understand, Danny, that my ass is on the line here. I've vouched for you. If you rabbit on me I'll help put you away rather than try to save your ass. We clear on that?"

"You can trust me, Mr. Montgomery. I'll do exactly what they tell me to do."

"Good. Now for the bad news. Unless you are willing to accept a plea she's going to take this thing to trial. If that happens I don't see how the outcome can be anything but a bad one."

"What kind of a plea?"

"I don't know. We haven't discussed that."

"It was just a thirty-dollar sale. And that kid was begging for the stuff. He'd have paid a hundred smackers if I had asked for it. Why does the D.A. have such a hard-on to send my ass to prison for ten years?"

"Bad luck, Danny. The kid you sold the Ritalin to shared it with three of his friends. One of those friends, a sixteen-year-old girl, had a serious allergic reaction. Convulsions, to be precise. They had to take her to the ER, and from what the D.A. told me it was touch and go for a while. Thankfully, she did pull through. If she hadn't you'd be looking at a far more serious charge. But here's where your bad luck really comes into play. The girl's father is a deputy sheriff. If it were left up to him he'd probably shoot you. However, since he can't take that action he's determined to press charges to the fullest extent possible."

"I ain't taking a plea, Mr. Montgomery. No way."

"Haven't you been listening to me, Danny? This isn't winnable in a court of law. That's not a road you want to travel. Trust me on that."

Danny thought for a few moments, then said, "Tell your lady D.A. friend that I want to make a deal."

"What kind of a deal?"

"A straight-up trade."

"What does that mean?"

"I give her information about a crime, she drops all charges against me."

"What crime? What are you talking about, Danny?"

"I ain't saying no more, not even to you, Mr. Montgomery. You just tell her I've got something really interesting that she'd love to hear. Tell her to come see me."

"It doesn't work that way, Danny. If you want a deal, if you have information to share, you need to tell me what it is, and then I take it to the D.A. Otherwise, if I walk in and say you want a deal but have nothing of substance to offer, she'll laugh me out of her office."

"A murder. One that would blow this town wide open."

"Whose murder? And when?"

"I ain't coughing up no more details until that lady friend of yours signs that piece of paper saying all charges have been dropped."

"You've got it backwards, Danny. She's not gonna sign anything until she hears what you have to say. And giving her information is not going to be enough. It's gotta be corroborated."

Danny stood. "You go see your lady friend. Tell her if she passes on this she's allowing a murderer to continue walking the streets of Lexington. More than one murderer, if you want the whole truth. Ask her which is more important, putting away a bunch of killers or a guy who made thirty lousy bucks selling two bottles of pills to some snot-nose rich kid. Way I see it, that's an easy call."

As Danny began walking away, Sean stood, crammed some papers into his leather bag, and thought about what he'd just been told. Danny Michaels was a hustler and a con man but he wasn't a liar. At least, he'd never lied to Sean in the past. Sean felt that had to count for something. Like giving him the benefit of doubt. But Danny's story was pretty far out there. And the timing made it somewhat suspect. A shrimp like Danny facing ten years in prison might come up with some very creative thinking in an effort to avoid serving serious prison time. Even to the point of concocting a wild story about a murder.

But . . .

Danny lived in a shabby three-room apartment but he existed on the street, a world unto itself, a place where plenty of information gets passed around on a daily basis. Maybe Danny knew what he was talking about. Maybe he'd heard something that was actually true. Maybe his preposterous tale wasn't so preposterous after all.

Maybe . . .

CHAPTER THIRTEEN

When Julie Bradley's alarm went off at six-thirty a.m., she reached over and turned the damn thing off. Three hours in the sack, which was all she'd had, simply wasn't enough. A few more minutes, she mumbled, maybe another hour, and then she would be ready to face the day. Closing her eyes, tugging at the covers, she immediately went back to sleep.

She finally climbed out of bed three hours later, still tired, groggy, and feeling more than a little grumpy. By eleven she had showered, dressed, and scarfed down the remaining cold fries from last night's dinner. Fifteen minutes later, standing in front of the big mirror, staring at her own face, all she could see were dark circles and bags under her green eyes. She sighed, picked up her laptop, and walked out the door.

Time to begin the hunt.

First on her list of men to speak with was Eddie Campbell. Finding his house turned out to be easy. He lived on Heather Way, in a small white wooden house that sat between two larger brick homes. There was a tiny front yard, a porch with a swing on it, and a covered parking space. A blue Dodge Caravan was parked there. If the station wagon was in its spot, Julie reasoned, that probably meant Eddie Campbell was at home.

As she walked toward the house she noticed there were two avenues onto the porch—wooden steps and a metal ramp. Access for an individual confined to a wheelchair was her first thought when she saw the ramp. Was Eddie handicapped, or was it his wife? Was Eddie married or single? She would get answers to those questions when Eddie or his wife opened the door.

Julie rang the doorbell, stepped back, and waited. Hearing nothing coming from inside, she repeated the process a second time. Again, she heard nothing. Opening the storm door, she knocked hard on the front door. Nothing but silence. Moving to her right, she peered in through a front window. The place was dark, save for a sliver of light coming from a back room off to the left. Obviously, no one was home.

Standing there, Julie thought about what she should do. She had three options—stick around until someone showed up, leave a note with her name and phone number, or take off and come back later. Waiting was ridiculous, she reasoned, because there was no way to know when someone might return home. Could be in thirty minutes, could be in five hours. Such uncertainty about when someone might show up was also why she wasn't inclined to come back at a later time. She had no guarantee that anyone would be here when she did make a return trip. That left but a single option—leave a note.

She was on the way back to her car to get pencil and paper when she heard a voice coming from her left. The speaker, a black woman dressed in coveralls and wearing a straw hat, was standing in her front yard holding a potted plant in her gloved hands. After placing the plant on a porch railing, she removed her gloves and walked slowly in Julie's direction.

"Missy, are you looking for Eddie?" she said.

"Yes, ma'am, I am."

"He's not at home. Someone came by to pick him up. That was about an hour ago."

"Any idea how long he might be gone?"

"Can't say. Depends on how long the funeral lasts, I suppose. Well, it's not really a funeral. More like a memorial service. That's what

Eddie told me, anyway. Said his friend has already been cremated. That cremation nonsense sure isn't for me, that much I can tell you. Bury me when I'm dead. Don't fry me."

"Was it someone close to Eddie?" Julie asked.

"I don't know if they were close or not. What I do know is they worked together."

"Eddie was a cop, wasn't he?"

"Sure was. Might still be one if he hadn't had that horrible automobile accident. Broke his back. Put him in that wheelchair."

"How long ago was that?"

"Well, when we moved here seven years ago Eddie was already crippled. So, it must've happened eight, nine years ago, at least."

"Eddie's friend, the one who died? Know his name by any chance?"

"Oh, Missy, let me study on that for a while. Eddie told me, but my memory ain't what it once was. Uh, I am so sorry, Missy. His name is on the tip of my tongue, but I can't remember it for the life of me."

Julie said, "There's no need for an apology, Miss . . .?"

"Ella Brown."

"Miss Brown, if I leave my name and phone number with you, will you see that Eddie gets it?"

"I suppose I can do that. Mind telling me why you need to speak with him?"

"I'm doing research for a book I plan to write. I need to interview him."

"You're a book writer?"

"Yes, ma'am, I am." Julie wrote down her name and phone number. Handing the paper to Ella, she said, "Ask him to contact me as soon as he can. It's important that I meet with him."

"I'll see that he gets this, Missy. But I can't promise that he'll get back in touch with you. Eddie's not exactly the chatty type."

Chatty type or not, Julie said to herself as she drove away, I have to talk to the man.

I *will* talk to the man.

⌃

Marianne Ramsey, an assistant district attorney, wore a look trapped somewhere between bemused and incredulous after listening to Sean deliver Danny Michaels's offer to make a deal. Sitting behind her huge oak desk, Marianne twirled an expensive ink pen in her fingers and stared across at Sean.

"Can I safely assume that Danny Michaels is a total imbecile?" she asked. "Or is he just plain stupid?"

"Danny's not stupid," countered Sean. "And he's no imbecile. In his own way he's a fairly intelligent guy."

"Not when it comes to matters of law," Marianne snapped. She placed the pen on her desk and leaned forward. "He's not really serious about this, is he, Sean?"

"My impression is that he's deadly serious."

"Did you enlighten him as to how such a process works? That he has to give me more—plenty more—than what he told you?"

"I did."

"And?"

"He wants to meet with you."

"About a murder, right?"

"That's what he said."

"No name, no location, no time frame, nothing? Right?"

Sean nodded.

Marianne leaned back in her chair, picked up the pen, and began the twirling action again. Following almost a minute of silence, she said, "You know what you have to do, Sean. You need to convince Danny that he has to give you more details—and they'd better be solid details—if he wants me to hear what he has to say. I'm not about to go waltzing blindly into the unknown. I don't have time for fruitless excursions. Being played for a sucker is not listed among my job duties."

"I'll see what I can do," Sean said, getting out of his chair. "But I have to tell you, Marianne. I think Danny is telling the truth. I do think he knows something."

"Sean, baby, you know I love you. I also trust your instincts. But I need more to work with. Make him understand that. Otherwise, there'll be no conversation."

_‿^‿_

As dusk was quickly giving way to night Julie sat in a small Mexican restaurant and thought about her first day of real investigative work. It had not gone well. In fact, it had been a dismal failure. She had come up with nothing at all, not a single thing that made her more informed today than she was yesterday.

The day was a dud.

After leaving Eddie Campbell's place she went to the homes of James Newman, Mike Perkins, and Alex Shannon. None of the men were home. Since she did have a number for Sean Montgomery's office, she phoned him there. Sean's receptionist informed her that he was out of town and wouldn't be back until Thursday morning. Two days away.

Julie paid her bill and walked out to her car. As she settled in behind the steering wheel an uneasy feeling ran through her bones. Mostly, her thoughts kept drifting back to Danny Michaels. Was she being played? she asked herself. Was she so hungry for a story, so desperate to write another book that she was allowing herself to be taken advantage of? Was she wasting her time looking for something that might not exist?

As Julie fired up the engine and drove toward the Embassy Suites, one question kept churning over and over in her head:

What the hell am I doing here?

_‿^‿_

Dantzler was sitting on his back deck, glass of Pernod and orange juice in hand, when his doorbell rang. Always suspicious that a late-night caller might be a revenge-minded scumbag he helped send away to prison, Dantzler's initial thought was to grab his Glock before opening the door. Better safe than sorry. No, better safe than dead. His holstered weapon was on the kitchen table. He went into the kitchen, looked down at the gun, and decided to take his chances, knowing the odds of his nighttime guest being a convicted felon were slim at best.

He was right. The caller was Richard Bird.

Dantzler was surprised by a visit from his captain; that hadn't happened more than two or three times in all the years they worked together. Richard Bird wasn't a late-evening guy. But Dantzler knew why his boss showed up on this night. He was here to deliver some news. And Dantzler had a pretty good idea what his long-time boss was going to say.

"Want a beer, Rich?" Dantzler said, as they made their way into the kitchen. "I'm having Pernod, which I know you would hate. But I have Smithwick's, Guinness, Beck's Dark. Any of those sound good to you?"

"What about Scotch? Got any of that?"

"I most certainly do. Mccallan. Top of the line stuff. James Bond drinks it, so it has to be good. How do you want it?"

"Straight up, no ice."

"You're a man's man, Rich."

"That's what all the ladies say."

Drinks in hand, they went back out onto the deck. The night was cool, aided by a soft summer breeze. The crickets and frogs were strangely silent, but a few ducks had made their way into the lake and were squawking loudly. Dantzler sat in his usual wicker chair, Bird plopped down on a long wooden bench. For five minutes neither man spoke, content to sip their drinks and listen to the ducks.

As good friends, they were comfortable with silence.

Dantzler looked out at the lake while waiting for Bird to say what he had come to say. Bird took a sip of Scotch, keeping his eyes cast downward, unwilling—or perhaps unable—to speak the words. At last, he lifted his head and spoke. His voice was soft, low, heavy with emotion.

"I'm calling it quits, Jack," he said. "I've had enough. It's time to move on, do something different with my time. With my life."

This was exactly what Dantzler knew Bird was going to say. Rumors do sometimes turn out to be true. "You've earned it, Rich. If you're sure this is what you want to do, then I say go for it. You've paid your dues. But are you sure?"

"One-hundred percent." Bird took another sip of Scotch. "Been thinking about it for close to a year now, maybe even a little longer. Now just seems like the right time."

"When are you planning on doing it?"

"End of June. That should give the Chief plenty of time to name a replacement." After taking another drink, Bird said, "And we both know who that replacement should be."

"Don't even go there, Rich. I have zero interest in taking over that position."

"It has to be you, Jack. Who the hell else could it be?"

"Eric."

"He's not ready. Maybe a few years down the road he will be. But not now."

"Eric is ready, Rich. He can do the job. I'd stake my pension on it. But, if you don't think so, if the Chief doesn't think so, then you need to look elsewhere if you are serious about finding someone to fill your shoes. 'Cause I can promise you that it won't be me."

"Why not?"

"I'm an investigator, Rich, not an administrator. I catch bad guys. It's what I was put on this earth to do. And you know better than anyone how much I hate sitting in an office doing paperwork. I'm no good when it comes to the mundane side of the job."

"That's for damn sure."

"There's a second reason why I won't accept the job—I'm also thinking about pulling the plug and calling it quits. I don't know how much longer I'll be around."

"Where is this coming from, Jack? You quitting? I can't see it happening anytime soon."

"Rich, you aren't the only one who needs to make a life change."

"You have a date in mind?"

"End of the year, if I do decide to do it."

"Jesus, the way this conversation is going, I need another drink," Bird said. He went into the kitchen, refilled his glass, came back onto the deck, and sat down. Holding up his glass, he said, "Hell, Jack, I came here feeling pretty shitty. You've managed to make me feel worse. Thanks."

"Anytime, Rich," Dantzler said, clinking his glass against Bird's. "Have you told anyone up the line that you're intending to quit?"

"Not yet; I wanted to tell you first. I'll meet with Chief Douglas tomorrow. I suppose Mayor Anderson also needs to be informed."

"That'll mean a press conference at some point. Elizabeth loves nothing more than standing in front of all those TV cameras."

"No doubt." Bird stood and stretched his six-foot-six body. "Do you really believe Eric is ready to take my spot?"

"Wouldn't say so if I didn't."

"He'd have to be bumped up to captain. That would make him your boss."

"Not a problem for me."

"Eric is a far better detective than I ever was," Bird said, taking his seat. "A superior investigator. But is he ready to manage a department, one as important as Homicide?"

"Stop fighting it, Rich. Eric is ready."

"If he were to get bumped up, who would you want as his replacement?"

"Victoria Jefferson would be my first choice."

"She's Eric's cousin, isn't she?"

"She is. And like Eric, she is superbly talented. She would get my highest recommendation."

Before Bird could respond his cell phoned went off. He picked it up, listened intently, said he would make the proper notifications, thanked the caller, and ended the call. When he was finished he looked at Dantzler and shook his head.

"Seems we have another suicide, Jack," Bird announced. "Another ex-cop."

"Who?"

"'Iron' Mike Perkins."

CHAPTER FOURTEEN

Dantzler turned off Nicholasville Road onto Zandale and then made a quick right into a shopping center parking lot. It was almost midnight when he arrived, yet despite the lateness of the hour the lot was a buzz of activity. The onlookers were evenly divided between shoppers who were leaving one of the big all-night businesses, and those drawn to the scene by the lights flashing on a half-dozen patrol cars parked in the lot and up and down the street.

Across from the lot was a two-story apartment complex that had been around for decades. Dantzler had passed by it a million times without ever once giving it a second look. It was a non-descript, run-down and thoroughly depressing place. He doubted that any attempt had ever been made to improve or upgrade the structure during the years since it had been built.

As Dantzler strolled across Zandale he saw that all activity was taking place near a second-floor unit, the last one on the right as he faced the building. He climbed the stairs and slowly made his way toward the place where Mike Perkins had lived. And where, apparently, he died.

Two ex-cops dead within the past week, Dantzler thought to himself. *What were the odds?*

Dantzler stepped inside an apartment that was as depressing as the outside building itself. Maybe more so. It could best be likened to a third-world hovel. There was a small open space as you walked in, an even smaller kitchen, a bedroom, and a bathroom. The place was sparsely furnished—no sofa in the living room, just a pair of non-matching, worn-out recliners, and a small table stationed between them. An empty pizza box and two beer cans were on the table, along with a TV remote. Several cockroaches scurried away from the pizza box, their search for food interrupted by the intruders. There were no photos or posters on the grimy walls. The carpet had once been dark green but was now dirty brown and badly stained. Dantzler shuttered to think what was the source of those stains.

Mike Perkins had allowed himself a single luxury—a 50-inch Samsung TV that rested on a stand next to the right wall. That single appliance probably cost more than everything else in the place combined.

Mike was at the kitchen table, slumped over, his head on the Formica table top. The table was soaked in blood, much of which had dripped from the table and pooled on the floor. His arms were hanging down, and a weapon Dantzler recognized as a Glock lay on the floor beneath Mike's right hand. Another Glock. The same type of weapon Dantzler carried, and the same type Larraby used to take his life.

Arnie Edwards, the medical examiner, was kneeling next to Mike's body, while Jake was searching through kitchen drawers and cabinets. Eric could be heard rummaging through the bedroom off to the left of the kitchen. Dantzler eased around Arnie, careful to avoid stepping in blood, and took a closer look at the scene.

"A second suicide," Jake said, once he noticed Dantzler's presence in the kitchen. "Who'd a thunk it?"

"Would you be willing to bet dinner on that assumption, Jake?" Arnie asked, looking up, smiling.

"Why? Would it be a fool's bet?"

"Let me put it this way. I would be eating for free."

"What are you seeing that indicates something other than suicide?"

"It's what I'm not seeing that tells the story." Arnie motioned for Jake to come closer. "Describe what you're seeing, Jake."

Jake moved around Mike's lifeless body, carefully watching where he stepped. "A gunshot to the right side of his head, just above the temple, a through and through. I know this because the bullet is lodged in that wall over there. And the weapon, a Glock, is on the floor. I would also add that death was instantaneous."

"You've passed the initial part of your test," Arnie said. "Now, take a close look at the weapon and tell me what you see."

Jake knelt down and studied the Glock. After a few moments he looked up at Arnie and said, "A weapon, presumably Mike's, covered in blood."

"Where's the blood?"

Jake looked back down at the weapon, leaned closer, and said, "On the barrel, the grip, and the trigger guard."

"And where do you not see any blood?"

Again, Jake closely studied the Glock. "The trigger," he answered. "There's no blood on the trigger."

"Give the boy a solid A on part two of the exam. Now, for the third part. Come here, Jake, and take a look at this place on Mike's neck. Then tell me what you see."

Jake rose, moved around to Mike's left side, and immediately noticed a bluish circular spot on the back of the dead man's neck. "That's obviously a bruise," Jake said.

"Based on what you see, combined with the location of the bruise, what is the first thought that comes to mind?"

"Choke hold."

"Okay, Jake, now for your final exam," Arnie said. "Share with us your version of what happened here."

"The killer used a choke hold just long enough to cause Mike to pass out but stopped before ending his life. Then . . ."

"What's the basis for your theory that Mike was still alive when the fatal shot was fired?" Arnie interrupted.

"Because of the amount of blood on the table and the floor. If Mike was dead when the bullet was fired his heart would not have been beating. That means there would have been much less bleeding from the wounds. Since he was alive and his heart was still beating, that's why there is so much blood."

"Go on."

"Whoever did this put the Glock in Mike's hand, probably wrapped his own hand around Mike's, put the barrel of the weapon against Mike's head, and squeezed the trigger. The shooter wore gloves so as to not leave fingerprints. I would also bet that he put Mike's finger on the trigger, then covered Mike's with his own finger before firing the weapon. When the blood blew back from the wound, the trigger was covered by both men's fingers. That's why there is no blood on the trigger. I would also bet that you will find GSR on Mike's right hand. This was definitely a murder, not a suicide."

Arnie looked up at Dantzler, who was listening and watching with a bemused look on his face. "I do believe, Jack, that our young lad here is going to be a first-rate detective," Arnie said. "I have no choice but to give him an A-plus."

"He definitely has potential," Dantzler answered, smiling.

"Looks like you have a murder on your hands, Jack," Arnie said, removing the plastic gloves from his hands. "Young Jake pretty much nailed it on the head."

The exchange between Jake and Arnie had been interesting to Dantzler but it had not been enlightening. He didn't need to hear a detailed explanation to know that Mike Perkins had not taken his own life. He knew it from the very first second he observed the scene.

"Our killer did a fairly good job of making this look like a suicide," Dantzler told the two men. "Except that he made a huge mistake."

"What mistake?" Jake asked.

"Mike Perkins was left-handed."

Before Jake or Arnie could comment on that important tidbit Eric called out from the bedroom. "Holy shit, guys, you're not gonna believe what I just found."

Eric came into the kitchen holding a large leather bag in his hands. Once he, Jake, and Dantzler moved into the living room, Eric opened the bag. It was stuffed with money. Dantzler picked up a stack of bills and thumbed through them. All were hundred-dollar bills.

"That's a shit-load of cash, Jack," Eric stated. "I can't believe this belongs to Mike Perkins."

"If it was his money, why would he choose to live in a dump like this?" inquired Jake. "And if this money did belong to him, then I think we can safely rule out robbery as a motive for his murder."

Dantzler was every bit as puzzled as Eric and Jake. It didn't make any sense. None of it did. First, Larraby, now Mike Perkins. Both dead. Within a matter of days. Two guys who hadn't been on the job for years. Okay, Larraby's was a suicide; what happened here didn't change that ruling. But . . . Mike Perkins murdered? What was the motive? Couldn't be the cash, since the killer left it behind. So, if not for the money, then what? And what if the killer wasn't aware that the money was here? If he wasn't, what was his reason for murdering Mike? And, lastly, were the deaths of Larraby and Mike Perkins somehow connected?

They had to be, Dantzler quickly concluded.

But how? And why?

Dale Larraby knows.

In Dantzler's mind, those three words held the answers to his myriad of questions.

_-^-_

Sean Montgomery had gone to Knoxville for the purpose of reconnecting with a former girlfriend. She had invited him down, and Sean, recalling nothing but the good times they shared together, was quick to accept the invitation. Doing so turned out to be a mistake. A big mistake. The visit was an unmitigated disaster in every way. What Sean had failed to remember when agreeing to make the trip were the countless times that weren't so good. The many times they argued, were silent for hours, or ignored each other for days. Unhappy times when whatever relationship they did have veered badly off the rails.

Memory can be a sly trickster and this was one of those times when it had been. It didn't take long for Sean to reach that conclusion. After less than three hours together he knew it was time to hit the road. The woman, Alexis Butterfield, was in complete agreement. During that brief time span, Sean's feelings about the visit had gone from it is good to see you, to this might have been a mistake, to I think it's time for me to hit the road.

Alexis's response? It's way past time, Sean.

Sean couldn't help but laugh about it as he drove back to his motel. If nothing else it made for a colorful story to share with Dantzler and Bloom. No doubt they would find great humor in such a failed encounter. After all, what are good friends for if not to ridicule your failures?

Once he settled into his room, Sean phoned Susan Collins, his receptionist, unaware that it was past midnight. When he did realize how late it was he thought about hanging up. But he didn't. He was in a mischievous mood, and rousing Susan from a deep sleep seemed like the proper thing to do. Sometimes being a bad boy feels really good.

"Do you know what time it is?" Susan mumbled.

"No, tell me."

"Almost two in the morning."

"No kidding. I had no idea."

"You're an asshole, Sean. You do know that, don't you?"

"But you love me just the same."

"Not now, I don't."

"I just wanted to let you know that I'll be back in the office tomorrow by noon. Seems my latest tryst turned out to be a bust."

"And you had to tell me this now?"

"Sure. Like they say on TV, this is breaking news. I wanted you to be the first to hear it."

"You are an asshole, Sean."

"You're repeating yourself, Susan."

"Okay, then, you're a giant asshole."

Sean laughed, said, "Anything important happen while I was away?"

"No, nothing important attorney-wise. You did get a call from a woman who wants to speak with you."

"Speak to me about what?"

"She didn't say."

"You get her name and phone number?"

"Only her name. Julie Bradley."

"Julie Bradley? The author?"

"She didn't say, Sean. For all I know she could be the Virgin Mother herself."

"Nah, her name was Mary," Sean said. "What did you tell Julie Bradley?"

"That you would be back in the office on Thursday."

"Julie Bradley, huh? Interesting."

"Why? Do you know her?"

"She's written a couple of books I've read. True Crime stuff. She's pretty good."

"Well, I think it's a true crime that you woke me up at this hour just to tell me something that could have waited until tomorrow. Goodnight, Sean."

"Nite, Susan. And sleep well. But don't be late for work in the morning."

"Piss off, Sean," Susan said, ending the call.

Julie Bradley, Sean thought as he closed his phone. *Wonder what in the hell she wants with me?*

That question lingered as he lay on the bed, closed his eyes, and drifted off to sleep, still fully clothed.

_^_

While the crime scene folks were going over Mike Perkins's apartment, Eric and Jake stood next to Dantzler's new Mercedes counting the money found in the bag. It took more than half an hour to finish the task. The final tally: one-hundred-twenty-four thousand dollars.

"Guy has this much cash and the best he can do is a fancy TV?" Eric said, shaking his head. "And did you see Mike? Looked like he hadn't eaten in days. If I had this kind of cash I'd be eating steak every night."

"If you had that kind of money, Eric, you'd spend it all on clothes," replied Dantzler.

"You're probably right about that."

"Where do you think he got this much money, Jack?" Jake asked.

"Assuming that it's his money, I haven't a clue. If I did have to make a guess, I'd say it has something to do with drugs."

"You think Mike was selling drugs?"

"I don't know. But it's an area we need to look into."

Eric said, "I remember Mike when I first joined the police force. That was right before he started to go downhill. To remember what he looked like back then, and to see that skeleton upstairs, it's almost impossible to believe it's the same man."

Jake said, "I find it impossible to believe that no one heard the gunshot. A Glock's not exactly a silent weapon."

"There's probably a lot of noise in an apartment complex like this one," countered Dantzler. "When I arrived there was a party going on in the unit right below Mike's. The music was pretty loud. I would venture a guess that no one in that unit heard a gunshot."

"Vee and Sammy Hamilton spoke with all the residents," Eric pointed out. "Not one claimed to have heard anything out of the ordinary."

"There's a real shocker," Jake said. "And if they did hear something not one of them would admit it."

"Okay, guys, head home," Dantzler ordered, picking up the bag. "It's way past late. I'll take the money back to the station and book it into evidence. This is a murder, so we need to follow the rule book. Grab a few hours' sleep, then we'll get together tomorrow morning. Excuse me, make that later *this* morning. I have to meet with someone at nine-thirty, so I won't be in the office until around eleven. Until I get there, compare notes, process what we've seen tonight, and bring Captain Bird up to speed. One final point—do not tell anyone about the money. That detail stays with the three of us."

"What about contacting Mike's family?" Jake asked.

"I don't know if Mike had any family. Get Bruce to pull up Mike's file. See who is listed as his contact in case of an emergency. If you get a name, make the call."

"Roger that."

Eric said, "Two ex-cops dead in a matter of days. Both died under suspicious circumstances. What are the odds of that happening?"

"Don't know, Eric," Dantzler said. "That's what we've got to find out."

CHAPTER FIFTEEN

At nine the next morning, while on his way to Cathedral of Christ the King Church, Dantzler punched in Charlie Bolton's number. He was surprised when Charlie answered. Dantzler would have bet money that Charlie was out on his fishing boat, and had left his cell phone back in the truck. The man wanted no disturbances while on the hunt for those slippery water creatures.

"You're calling to tell me about poor Mike Perkins, aren't you?" Charlie asked, before Dantzler could say hello. "If you are, you're too late. I already heard."

"From Rawlinson?"

"From several of my spies."

"Did your spies tell you it was a homicide, not a suicide?"

"They did."

"Any thoughts on the matter?"

"An ex-cop, a drug user . . . that could make for a long list of suspects."

"Anyone in particular come to mind?"

"Hell, Jack, I haven't seen Mike Perkins in fifteen years, maybe more. I don't know anything about how the man lived, other than what

I've been told. Don't know any of his friends, or who he hung out with. If you want to know who might've done it you have come to the wrong man. I can't help you."

"Did your informants tell you how Mike died?" Dantzler asked.

"Single gunshot to the temple."

"His right temple."

"So?"

"Mike Perkins was left-handed."

"Well, there's your first clue that it was a homicide."

"What other bits of information did your spies share with you?"

"There was a bruise on Mike's neck, which, according to the medical examiner, likely resulted from a choke hold."

"And who uses a choke hold, Charlie? Cops, that's who."

"Maybe back in the day we had a few guys who used it a little more often and more enthusiastically than they should have. But not anymore. It's unacceptable in today's world. Ranks right up there with waterboarding." Charlie hesitated for a few seconds, then said, "What are you saying, Jack? That a cop killed Mike Perkins?"

"That thought had crossed my mind."

"Bullshit, Jack, total bullshit. What reason would a cop have to kill a poor bastard like Mike Perkins? Answer that, will you?"

"I don't know. Maybe one-hundred-twenty-four thousand reasons."

"The money, yeah, I heard about that. But the killer left it behind, didn't he?"

"He did."

"I'd say that eliminates the money as a motive."

"You're probably right, Charlie," Dantzler said. "Didn't Mike work for you when you headed the Missing Persons Unit?"

"For a couple of years before I retired."

"What kind of a cop was he?"

"A damn fine one when he worked for me. But after I left the job he went downhill fast. I don't know what happened to that boy. He ruined a promising career, that's for certain."

"You going fishing today?"

"Yeah, thought I'd leave sometime after noon."

"Thanks for chatting with me, Charlie. And good luck with the fish."

"I keep telling you, Jack. It's the fish who need good luck, not me."

We're all in need of some good luck, Charlie, Dantzler thought to himself as he closed his phone.

_^_

Following two unsuccessful scouting trips, Julie Bradley finally had her first piece of good luck. Eddie Campbell and James Newman were not at home but Alex Shannon was. Julie found him working in the backyard of his house on Chinoe. The two-story brick structure was a nicer, more-expensive place than the houses lived in by Campbell and Newman. For a man making a cop's salary, Shannon had obviously done well for himself.

As Julie opened a wire gate and entered the backyard Shannon glared at her with hard blue eyes that offered no hint of warmth or friendliness. Only menace. He was a man of medium height with thick, muscular arms, a shaved head, the makings of a beard, and that unflinching stare. Alex Shannon gave off a vibe that said he was permanently angry.

She smiled and started to speak but he beat her to the punch.

"What can I do for you, little lady?" he said in a voice as unfriendly as his eyes. "If you're here to sell me something you can go ahead, do an about-face, and march on back to your vehicle."

"Rest easy, Mr. Shannon. I'm not here to sell you anything. I'm . . ."

"Then why are you here?" Shannon interrupted.

"To ask you a few questions, if you don't mind."

"You a cop?"

"No, I'm not a cop."

"Then I do mind. I have nothing to say to you."

"Shouldn't you at least hear what I have to say before you dismiss me outright?"

"You're changing your tune, aren't you, little lady? First, you want to ask me questions, and now you tell me you have something to say. Which is it?"

"Questions?"

Shannon removed a red bandana from his hip pocket and wiped perspiration from his face. Then he dug out a pack of Camels from his shirt pocket, extracted a cigarette, lit it, and inhaled deeply. After exhaling a cloud of smoke he sat on a marble bench, took a second long drag, and looked up at Julie. He did not offer her a seat.

"Who are you and what's your racket?" he said, blowing out another smoky cloud.

"My name is Julie Bradley. I'm a writer."

"A writer, huh? What the hell do you write? And who do you work for?"

"Books. And I don't work for anyone. I'm a free-lance writer."

"What kind of books do you write, little lady? That mushy romantic crap?"

"Would I be talking to an ex-cop if I wrote that kind of shitty stuff?"

"Now, that's a helluva good answer, little lady. And just because I liked it so much I'm going to answer a few of your questions. But before I do I have one for you. What possible reason could you have for asking me questions having to do with anything you are writing?"

"Because you were a cop in Lexington."

"Lexington has had lots of cops. Still do. Why me?"

"Your name was given to me by a source."

Shannon finished his cigarette, tossed it onto the stone sidewalk, ground it with his boot, withdrew a new one, and lit it up. "Now here's where I ask you the name of the source and you tell me you can't reveal it, right?" he asked.

"Right."

"Little lady, if . . ."

"Julie. That's my name. Julie Bradley."

"Okay, *Julie Bradley*, here's the deal. If you don't tell me what this is about, or give up the name of your source, then we have nothing to talk about."

"Look, Mr. Shannon, I'm not here to point fingers or cause you any trouble. My only goal is to gather information."

"Information about what, specifically?"

"A murder that took place in Lexington fifteen years ago."

"You're asking me about a murder? Honey, you're barking up the wrong tree. I never worked Homicide a day in my life. My entire career was spent working Vice."

"You weren't in Missing Persons?" Julie said.

"Not for a single day."

"What about Eddie Campbell, James Newman, Dale Larraby, Mike Perkins, and Sean Montgomery? Did they work in Missing Persons?"

"Eddie, Jim, and Mike worked it exclusively. Larraby was in the unit for several years before he went over to Homicide. Montgomery was with us for about a year before he got bumped up to Homicide. Why are you inquiring about those guys?"

"Those five names, along with yours, were given to me by my source."

"If your book is about a murder then your time would be better spent speaking with the guys in Homicide?" Shannon said. "Missing Persons personnel don't investigate murders."

"The problem is, I was given the names of men who worked Missing Persons, not Homicide."

"That's not entirely accurate. Larraby and Montgomery did work in Homicide."

"And I plan to interview both men."

Shannon laughed out loud and tossed his cigarette to the ground. "You ain't talking to Dale Larraby, that much I can assure you," he said. "Larraby checked himself out last week."

"He's dead?"

"Well, if he wasn't before they cremated his ass, he damn sure is now."

"What happened to him?"

Shannon shaped his right hand into a pistol, put his forefinger under his chin, and pantomimed pulling the trigger. "And I've got more bad news for you, miss book writer," he said. "Jim Newman ain't among the living either. Had a massive heart attack about three years ago. Stupid bastard was training for some damn charity run. At his age. Keeled over in the kitchen while serving Fruit Loops to his grandkids. A damn shame."

Shannon lit a third cigarette, said, "Looks like your interview list ain't as long as it once was. I'd say you ought to have some serious concerns about that source of yours."

Julie stood there, not sure what to say.

"Since we are both in complete agreement that your source leaves a lot to be desired in the accuracy department, why not give me his name?" Shannon said. "It's not like you're an attorney or a priest, for Christ's sakes. There's no binding confidentiality agreement in play here."

"Danny Michaels."

"Oh, fuck me. Danny Michaels is your source? You have to be joking. Tell me you are joking."

"I'm not joking."

"Have you ever met Danny Michaels?"

Julie shook her head, said, "Only spoke to him over the phone one time."

"Well, miss book writer, I know Danny Michaels. Known him for many years. And what I can tell you about him is that he's a world-class hustler and con man. He's been in trouble with the law so many times I wouldn't be surprised if he has a defense attorney on retainer. Except he's too damn poor to afford an attorney. If you believe a single word that tumbles out of his mouth you're the biggest sucker on this planet."

Once again Julie really didn't know what to say.

"What exactly did Danny Michaels tell you?" Shannon asked.

"Just what I've already told you. That a woman was murdered fifteen years ago, and that I needed to speak to you six men about it."

"And what did Danny want for his information? I'm sure he wanted something."

"He didn't ask for anything."

"Eventually, he would have. A guy like Danny is always working some kind of a scam." Shannon started to reach for the pack of cigarettes but decided not to. "Did he give you the name of the woman who was allegedly murdered?"

"Gloria Nash."

Shannon chuckled, those cold, hard eyes continuing to bore in on Julie. "Most likely she was one of Danny's old girlfriends who dumped his sorry ass and disappeared," he said. "But if you're stubborn enough to continue your quest, then my advice would be to speak with someone in Homicide. Sean Montgomery should be your first stop, since he worked in Missing Persons and Homicide. Maybe he can help you, maybe he can't. He's now an attorney, and hasn't been on the force for several years, so talking to him may end up taking you down a dead-end street. If it does, go see Jack Dantzler. He's the big Homicide ace."

Having said his piece, Shannon walked past Julie and disappeared into his garage. Julie didn't have to be told that the conversation had ended. She quickly went back around the house, got into her car, and drove away.

Her thoughts were moving at warp speed. Questions swirled like they were trapped in the middle of a tornado. Once again she kept asking herself if she had been played by Danny Michaels? All indications were that she had been. And yet . . . she simply could not shake the feeling that what he told her was the truth. At the very least, his story was partially true. And what to make of the fact that two of the six men on the list Danny had given her were now deceased? If nothing else it certainly had to rank high on the list of strange coincidences. And what about Alex Shannon? He was a classic hardass, that's for sure. Nothing warm or fuzzy about him. Especially those eyes of his. They were harder than diamonds, among the coldest Julie had ever seen on another human being. They were eyes that gave nothing away, eyes impossible to read. But . . . even though he didn't appear to be lying or dodging the questions there was something troubling about him. What, exactly? Maybe it was his insistence that she give him the name of her source. And she did give it up, something she'd never done in the past. Was that a mistake? She hoped it wasn't.

Driving away from Shannon's house, she silently made the decision to press on with her investigation. Quitting wasn't an option, no matter what Alex Shannon or anyone else advised. If there were answers out there waiting to be uncovered, she would dig them up. She hadn't become a success by walking away. Only cowards and losers refuse to face a difficult challenge head on. And she didn't belong in either of those categories.

Shannon had advised her to meet with Sean Montgomery, and that's exactly what she planned to do. Maybe he would be more helpful than Alex Shannon had been. And, hopefully, more friendly.

CHAPTER SIXTEEN

An unpleasant three hours with a former girlfriend and a restless night's sleep were not good reasons for skipping a solid, tasty breakfast. So at a little past eight Sean pulled into the parking lot of a small mom-and-pop restaurant just past the Kentucky-Tennessee state line. It was a place he had frequented many times over the years. There was a well-established reason why the parking lot was always full of cars, trucks, and SUVs—small, dinky restaurants like this one invariably served terrific food. Truckers, in particular, know the best places to eat.

Sean wolfed down a breakfast consisting of an omelet, a stack of pancakes, link sausage, hash brown potatoes, toast, and a huge glass of orange juice. It was easily the biggest breakfast he'd consumed in years. And he had certainly not been disappointed. His judgment had been on the money—the food was outstanding.

Sean paid, left a nice tip, and stepped outside. As he was leaving four truckers were on their way inside the restaurant. They nodded but moved past him without speaking. Sean climbed into his car, turned on the AC, took out his phone, and punched in Danny Michaels's number. Sean knew the number, because he purchased the phone for Danny after learning that his client was being placed on house arrest.

Danny answered after four rings. "Hey, what's up, Mr. Montgomery?" he said, his raspy voice that of someone just rousted out of a deep sleep. "Kinda early for a call, isn't it?"

"It's never too early to speak with a charmer like you, Danny-boy."

"Well, all I can say is it's kinda early."

"Are you following the rules, Danny? Staying at home like you're supposed to?"

"Yeah, I am. And it really sucks, if you want the truth. I mean, if I want to walk up to the Minit Mart on the corner and buy a hot dog I have to call and get permission. That's just not right, Mr. Montgomery. I don't care what anyone says."

"Your other option is to have the bracelet removed. I can get it done today. All I have to do is make one phone call. If that's the option you choose you get sent back to the detention center. How does that sound to you?"

"I don't want no part of the detention center."

"Then option A is your best play here. I seriously doubt those hot dogs are all that scrumptious, and they're definitely not worth a violation. However, if you are intent on getting one, make the call and get permission to leave the apartment. Be smart, Danny."

"You're dead wrong, Mr. Montgomery. Those hot dogs are delicious."

"That's lovely to know, Danny, but I didn't call to chat about ankle bracelets or hot dogs. My reason for calling is to let you know that I did meet with Marianne Ramsey, the assistant district attorney. While she didn't exactly turn her nose up at your suggestion of a deal somewhere down the road, she reiterated to me exactly what I told you—that you had to offer more information than what you've already given. You ready to do that?"

"No."

"You sure about that, Danny? You're positive this is the road you want to travel? Because if it is she will not meet with you. She's adamant about that. That means no deal. It also means she's going to prosecute you to the full extent of the law for those charges against you. If that happens you're going away for a long time."

"Gloria Nash," Danny whispered. "Her name was Gloria Nash."

"Who is Gloria Nash?" Sean said, taking a pen and scribbling the woman's name on the back of his left hand.

"The girl who got murdered."

"Who murdered her, Danny? And when?"

"I ain't saying nothing else, Mr. Montgomery. You just give that information to your district attorney friend. When she hears that she'll agree to meet with me."

"Do you know who murdered her, Danny?"

"I ain't saying no more. Talk to that woman, tell her I'll spill everything I know once she agrees to a deal. And her promise to place me in the Witness Protection Program."

"Witness Protection? Where the hell did that come from?"

"I tell you what I know my life won't be worth a can of beans."

"Let me clue you to why I'm having trouble believing your story, Danny. And why Marianne Ramsey will also have trouble believing it. I worked in Homicide for a couple of years and I can't recall an investigation involving a woman named Gloria Nash. That in itself is only a minor reason for my disbelief. But the big reason is, there's a guy in Homicide named Jack Dantzler. Great cop, best I ever saw. Been on the job for twenty-five years. And you know what, Danny? He's never failed to solve a murder case. Not one. I'll bet you two of those hot dogs you love that if I phone him right now he'll tell me he's never had a case involving Gloria Nash."

"That's because nobody knows about the murder."

"Except you."

"Well, yeah, me and them that did it."

"And you are adamant about not giving me those names?"

"Yeah, I am."

"Okay, Danny, here's what I'm going to do, insane as this probably is. I'll pass along this woman's name to Marianne. Once I do all bets are off. I can't begin to tell you what her response will be. I'm just hoping she doesn't pull out a pistol and shoot me."

"That's what happened to Gloria," Danny said, just before ending the call.

Sean tossed his phone on the passenger's seat, started the engine, pulled out of the parking lot, and got back on the interstate heading north to Lexington. Taking the steering wheel with his left hand, he saw Gloria Nash's name written in dark blue ink. Like a cheap tattoo.

An odd thought suddenly crossed Sean's mind: Did Gloria Nash have any tattoos?

Damn, if I'm thinking that, then I must really believe Danny's story.

_^_

Father Steven Mulaney sat on a front-row bench in Cathedral of Christ the King Church holding a single rose in his left hand. Dantzler took the seat next to Father Mulaney, a diminutive man who happened to remind Dantzler of Barry Fitzgerald, a wonderful old character actor who won an Oscar for playing a priest in *Going My Way*. Like the late Irish actor, Father Mulaney had a warm smile and a twinkle in his eyes. Dantzler judged him to be an easy man to speak with.

Before Dantzler could kick off the conversation, Father Mulaney said, "I know you are here to talk about Declan, and I will be more than happy to do just that. Declan was a special human being in every way. Kind of spirit, generous, warm, witty, compassionate, intelligent, and a true believer. Having said that, he was also tough when he had to be. If you were in the wrong he held you accountable. No one got a free pass. Declan was my mentor. Whatever I am as a priest I owe to that man. When I was young I had moments of doubt, times when I struggled, when my faith was put to the test. In each of those instances it was Declan who steered me back to the right path."

Dantzler remained silent, sensing that Father Mulaney wasn't quite finished with his assessment of a friend, mentor, and fellow priest.

"Declan was exactly twenty-five years older than me," Father Mulaney continued. "He acted young but he had a very old soul, if that makes any sense. In some ways, to me at least, he seemed almost time-less. Or maybe he seemed out of time in some strange way. The Book of Job asks the age-old question, *where shall wisdom be found?* I can tell you where—in Father Declan Riley, may his eternal soul rest in peace."

Father Mulaney crossed himself and kissed the gold cross hanging from his neck.

"I recently spoke with Father Riley's sister," Dantzler said. "She . . ."

"Mary Farmer."

"Yes, Mary. She . . ."

"A wonderful woman. She and Declan were very close."

"Mary told me that right before Father Riley passed away he opened his eyes and spoke three words in a loud, clear voice. He said, 'Dale Larraby knows.' Any idea what he might have meant by that?"

"No, I don't. Isn't he the former police officer who committed suicide recently?"

"Yes. I take it from your question that you weren't familiar with Dale Larraby. Do you know if Father Riley knew him?"

"I have no idea. But just because I don't know the answer to that question doesn't mean Declan didn't know the man. He very well could have. Was Dale Larraby a Catholic?"

"Baptist."

"I have many friends who are Baptists, and I'm sure Declan did as well. But I'm afraid Dale Larraby wasn't among those I'm familiar with. Sorry."

"Don't apologize," Dantzler said, standing. "It was a longshot at best. Thanks for your time, Father Mulaney. I appreciate it."

"You know, Detective, I could have been more helpful had you inquired about the poor man who took his own life last night," Father Mulaney said. "Him, I was acquainted with."

Dantzler was thrown off by those words. Looking puzzled, he sat back down, and said, "What poor man are you referring to?"

"Mike Perkins," Father Mulaney answered, again crossing himself.

"How did you know about that? Details of his death haven't been released yet."

"Well, I don't know the details, other than he took his own life. As for where I got the information, one of my parishioners works in the morgue. He told me. It's very sad when someone reaches such a level of hopelessness that he chooses to take his life."

"Mike Perkins didn't commit suicide, Father. He was murdered."

"For his money, I assume," Father Mulaney said, as though it was common knowledge.

Once again Dantzler was stunned by the priest's words. "How did you know he had money?" he finally asked. "Only three detectives are aware of that detail."

"I know because he donated one-hundred thousand dollars to the church. He told me there would be further donations sometime in the future."

"When did he make this donation?"

"*Donations*. He made four, each one totaling twenty-five thousand dollars."

"Father Mulaney, when was the last time you saw Mike Perkins?"

"Oh, must've been about two weeks ago."

"Did he look like someone who had large amounts of money to give away?"

"Outside appearance is rarely an accurate gauge of a person's inner soul."

"Or his financial status, apparently. Do you recall when these donations were made?"

"I would have to review the records to be completely accurate, but I can say with confidence that the first one was made eight years ago. And if I'm not mistaken, each of the other three came after two-year intervals. I can also tell you that all four were made on the first day of June, and that they were facilitated by an attorney named Lawrence Brady. The last time Mike and I spoke, he indicated that another check would be sent out on June first, which is two weeks away. Should I expect to receive that check, Detective?"

"That money isn't going anywhere until this is all sorted out."

"It will go where God intends it to be," Father Mulaney said. "As for the other matter, give me a day or two and I'll have the exact years of the subsequent donations."

"Yes, I will need that information," Dantzler said. "How well did you know Mike?"

"Primarily, I knew him through Declan. They were fairly close. In fact, Declan often heard Mike's confession."

"Often? How often?"

"Mike was a tortured soul, a man carrying a very heavy burden. He met with Declan on numerous occasions, sometimes two or three times a week. There were times when Mike confessed, and other times when he and Declan just talked."

"Any idea what they talked about? Or why Mike was carrying a heavy burden?"

"Only Declan could answer those questions for you, Detective."

Dantzler leaned back, silent, thinking, completely startled by what he'd just learned.

"A shekel for your thoughts, Detective," Father Mulaney said.

"Keep your shekels, Father. At the moment I'm more confused than anything. I have no idea what to think."

"You don't suspect robbery as a motive for Mike's murder?"

"We found more than one-hundred-thousand dollars in his apartment, so, no, robbery wasn't why he was killed."

"Why kill Mike, then leave so much money behind?"

"Good question, Father."

"Is it possible that Mike was murdered because he spoke with Declan?"

This was a path Dantzler hadn't considered. Thinking about it now he concluded that it was a theory that lacked plausibility. But then, didn't most theories lack plausibility at a certain stage along the way?

"If that were the case then the killer must have known that Mike shared important information with Declan. And maybe Declan shared this information with the killer. That's why the killer felt the need to silence Mike."

"Declan was a priest, Detective. I can assure you that he didn't share the contents of those talks with anyone. Declan didn't 'spill the beans,' as they say in the movies. And if I am to buy into your theory, then I have to ask, why didn't the killer murder Declan?"

Dantzler shrugged, said, "Get me those records of Mike's donations as soon as you can, Father. And if you think of anything that might be helpful, please let me know." Dantzler handed Father

Mulaney a card. "I can be reached at either of those numbers. Call anytime. I'm on the job twenty-four/seven."

"As am I, Detective." Father Mulaney extended his hand. "I will do everything within my power to help you, Detective Dantzler. Poor Mike Perkins deserves nothing less than our best effort."

Dantzler shook the man's hand, said, "He'll get our best effort, Father. You can count on that."

On the way back to his car Dantzler took out his phone and punched in Sean Montgomery's number. The call was answered immediately, and Dantzler could tell Sean was on the highway.

"What's up, Jack?" Sean asked.

"Where are you?"

"About thirty miles from Lexington. Why? Something going on?"

"Mike Perkins is dead. Murdered late last night or early this morning. In his apartment on Zandale. Gunshot to the head. The killer tried to make it look like a suicide but botched it."

"You're positive it wasn't a suicide. Mike did seem depressed when I ran into him."

"The killer made the mistake of placing the gun on the floor under Mike's right hand. Mike was left-handed."

"Does this change your mind about Larraby?"

"No. Larraby committed suicide. I do, however, think the two deaths are connected in some way. I just can't seem to make that connection."

"Two guys who worked in Missing Persons around the same time. That might be the place to start."

"There's more, Sean. We found a bag in Mike's apartment with one-hundred-twenty-four-thousand dollars in it."

"And the killer left it?"

"Either left it, or didn't know it was there."

"Jesus, the way Mike looked when I saw him I wouldn't have thought he had ten bucks, much less one-hundred grand. Do you think the money was Mike's?"

"Yes. And here's why. I just spoke with Father Steven Mulaney and he told me Mike had donated one-hundred-thousand dollars to Christ the King Church. Four donations, each one twenty-five grand, made at two-year intervals. So, yeah, he had plenty of money."

"This is insane, Jack. Where could Mike Perkins come up with a bankroll that substantial? And how did he manage to get it?"

"Don't know, Sean. But you've just added two more to a growing list of questions that need to be answered."

CHAPTER SEVENTEEN

When the front door opened Julie immediately realized that the information given to her by Ella Brown had been accurate. Eddie Campbell, the man Julie had come to see, was confined to the wheelchair. One small mystery solved.

Eddie, tall and overweight, held up his right hand to block the sun that was hitting him directly in his eyes. After scanning Julie from head to toe he lowered his hand and rolled the wheelchair back into the living room. Unsure what to do, Julie stood there, waiting to either be invited in or told to get the hell away.

Following several uncomfortable seconds, Eddie waved her inside. Turning the wheelchair around until he was facing Julie, he said, "You're the book writer who spoke with Alex, aren't you?"

Word sure travels fast in Lexington. "Yes, that would be me," Julie answered, trying not to sound annoyed. "The name on my birth certificate is Julie Bradley, not book writer. So if it's not too much trouble, please call me Julie."

"Alex failed to mention that you're a smartass."

"Normally, I'm not."

"Some people just bring it out, right?"

"Exactly."

"I know the feeling. Had to deal with plenty of smartasses in my time."

"Look, Mr. Campbell, I didn't mean to get off on the wrong foot with you. I apologize if I did. I'm just here to ask you a few questions, that's all."

"Yeah, Alex told me to be on the lookout for you. Said you wanted to talk about a murder that allegedly took place a few years ago. The victim was a young woman, if I'm remembering Alex correctly."

"Gloria Nash."

"Never heard of her."

"You sure about that? Gloria's sister filed a notice with Missing Persons."

"If she did, and she very well might have, I'm not aware of it." Eddie picked up a cup and took a drink. "Plenty of shit gets lost in all that bureaucratic red tape. Maybe that's what happened in this instance."

"According to Gloria's sister the case was investigated."

"Not by me." Eddie rolled the wheelchair closer to Julie, said, "Alex tells me Danny Michaels is your source for this book you are hoping to write. Is that correct?"

"It is."

"Well, *Julie Bradley*, you couldn't have put your money on a more untrustworthy or a more unreliable source if your life depended on it. There are two hard, cold facts you need to know about Danny Michaels. First, just about every word that comes out of his mouth is a lie. Second, there is no way in hell that Danny Michaels could begin to know what goes on inside the police department. He can tell you what goes on behind bars, but not what happens on the other side of those bars. You need to find a better source."

"That seems to be the consensus," Julie said.

"If Danny was so knowledgeable, why didn't he let you know that Jim Newman was dead? Why did he include Jim's name on that list he gave you? But he did, didn't he? And that ought to tell you everything you need to know about Danny's credibility."

Eddie took another drink, set the cup down, looked straight at

Julie, and said, "Speaking of that list, it seems to be shrinking every day, doesn't it? Half of those six men aren't around anymore."

"Where do you come up with half?"

"Well, Jim's gone, Larraby's gone, and now Mike Perkins is gone. Unless my math fails me, three is half of six."

"What do you mean Mike Perkins is gone?" Julie asked, more than a little bewildered. "Gone where?"

"Dead." Eddie laughed out loud. "You didn't know about that, did you?"

"When? How?"

"Sometime last night. Put a gun to his head and blew his brains out. Same as Larraby."

Julie was speechless, unable to slow the speed of her thoughts to a degree that would allow those thoughts to become actual, intelligible words. She was beyond shocked; she was stunned into silence. But silence is often the place where truth is found hiding, waiting to be discovered. Yes, three of six men were now deceased, and the dead cannot be interviewed. Their voices have been silenced forever. But sometimes the dead do speak. They have their own tale to tell. And Julie was now more certain than ever that there was a truth to be uncovered related to the deaths of Dale Larraby and Mike Perkins. There had to be a reason why the dominos had suddenly started to fall.

Was she that reason?

Julie said, "Thanks for your time, Mr. Campbell. I can see my way out."

"Find a better source than Danny Michaels," Eddie yelled, as Julie walked out the door.

Don't worry, Eddie, I will. You can bet on that.

_^_

Mike Perkins's personnel file listed an aunt named Dana Perkins as his only contact in case of an emergency. Eric called and gave her the grim news about Mike's death, omitting all specific details. He asked if she would meet with him; she agreed. Eric could tell by the quiver in her voice that the news had delivered a hard blow.

Dana Perkins lived in an expensive home in a neighborhood off Harrodsburg Road. She was a tall, angular woman with sharp features, jet black hair she had tied back in a ponytail, and eyes even darker than her hair. She wore a pair of Levis, a blue University of Kentucky T-shirt, and flip flops. A sad smile creased her face when she invited Eric and Victoria Jefferson into her house. The puffiness around those dark eyes was an indicator that she had been crying.

"The place is a mess, I know, and for that I apologize," Dana said. "I keep my nephew's two kids—boys ages three and five—and they are natural-born destroyers. They can tear a room apart in a matter of minutes. I call them my two little cyclones."

She led Eric and Vee into the den and motioned for them to have a seat. Eric waited until both women were settled in before he sat.

"I'm Eric Gamble and this is Vee Jefferson," Eric said. "We're with the Homicide Unit. First off, let me say how sorry we are for your loss. We . . ."

"Homicide? Are you saying Mike was murdered?"

"Yes, ma'am, he was."

"My lord, I just assumed he took his own life. I mean, he was so depressed and so disappointed in how his life had turned out. He lived under a dark cloud. So when you informed me that he was dead I figured he had decided to end his misery."

"The evidence makes it clear that his death was the result of a homicide."

"Do you have any suspects?" Dana asked. "Any idea why someone would want to kill Mike?"

"That's what we're trying to find out," Eric answered, before looking at Vee and nodding.

"Mrs. Perkins, what can you tell us about Mike's financial situation?" Vee said.

"What financial situation? Mike had no money. He lived like a pauper. He *was* a pauper."

"We found a bag in Mike's apartment containing well in excess of one-hundred-thousand dollars. Plus, we know he donated one-hundred grand to the Catholic Church. No pauper has that much money."

Dana seemed incredulous. "That's preposterous," she stated. "Where would Mike come up with a small fortune like that? And if he had all that money, if it really was his, why continue to live the way he did?"

"Those are questions that need to be answered." Vee shifted in her seat and surveyed the room. "You have a very nice house, Mrs. Perkins. Very impressive."

"Thank you, Detective. And, please, call me Dana."

Vee said, "Do you own the house, Dana?"

"Well, it's paid for, if that's what you're asking. My brother Jerry and his wife bought the place seventeen years ago. Jerry was Mike's father. Jerry's wife Sandy died two years after they moved in. Ovarian cancer. Then six years ago Jerry passed away. He left the house to me. I've lived here ever since."

"What line of work was Jerry in?" Eric said. "To pay off the mortgage for a place like this in such a short period of time indicates that he must have been very successful."

"Jerry was an orthodontist, so, yes, he did very well. And Sandy had a life insurance policy worth quite a bit. I know Jerry used some of that money to pay off the mortgage."

"Do you live here alone?"

Dana nodded.

"Big place for one person," Vee said.

"My two nephews are here five days a week, so I have plenty of company during the day. Occasionally, they'll spend a Friday or Saturday night with me. I don't know what I'll do when they start school."

Eric said, "When was the last time you saw Mike?"

"This past Monday. I picked him up at his apartment and drove him to the memorial service for Dale Larraby. They worked together as police officers."

"How did Mike seem to you?"

"Same as he always did. Down, depressed, despondent."

"Do you know if Mike had any enemies? If he was having trouble with someone?"

"Sadly, Detective, I wasn't privy to Mike's personal life. Hadn't been for many years. Not since he began to go downhill. When that happened he shut us all out of his life."

"I knew Mike back in those days," Eric said. "He was a truly formidable dude, one of the strongest guys I've ever been around. No one dared mess with him. And then one day the Mike we all knew was gone, replaced by this whole other person. Do you have any idea what happened to cause such a drastic transformation?"

"No, I don't. But what I can tell you is it happened almost overnight. I asked Mike about it a hundred times and all he would do was shrug. He never once ever attempted to give me an answer."

"Could it have been because his parents died?"

"No. I think it's the other way around. His downfall contributed to their deaths."

Eric stood, followed by Vee. "If you think of anything that might be helpful, don't hesitate to let us know," Eric said, handing Dana one of his cards. "And I give you my word that we'll do everything within our power to find the person or persons responsible for your nephew's death."

"Thank you, Detective. Thanks to both of you."

As they stepped outside and were heading to Eric's car, Vee said, "I like that woman. Want to know why?"

"Okay, I'll bite. Why?"

"Because she didn't inquire about what happens to all that money. The average person would. They'd want to know if some of it—maybe all of it—was coming their way. She never gave it a second thought."

"Don't be too quick to make that judgment, Vee. Once she gets over the initial shock of losing her nephew and starts thinking about the money, she might develop an interest. And you know what? There's a possibility she might end up getting it all."

_˄_

Two men, one short and muscular, the other tall and overweight, sat across from each other at the same back table in McDonald's. This time, however, they were joined by a third man. He was much older than his two companions, both of whom appeared to be slightly nervous in his presence. And for good reason. They had known the older man for decades, and were keenly aware of how draconian his judgment could be for anyone unlucky enough to incur his wrath.

"I said no fuck-ups," the older man whispered in a harsh tone. "And what happens? A major fuck-up. I might as well have sent an amateur to handle the job."

"Shit happens," the short man replied.

"*Shit happens?* That'll be a sorry defense when you're standing trial for murder." The older man leaned back and crossed his arms. "How could you screw up like that? Everybody knows Mike Perkins was a lefty, yet you leave the weapon beneath his right hand. How stupid are you?"

"Why are you bitchin' like this? The problem has been eliminated."

"Wrong, my stupid friend. The problem is just beginning. Now you have Dantzler involved. That's like having the proverbial bug up your ass."

"If Dantzler becomes too big a problem, we'll eliminate him."

The older man looked at his tall companion, and said, "Do you hear this fool? Eliminate Dantzler, he says. This guy is a comedian. He should have his own comedy show on TV."

"Look, all I'm saying is we have more immediate concerns than Dantzler," the short man said, trying to salvage what remained of his dignity. "One isn't such a big problem, but the other one is."

"The female writer you told me about?" the older man said.

"Yeah, her. Should we take her out?"

"More bodies falling all around us? Is that what you want?"

"I want to do what needs to be done, that's all."

"I've already told you what needs to be done, and it doesn't include the girl. Not yet, anyway. That decision won't be made until we see how things shake out." The older man stood. "This time try not to fuck-up. Okay?"

After the older man had departed, the short one looked at his tall friend, and said, "You sure added a lot to the conversation. Thanks for nothing."

"I learned a long time ago to keep my trap shut when he's in one of those moods. Last thing I want is to get on his shit list."

CHAPTER EIGHTEEN

Dantzler nailed it when he predicted that Mayor Elizabeth Anderson would hold a press conference to announce that Captain Richard Bird, head of the Homicide Unit, was retiring after thirty-two years on the job. Mayor Anderson, like virtually all politicians, did not shy away from standing in the spotlight or in front of a TV camera. Publicity was the nourishment that kept them going. Though small in stature, the mayor was feisty, fearless, outspoken, and super intelligent. Few could go toe to toe with her and walk away the winner.

Along with Mayor Anderson, others standing in front of the media mob included Bird, Chief of Police Tyrone Douglas, former Chief Robert Vincent, Charlie Bolton, Dantzler, several members of the city council, and a state senator. Only the elected officials appeared to be comfortable in this situation; the cops all looked like they would rather be anywhere but here.

The mayor got it started by saying a few kind words about Bird, praising him for his long years of service to the city of Lexington. Douglas and Vincent, the current and former police chiefs, were next to speak. Both men echoed what Mayor Anderson said while also tossing in a few anecdotes, all of which would have been far more colorful had they been told in front of a different crowd. The state senator was next to praise Bird, which surely came as a surprise to him, since he had met the man exactly one time. No one asked Dantzler or Charlie to speak, and that was fine with them. They had no problem serving as window dressing.

Once all the speakers had their say Bird was presented with a couple of nice plaques, his gold shield in a glass case, a key to the city, and a framed charcoal drawing of him done by a talented local artist. It was all small stuff. Nothing big like a new automobile, lifetime season tickets to University of Kentucky basketball games, or an all-expenses-paid trip to some exotic country. On balance, Bird received nice gifts, but not too nice.

To no one's surprise Mayor Anderson said she had time to take a few questions from the local reporters on hand to cover the ceremony. Upon hearing that the other dignitaries took this as their cue to exit stage right, which they all happily did. They had better things to do than watch Mayor Anderson juke and jive with the media folks.

"Damn, I'm glad that's over and done with," Bird said, handing the framed drawing to Dantzler. "Totally unnecessary, if you want my opinion."

"Be a good sport, Rich," Dantzler said. "Truth is, you deserve a helluva lot more than you got."

Charlie slapped Bird on the back, said, "I agree with Jack. You got shortchanged, Rich."

"My wife says she got shortchanged every time she sees me in the nude."

"Hell, isn't that what all women say?" Charlie said.

When the three men entered the police station every cop in the place stood and applauded. Dantzler and Charlie stepped away from Bird and joined the celebration. After the clapping and whistling subsided, Bruce Rawlinson strolled forward and handed Bird a bottle of Dom Perignon.

"Only the best for the best, Captain," Rawlinson said, his voice sounding close to breaking. "From all of us, with our respect, appreciation, and admiration. We'll always be your guys."

Bird held up the bottle of champagne, and said, "I'm deeply moved by this, and I'm honored to have worked with each and every one of you. But I'm not out of your hair for another three weeks. Regardless of how much you kiss up to me, you aren't getting a raise, so knock it off and get back to work."

Bird's order to his troops was met with the usual chorus of boos and false cries of disappointment. He expected nothing less when he shouted the order. It was all in good fun and everyone knew it. Brothers and sisters in blue, comrades through good and bad times. Only firefighters and those in the military could understand and appreciate such bonding.

Dantzler had started for the door when he felt a hand on his shoulder. It was Charlie Bolton. "What's up, Charlie?" Dantzler asked.

"Making any headway on the Mike Perkins murder?"

"Haven't moved the needle one inch."

"You will."

"You got that right, Charlie."

On his way outside Dantzler's cell phone went off. He checked the caller ID and didn't recognize the number. Opening the phone, he identified himself and said hello.

"Detective Dantzler, this is Carole Perkins. I hate to bother you this late in the afternoon, but I really need to meet with you. Do you think that's possible?"

Hearing her voice reminded Dantzler of something that had completely slipped his mind—this poor woman's two ex-husbands had died within the past week, one by his own hand, the other a homicide victim. With so much going on he had forgotten all about her.

"Sure, Carole, I can meet with you whenever it's convenient. Did you have a time in mind?"

"Right now," Carole said with urgency in her voice.

"Are you at home?"

"No, I'm at Dale's condo."

"That's on Waller Avenue, right?"

"Yes, Waller Avenue."

"Give me twenty minutes and I'll be there."

Dantzler ended the call, went back inside, and found Jake talking to Bruce Rawlinson. "Come on, Jake," Dantzler said, "we're going for a ride."

Seventeen minutes later Dantzler and Jake pulled off Waller and saw Carole standing in front of the condo complex. Dantzler whipped the Mercedes into the lot, parked next to a white BMW, and cut the engine. He and Jake exited the car and headed in Carole's direction.

"Thank you for meeting with me, Detective," Carole said, turning quickly and opening the ground-floor condo door. "I think it's important that you see what I found inside."

"What did you find?" Dantzler asked.

"It's better if I just show it to you." Carole hurried across the living room and entered a bedroom off to the right. "I came by to check on the place, just to see if everything was all right. When a place is vacant for an extended period of time it tends to attract people with bad intentions. I wanted to make sure the place hadn't been broken into or vandalized in any way."

Carole was speaking rapid-fire, almost to the point of babbling, as she moved closer to the bed. Jake glanced at Dantzler and gave one of those what-the-hell-is-up-with-her looks. Dantzler shrugged and shook his head. He had no idea what was on her mind, but something had shaken her to the core.

"It's there," Carole said, pointing to the bed.

Dantzler saw nothing but a perfectly made-up bed. He looked at Jake, then back at Carole, and said, "What am I looking for?"

"Under the bed," Carole said. "I found it, saw what was inside, put it back under the bed, and then I phoned you."

Jake knelt down and shone his flashlight under the bed. Two suitcases were side by side, and behind them was a green army duffel bag. Jake put the flashlight on the floor next to him, dropped down onto his belly, and crawled under the bed. The two suitcases came out first, followed by the duffel bag.

"Those suitcases are empty," Carole said.

Jake stood, picked up the duffel bag, tossed it onto the bed, unsnapped the top flap, opened it, and turned it upside down.

Stacks of hundred-dollar bills landed on the bed.

"That's got to be more than we found in Mike's place," Jake noted. "Way more."

Dantzler picked up a couple of the stacks and fanned through them. "I'd say there's at least twice as much here," he said, tossing the money back onto the bed. "Easily a couple hundred thou."

"Didn't Eric and Vee toss this place after Larraby died?"

"Call Eric, tell him what we found. Ask him if they looked under the bed."

As Jake moved into the living room to make the call, Dantzler picked up the duffel bag and looked to see if a name was stenciled on it. There was none. Looking at Carole, he said, "Did Larraby serve in the military?"

"No. Dale worked in the steel mills up near Chicago before coming back to Lexington and joining the police force."

Jake came back into the bedroom, said, "According to Eric, Vee checked the bedroom and did mention finding two suitcases, both of which were empty. Eric said he spent most of his time in the other bedroom, the one Larraby used as his office. That's where he found a copy of Larraby's will."

"Vee made the classic rookie mistake—she gave up too quick She just assumed the duffel bag was also empty."

"In her defense, the duffel bag was partially hidden by the suitcases. And it was pretty far back there, up against that wall. The suitcases were easy to bring out; the duffel bag wouldn't have been."

"You'd make a fine defense attorney, Jake," Dantzler said, adding, "relax, I'm not upset with Vee. She and Eric weren't here to find hard evidence; after all, we knew from the start that this was a suicide, not a homicide. They were primarily here to find something that would give us a reason why Larraby did what he did."

"Why do you think Dale took his own life?" Carole asked.

"I can't answer that, Carole. But what I do know is that his suicide and Mike's murder are both connected to the money we found. Unless we can find out how they got all this cash I'm afraid we're going to keep stumbling around in the dark."

CHAPTER NINETEEN

J ulie finished off her taco salad, pushed the plate away, took her notebook out, opened it, and began scanning the notes she had recorded. She still didn't have nearly as much information as she'd hoped to have after three days of investigating, but at least she had come up with more today than she did yesterday. Progress was the goal, even slow progress. Always keep moving forward, she reminded herself. Advance, advance, advance.

Julie paid her bill, got into her car, and drove to the Embassy Suites. She stood in front of the elevator for a few minutes, then decided she would go to the bar and have a drink. Maybe several drinks. She needed fortification, a good dose of liquid courage. Because once she went to her suite she had to make a call to Darvis Bernstein and Nancy Sloan. Putting off updating them any longer wasn't a wise move. She had promised to keep them informed, and promises made must be kept.

Pissing off the boss is never a good thing, especially when he controls the purse strings.

Julie took a seat at the bar, thought about ordering a glass of wine, but opted instead for something stronger. This was not the time for a weak, girly drink. Tonight, she'd go with a gin and tonic. So, she ordered one, telling the bartender to make it strong. He complied. Three of these babies ought to be enough to get the job done, Julie said to herself, after taking the first sip. Nothing weak or girly about this drink. Holding up her glass, she saluted the bartender for a job well done.

She never made it to drink number three. After the second one she was already feeling a strong buzz. And a bit woozy. One more and she would be falling down drunk, certainly in no condition to have an intelligent conversation with Darvis and Nancy. She would be slurring her words, saying God knows what. If that happened Darvis would tell her no more money, just get your ass home. Our deal is off.

And who could blame him?

Julie made it to her room, sat on the bed, and opened her cell phone. Then she tossed it on the bed. Picking up her bag she pulled out the notebook and looked through her notes. *Damn, I wish I had more before I make this call*. That thought ran wild in her mind. Darvis needed more than this. Hell, he expected more than this.

Suddenly, Julie felt sick at her stomach and it wasn't from the alcohol. A legion of butterflies was swarming deep in her gut. She'd had moments of doubt, moments of fear in the past, but none of those began to compare with how she was feeling right now. This was different, something else entirely, and she didn't like it.

"*Get a hold of yourself*", she said out loud. "*You can do this. You know you can. You've done it before.*"

Julie picked up the phone and punched in Darvis's number. While waiting for him to answer she made the decision to be as honest with him as possible. Being on the up and up was always her primary goal. But . . . if she felt the need to stretch the truth a few degrees, that's what she would do. That plan of attack couldn't be implemented until she got a read on Darvis's reception to the facts she was relaying to him. If he didn't appear to like what he was hearing, and if she felt things were going badly, that's when she would fudge the facts.

Maybe not fudge them so much as finesse them.

"Julie, dear, we were beginning to wonder if you had deserted us," Darvis said. Then: "Hold on a second while I put you on speaker. Nancy's here with me."

"Hello, guys," Julie said. "No, I didn't take your advance money and head off to the beach. I've just been really busy."

"That's what we wanted to hear," Darvis said. "Would I be correct in assuming that your source got back in touch with you? What was his name again?"

"Danny Michaels. And no, I haven't heard from him."

"That can't be good. So, what has been keeping you busy?"

"Julie, this is Nancy. I hate to sound like the skeptic here, but is it realistic for us to continue to believe in this project? With no source, where do you turn?"

Julie said, "To be perfectly honest, I don't think I need Danny Michaels anymore. Regarding your question about continuing with the project, my answer is a stern yes. There is more reason now than ever to keep going."

"On what basis?" asked Darvis.

"When I did speak with Danny he gave me a list of names. He . . ."

"A list? What list?"

"The names of six men who were on the Lexington police force when Gloria Nash disappeared."

"Why are we just now hearing about this list? Why weren't we told about it during our previous meeting?"

Finesse time. "I held off telling you until I could do some research," Julie said. "I wanted to make absolutely sure these men existed and did in fact work in law enforcement."

"And did they? Was Danny truthful?"

"Yes. And here's where things become quite intriguing. One of the six men died several years ago from a heart attack. Danny must not have been aware of that. However, within the past week two more of those men died. Both of them committed suicide."

"Hmm, that does sound suspicious, to say the least. Were they aware that you wanted to speak with them?"

"No. One killed himself before I got to town, the second one died yesterday. But I have spoken to two of the men, neither of whom was helpful or forthcoming. In fact, if stonewalling was an art form they would both be great artists."

"Stonewalling or hiding something?" Nancy asked.

"I don't know if they were hiding anything, but they were both quick to tell me I was wasting my time. That I needed to forget about it and move on."

"Perhaps they know something you don't," said Darvis.

"I don't think there's any doubt about that. I believe they are guilty of something, and that it just might have to do with Gloria Nash's murder. The last thing they want is for me or anyone else to go snooping around."

"You don't know for a fact that Gloria Nash was murdered."

"But I do know for a fact that she went missing and hasn't been found."

"Are the two you spoke with still on the job?"

"Both are retired. One is in a wheelchair, the result of a car crash."

"Did his accident happen after Gloria went missing?"

"I'm pretty sure it did."

Darvis paused briefly, then said, "You said there were six names on that list. Three are dead and you've spoken to two. What about the sixth man?"

"Sean Montgomery. He's an attorney here in town. I'm scheduled to meet with him tomorrow afternoon."

"Okay, Julie, it does sound like you might be onto something. But if you don't hear from Danny Michaels, or if your interview with this lawyer is a bust, what would be your next step?"

"Do what I always do, Darvis. Just keep turning over rocks until I find something that leads to the next rock. Sooner or later I'll find the truth."

Nancy said, "Type up your notes on what you have and e-mail them to me. And please be very careful. If these men have committed one murder they won't hesitate to kill again. If you are threatened, or if you feel your life is in danger, tell the authorities. Let them deal with it. No book is worth your life."

"Don't worry guys, I can take care of myself."

Ending the call, Julie wasn't truly convinced that she believed her own words.

The short, muscular man sat in his car thinking about his two companions, neither of whom he had much use for. Never had, never will. He disliked them for very different reasons, but in the end did reasons really matter? No, they didn't.

He had long ago realized that one of the men was little more than a chicken-shit coward. Oh, sure, he always talked a big game, let on like he could really handle himself in dire situations, but that was far from the truth. The man would crap his pants at the first sign of real danger. Gutless, useless, worthless . . . those were words that best described him.

The second man, the older one, was a different story altogether. He didn't lack for courage or bravery. Those were qualities he had in abundance. And he'd proved it many times over the years. He didn't back down, never avoided a fight. He seemed to thrive on danger. When the guns came out he was always in the middle of the action.

Why, then, did the short, muscular man hate him so much? That was a great question, one the man had asked himself many times over the years. His answer was more complicated than he cared to admit.

He appreciated true toughness, and heaven knows the old man was plenty tough. But the old man was also someone who had to dominate. Everything had to be his way and there was no arguing or debating. Never. Disagreeing with him could get a man shot. That had happened in the past. One of the first lessons to learn was never cross this man. Under any circumstances.

Sitting in his car, with midnight rapidly approaching, the short man pondered what he might have to do before all this played out. The situation, he knew, was fairly simple. He'd have to take out those two bastards. He couldn't do it now; he had a more pressing issue to deal with first. Also, too many bodies popping up in such a short period of time would invariably bring on a tremendous amount of heat. He didn't need that.

But sometime down the road, who knows? They might have to go.

And so, too, that damn female writer who has been snooping around.

She was a loose thread that might have to be clipped.

_^_

Danny Michaels craved one of those hot dogs he loved so much. Truth is, if he could get to the Minit Mart he'd buy two, maybe three. Lather on the mustard, add some relish, and down they would go. Follow up with one of those Big Gulp drinks that are cool and refreshing.

Damn, I want those hot dogs.

But it was shortly past midnight, so a trip to the Minit Mart, although just down the street, was out of the question. No way he could call and ask for permission at this late hour. And for a hot dog? Hell, if he woke someone up with that request they'd probably haul his ass to jail tonight. And he damn sure didn't want that to happen.

Another option was to remove the ankle bracelet, which he was certain he could do. But then what? Getting the blasted thing back on and in perfect working order might not be such an easy thing to do. If he screwed up the bracelet then it was back to jail for sure, no questions asked.

Better to sit here and starve rather than take unnecessary chances. He had given his word to Mr. Montgomery that he would follow the rules, and that's what he would do. Mr. Montgomery was an ally, and at a desperate time like this the last thing you want to do is alienate your friends.

Danny just wished that Mr. Montgomery would talk to his lady pal in the district attorney's office and get the ball rolling. If she would listen to his story, really take him seriously, Danny was convinced he could get out from under this mess he was in. He was in trouble because of crappy luck more than anything. Who knew that rich little prick who bought the pills was going to hand them out like M&M's to his friends? And that one of the friends would get sick and almost die?

And that her old man was in the sheriff's department? Talk about a trifecta of shitty luck.

Still . . . if the D.A. would just meet with him for fifteen minutes, and if she would agree to drop the charges and put him in the Witness Protection Program, he'd tell her a story that would blow her mind.

Danny dug into his pants pocket and pulled out a wadded ball of bills. He smoothed them out and counted them. Six bucks. All the money he had in the world. Not much, to be sure, but enough to buy a couple of those hot dogs, if only he could get to the Minit Mart. Wasn't going to happen, he decided, so put the damn things out of your mind.

Danny reached into the other pocket and came out with a small scrap of paper. On it were Julie Bradley's name and cell phone number. He had promised to call her at some point, but when all this other shit happened he simply didn't have the time. Nor was calling her a big priority. Keeping his ass out of jail for the next ten years, *that* was a big priority.

Danny silently made a promise to phone her sometime later today. After all, he did have more information to pass along. Information she could definitely use.

Another name that belongs on that list he'd given her.

CHAPTER TWENTY

David Bloom had just ended the first session of the day, working with a reed-thin fifteen-year-old girl who saw herself as being at least fifty pounds overweight. She was all skin and bones, and she looked as if she hadn't had a meal in two weeks. And after the last one she had consumed she probably ran straight to the bathroom and sent all that nutritious food straight into the toilet. Like far too many young women—especially those in the celebrity-mad United States—self-image was becoming a more and more serious issue each year. Self-image was, unfortunately, closely linked to self-worth. If a young woman's body didn't resemble those of the movie stars and models she idolized, self-hatred was the inevitable result.

To Bloom's way of thinking, whoever was perpetuating this thin-is-in image, be it Hollywood or the fashion industry, they should be ashamed of themselves. They were doing far more harm than good, regardless of how much money they raked in. More to the point, what they were really doing was making a farce out of the old belief that beauty is only skin deep.

If it were left up to him Bloom would gladly send them all to hell.

When Bloom followed the young woman out of his office he was surprised to see Richard Bird talking with Emily Stern, Bloom's long-time receptionist. Although he had known Bird for many years, and had consulted for the Homicide Unit on numerous occasions, he had never met with the man in a one-on-one situation. Especially not in his office, and not in a professional capacity.

"It's good to see you, Richard," Bloom said, adding, "and something of a surprise. Is everything all right?"

"Everything is fine. I know you are busy, and I'm barging in without giving you a heads-up, but if you can spare a few minutes, I'd like to talk with you about something."

Bloom looked at Emily, said, "When is my next appointment?"

"You have Eileen Mattingly in twenty minutes."

"Does that give us enough time, Richard?" Bloom asked.

"More than enough. Ten minutes is about all I need."

"Then step into my humble office and tell me what's on your mind."

"Actually, I need to know what's on your mind, Doc."

"Ah, the shrink being shrinked. Should be interesting."

Bloom sat in the leather chair behind his desk and motioned for Bird to take the seat opposite him. When both men were settled in, Bloom said, "What can I do for you, Richard?"

"Has Jack informed you that I'm retiring in three weeks?"

Bloom nodded.

Bird continued, "That means there will soon be a vacancy that has to be filled. We both know who my replacement should be—Jack. But he insists that he's not interested in taking over the Homicide Unit. Claims he wouldn't be good at it. Do you agree with that?"

"Yes. Jack is a born hunter and the bad guys are his prey. If they are out there he's going to get them. He always does. You can't put a hunter behind a desk in an office. That's not his natural habitat, not where he can best be utilized. Jack doesn't have an administrator's mentality."

"That's what he says."

"There's another matter to take into consideration—Jack is also thinking about retiring. Has he shared that with you?"

"Yeah, he dropped that bomb on me a few days ago. You think he's serious?"

"He wouldn't have said it if he weren't."

Bird was quiet for a few seconds, then said, "Well, that brings me to the real reason why I'm here. I have two options when it comes to filling my position—bring in someone from the outside, or hire from within. Chief Douglas and I prefer the latter option. Bringing in a stranger invariably means a time-consuming learning curve for that individual. Getting familiar with the lay of the land doesn't happen overnight. It can also translate into low morale for the rank-and-file, most of whom would rather stick with a devil they know than have to deal with a devil they don't know. If I were in their shoes, I'd feel the same way."

"What you're really asking me is, do I think Eric Gamble is ready to lead the Homicide Unit? Am I right?"

"I know you've never worked with Eric, but you have been around him on many occasions. I need your assessment on his suitability for the position."

"Jack is convinced Eric is ready. Isn't that good enough for you?"

"Maybe. Probably. But when I meet with Chief Douglas next week I'll need as much ammunition as I can get. He'll want Eric, but he will have to be convinced before he signs off on it. That's as it should be. Jack's recommendation will help, no question about it. But your opinion might count for even more, because it will come with no politics or favoritism attached."

Bloom leaned back in his chair, took off his glasses, and stared up at the wall. "Here's what I think," he said, turning his gaze back to Bird. "From what I've observed, and from everything I hear, Eric Gamble is more than capable of handling your job. He's a sound thinker, he's professional, he's brave, he's compassionate, and he's fair. Those are qualities required for anyone hoping to be a successful leader. Another attribute Eric possesses is common sense. And that's something *every* successful leader must have. I don't give a crap how intelligent or brave a person is, if that individual lacks common sense, failure will be the outcome. Let me go one step further, Richard. Common sense may be the most important of all those attributes.

That's because at the heart of common sense is the understanding that you don't have all the answers, that you have to listen to voices and opinions from all sides of an argument, then gather the advice you've been given and make the decision you feel best serves the cause. That's where Jack might not be quite as good a leader as you think he would. He has plenty of common sense, but sometimes his voice is the only one he hears."

"So, in your judgment, Eric can handle the job?"

"If my opinion counts for anything when you meet with Chief Douglas you can tell him that I give Eric my blessing."

"Trust me, your opinion will count, Doc." Bird stood and stretched. Walking over to a wall, he studied an old black and white photo of Bloom and Dantzler, both of whom were holding trophies. "Looks like you guys took home the hardware."

"We had just won the NCAA doubles championship," Bloom said with pride. "I was a junior, Jack was a freshman. He was fifteen-years-old at the time. He won the singles title the next three years. Damn, he was good."

"Helluva detective, too. I suppose some people are blessed more than others."

"You've been a helluva detective yourself, Richard. You can walk away with your head held high."

"Thanks again for offering your advice, Doc. Looks like Eric gets the big seat at the table."

"Does he want it?"

"No one's mentioned it to him yet. We didn't feel the need to bring it up until we concluded he was the man for the job. Of course, what I say to Chief Douglas will only be a recommendation. He'll make the final call."

"You can tell the Chief that Eric has my highest recommendation."

"I will," Bird said, shaking Bloom's hand. "And thanks again for providing me with more ammunition. A man can never have too many bullets in the gun when he meets with a superior."

CHAPTER TWENTY-ONE

Dantzler and Jake walked into the small bar located on Versailles Road. The place was dark, music blared from an old jukebox, a mounted TV was on but the volume was either off or drowned out by the music, and although Lexington had enacted a smoking ban in public places, a hazy cloud of cigarette-smelling smoke floated near the ceiling.

This was Dantzler's first visit to the bar, which was owned and operated by Robbie Newcome. Robbie had once been on the job, and in Dantzler's memory he had been a decent cop. His career ended when he was involved in a serious automobile accident several years ago. Both of Robbie's legs were badly broken. Shattered, to be more precise. Initially, the doctors said he might never walk again, but after two years of extensive physical rehab he was able to do so. But he wasn't physically capable of handling the demands that go along with the job of a law enforcement officer. He was offered a full-time desk position but he declined. With money received from the settlement after the tragic accident he purchased the bar.

Robbie sat on a stool behind the bar but stood when he saw Dantzler and Jake enter. Standing, he was a tall man, on the thin side, and his head was shaved completely bald. Both forearms were heavily tattooed. Although he had come a long way since his accident, he still walked with a noticeable limp.

"Detective Jack Dantzler, to what do I owe this visit?" Robbie said, grinning. "Hope you don't think I've murdered anyone."

"The thought never crossed my mind, Robbie. I'm surprised you remember me."

"Hell, everybody knows you. You're famous. Who's your sidekick?"

"Jake Thomas," Jake said, extending his hand.

"Please to make your acquaintance, Jake. You also work Homicide?"

"I do."

"It's where I eventually wanted to end up," Robbie said, unable to hide the sadness in his voice. "But . . . things don't always turn out like you want them to."

Dantzler said, "I remember when you were on the job, Robbie. You were an excellent cop. I think you could have made it to Homicide."

"Yeah, well, a drunken driver ended that dream. Turned me into a bartender rather than a cop. A lousy exchange, if you want the truth."

"Bruce Rawlinson told me you own this place. Is he right?"

"Yep, it's all mine, for what it's worth. How is Bruce doing these days?"

"Bruce is Bruce. He'll never change, you know that." Dantzler looked around the place. No customers sat at the bar but a half-dozen or so were seated at tables. "How is business here?"

"We have a good group of regulars who come in, so I make a living. Things will really begin to pick up after the dinner hour." Robbie looked at Jake, then back at Dantzler. "But two homicide detectives didn't come in here to inquire about how the bar was doing, did they?"

"Bruce reminded me that you were close pals with Mike Perkins when you were on the job," Dantzler said. "That's why we're here."

"Mike Perkins, the iron man. Heard what happened to him, that he committed suicide. First Larraby, then Mike. What the hell is going on?"

"When was the last time you saw Mike?" Jake asked, ignoring Robbie's question.

"Last Thursday. He came in to say hello. Looked like he hadn't eaten in months, so I offered to buy his lunch. We have great hamburgers here. Told him I'd get him one and throw in some fries along with it. He declined my offer, said he wasn't hungry. Damn near made me cry, seeing how bad he looked. I probably shouldn't have been all that shocked when I heard he offed himself. He looked like a man who had reached the end of the road."

Dantzler had come here in search of information, but in this instance, getting it meant giving up details unknown to the public. Details known only to the cops and to Mike's killer. Keeping certain facts hidden from the public was standard procedure in most homicide cases. Dantzler's decision now was whether or not to share those details with an outsider, even one who once wore the uniform.

"Robbie, do you still have any of the cop left in you?" Dantzler asked, after a minute or more of silence.

"I'm not following you," replied Robbie, genuinely puzzled.

"If I share with you details about Mike's death that are not known to the public, can you keep it to yourself?"

"If that's what you want, then, sure, you know I will. You can trust me."

"Mike didn't commit suicide. He was murdered."

"For real? Are you sure about that?"

"Was Mike right-handed or left-handed?" Jake asked.

"Mike was a lefty."

"The killer tried to make it look like a suicide but he made two crucial mistakes. He shot Mike in his right temple, and he placed the gun on the floor under Mike's right hand," Jake said. "That's how we know it wasn't a suicide."

Dantzler said, "That's just one unknown detail we'll share with you. Here's the other one: in Mike's bedroom we found one-hundred-twenty-four thousand dollars stuffed in a bag. All in hundred-dollar bills."

"You think it was Mike's money?"

"It was in his apartment, so, yeah, I have to believe it was his."

"No way Mike could have had that much money," Robbie said.

"Oh, he had way more than that," said Jake. "Over the past eight years he donated one-hundred-thousand dollars to Christ the King Church."

"Are we talking about the same Mike Perkins? The one who came in here last Thursday looking like a starving homeless person?"

"One and the same," Dantzler replied.

"How do you think he got that much money?" asked Robbie.

"Good question. How long did you work with Mike?"

"Almost four years. You know, up until he sorta went bonkers."

"What's your best guess as to what caused him to change so suddenly."

Robbie thought about the question, then said, "Honestly, I can't answer that. All I can say is that he did. And it was like overnight."

"Who else did he hang out with back then?" Jake asked.

"You know, mostly the guys in Missing Persons. We had a bowling team back then, called ourselves the Pin Pricks. Me, Mike, Larraby, and Eddie Campbell, mainly. Jimmy Newman would show up sometimes and keep score. I don't recall him ever bowling with us. Damn, three of those guys are dead now. And Eddie, well, you know about him. He was driving the car when that drunk son-of-a-bitch rammed us head-on at eighty miles an hour. Put Eddie's ass in a wheelchair for life."

"I'd forgotten the two of you were together when that happened," Dantzler said.

"Oh, almost forgot. There was another fellow who sometimes bowled with us. A lawyer named Brady."

Dantzler's eyes lit up. "Lawrence Brady?" he asked.

"Yeah, that's him. He was big buddies with Larraby and Eddie. Me, I never cared much for the man. Came off as a little on the sleazy side, if you want my opinion."

"Did Mike have any dealings with Brady?" inquired Jake.

"If he did I have no knowledge of it."

"Did Mike say anything that might be of interest to us?"

"Not that I recall."

"Robbie, please keep this info on the QT," Dantzler reminded.

"You got it, Detective Dantzler. But before you go I have a question for you?"

"Shoot."

"Why murder a guy and then leave all that cash behind?"

"Two reasons, Robbie. Either the killer didn't know the money was there, or if he did, he had no interest in taking it. He wasn't there to commit robbery; he was there with a single goal in mind—silence Mike Perkins."

"Silence Mike? From saying what? To who?"

"I don't know, Robbie. But whatever it was it had to be very important."

As Dantzler and Jake were leaving Robbie's bar, Dantzler saw that he had a missed message on his phone. The call was from Father Steven Mulaney.

"Detective Dantzler, I have those dates when Mike Perkins donated money to the church. He made them in two-thousand nine, two-thousand eleven, two-thousand thirteen and two-thousand fifteen. As I previously told you, all donations were made on June first. And like I also told you, we were expecting another donation in a couple of weeks. If you have further questions, feel free to contact me at any time. Happy to be of assistance. Have a good day, Detective."

"Anything important?" Jake asked, as they got into the car.

"Not really," Dantzler answered. "It was Father Mulaney confirming the dates when Mike made his donations to the church."

"I'm still having a difficult time believing Mike had that kind of cash."

"Well, believe it, Jake, 'cause he did."

-^-

Julie showed up a half-hour early for her meeting with Sean Montgomery. Arriving ahead of the appointed meeting time was standard procedure for her. Many times in the past, the individual she had come to see ended his or her meeting ahead of schedule and was able to take Julie right in. She had come early today hoping that would be the case.

It wasn't. Susan Collins, Sean's receptionist, informed Julie that Sean had several important phone calls to make and likely wouldn't be available before the scheduled meeting time. Susan asked if Julie wanted some coffee or a bottle of water but Julie said she didn't.

Sitting there, Julie thought about what she wanted to ask Sean. She scribbled several questions in her notebook, looked them over, and then added a couple more. Of course, Julie realized, questions were like the jump ball in basketball or the kickoff in football. They only served to get the real action underway. In this situation, Sean's response to her questions would, hopefully, lead not only to important information but to follow-up questions as well. That's how a serious question-and-answer session worked.

The deeper you delve the more you come up with.

Julie was also aware that for this to happen Sean needed to be a more willing and more forthcoming subject than Alex Shannon and Eddie Campbell had been. She learned nothing of importance from either man. All she got from them was scorn and ridicule.

Assholes.

Julie looked at her watch; ten more minutes until her meeting time with Sean. Opening her notebook, she again looked at the questions she had prepared for the interview. Number four on the list asked Sean to offer his opinion on Shannon and Campbell. She quickly drew an arrow, moving that question up to number one.

But she never got the chance to ask it.

Sean burst out of his office with such force that it startled Susan Collins, causing her to nearly come out of her chair. "What's the matter, Sean?" she practically screamed. "What's going on?"

"Danny Michaels was found dead in his apartment," answered Sean, as he moved quickly toward the door. "I need to get over there and see what happened."

As he neared the door he looked over and saw Julie standing there, eyes wide, mouth open, as though she had something to say but couldn't get the words out. Sean shifted directions and came over to her.

"Julie, I'm Sean Montgomery," he said. "Something has come up that needs my immediate attention. I'm afraid we're going to have to postpone our talk. I'm terribly sorry about running out on you, but this matter takes priority. Get with Susan and schedule a time for tomorrow afternoon. You have my promise that I will be here."

Having finished his apology he gave Julie a gentle tap on the shoulder and took off for the door.

"Sean, I think you need to listen to what I have to say," Julie yelled.

"Tomorrow, I will. You have my word," Sean replied, not looking over his shoulder at her.

"Danny Michaels is the reason I came to see you in the first place."

That announcement stopped Sean in his tracks. Turning, he walked up to Julie, and said, "You knew Danny Michaels?"

"No, I only spoke to him once on the phone. He gave me a list of names, six men, and said I needed to speak with them. Your name was on the list."

"Speak to those six men about what?"

"A murder."

"A murder?"

"Yes."

"You sure about that?"

"Absolutely."

"Come with me, Julie."

Sean left the office with Julie following close behind.

CHAPTER TWENTY-TWO

Danny Michaels's lifeless body lay sprawled in an old recliner that had springs and white stuffing coming out of both sides and underneath. His head lolled to the right, his glassy eyes open and staring into nothingness. Dried vomit was on his chin and the torn T-shirt he had on. A clear rubber tube was tied tightly above his left elbow, and a syringe lay on the floor beneath his right hand.

Dantzler was standing off to Danny's left as Arnie Edwards examined the body. Jake drifted through the rest of the tiny apartment searching for anything that might be of interest.

Sean entered, took one look at Danny, and knew this was all bullshit. "This is another homicide, Jack. I don't give a shit how it looks." Sean moved closer to the body. "Danny Michaels never did drugs, not even pot. Plus, he was terrified of needles. He would never stick something like that in his arm. Never."

"You are preaching to the choir, Sean," Arnie said. "We've already concluded that this poor young man did not take his own life."

Dantzler motioned for Sean to come even closer to the body. Pointing at a place on Danny's neck, he said, "What's that look like to you, Sean?"

"A bruise. Probably resulting from a choke-hold."

"Almost identical to what we found on Mike Perkins," Arnie added.

"When was the last time you saw Danny?" asked Dantzler.

"Two days ago," Sean answered. "But I spoke with him on the phone yesterday."

"How did he sound to you?"

"Normal. He bitched about not being able to walk up to the Minit Mart on the corner and buy a couple of hot dogs, but otherwise he was fine."

Jake pointed at Danny's right foot. "Why the ankle bracelet, Sean?"

"This past weekend Danny was arrested for selling drugs. He . . ."

"Thought you said Danny didn't do drugs," interrupted Dantzler.

"He didn't."

"What about selling them? Is it possible that his death is somehow related to the drug world?"

"Hell no, it isn't. Danny sold two bottles of pills to a kid up in Woodland Park. Ritalin. Sold 'em for thirty bucks. Money he needed for food. The kid he sold them to then gave some to a couple of his friends, one of whom, a girl, had a serious reaction. Almost died. Her father is a deputy sheriff. He's going full bore on prosecuting Danny."

"A street kid like Danny could have some enemies. Can you think of anyone who might fit that category?"

"Most everyone liked Danny, which was easy to do. He was a likable guy."

"Well, at least one person didn't like him," quipped Jake.

Sean said, "Jack, there's a lady outside who you need to speak with ASAP."

Dantzler frowned, pointed at Danny's body, and said, "In case you haven't noticed, Sean, I'm looking at a second homicide here. I am kinda busy. Can't this wait?"

"No. You need to hear what she has to say."

"Who is this woman?"

"An author."

"Are you kidding me, Sean? I don't have time . . ."

"Just come with me, Jack. What she has to say is important."

"Does it relate to Danny Michaels's death?" Dantzler asked, in a somewhat sarcastic tone.

"Yes, it does."

"Okay, then lead the way."

_^_

Julie was standing in the shade, safely protected from the hot after-noon sun by an old elm tree. Sean hurried across the street several steps ahead of Dantzler, who still had his doubts about choosing to speak with an author he was unfamiliar with rather than continuing to work an active crime scene. Solving two homicides didn't allow for wasted time.

This better be good, Sean, or I'll kill you.

When the two men reached Julie, Sean made the introductions. Dantzler nodded but didn't extend his hand.

"Sean says you have information that might be of some value to me," Dantzler said, bypassing the usual first-meeting niceties..

"I have information that I know for a fact will be valuable," Julie said without hesitation.

Dantzler said, "It's pretty warm out here, even under this tree. It will be more comfortable if we talk in my car with the AC on."

They walked over to the Mercedes and got in, Dantzler and Julie in the front seats, Sean in the back. Dantzler started the motor, turned on the AC, and cranked it up to the max. Frosty air quickly began to successfully drive out the heat.

"All right, Julie. Let's hear what you have to say," Dantzler prompted. "Take it from the beginning."

"I don't know how much Sean told you, but I've written a couple of books. True Crime is the category my books fit into. After my second book came out I began looking around for a crime that might be worthy of the time and effort it would take me to write a new one. I wasn't having much luck. Then one day, about two weeks ago, out of the blue I received a phone call from Danny Michaels."

"How did Danny Michaels get your phone number?" Dantzler inquired.

"He must have read one of my books. My website is included in the author's bio section on the back cover. My phone number is listed on the website. I can only assume that's how he got the number."

"Okay, so two weeks ago Danny Michaels phones you," Dantzler said, picking up the story. "What was his reason for contacting you?"

"To tell me about a murder that took place in Lexington fifteen years ago."

"Who was the victim? Did he tell you that?"

"Gloria Nash."

Dantzler turned and looked over his shoulder at Sean. Then he looked back at Julie. "I've never worked a homicide case involving anyone named Gloria Nash," he said.

"That's because no one knew she had been murdered," Julie replied.

"And Danny Michaels knew this, how?"

"I can't answer that . . . only Danny can." Realizing what she'd just said, Julie whispered, "Sorry, I spoke before I thought."

"So, we have a murder victim that no one but Danny Michaels knew was murdered? Is that what you're telling me?"

Julie nodded, said, "Yes. Danny told me that Gloria's older sister reported her missing, and that Missing Persons briefly looked into it. Gloria wasn't located and the matter was soon dropped."

"When did this supposed crime take place?"

"All Danny said was fifteen years ago."

"How many times did you speak with Danny?"

"Just that one time. He promised to call again but he never did."

"And that's all he told you? This story about Gloria Nash being murdered? Is that correct?"

"No, there's more. Danny also gave me the names of six men, all of whom worked in Missing Persons, and told me to go speak with them. He said they would be at the heart of my story."

"Do you have those names with you?"

Julie ripped out a piece of paper from her notebook and handed it to Dantzler. "Those are the names he gave me," she said.

Dantzler studied the list of names, then said, "Why is your name on here, Sean?"

"I worked Missing Persons."

"You were in Homicide fifteen years ago," Dantzler pointed out.

"Danny didn't know that, obviously. But the better question is, why is that last man on the list at all?"

"Alex Shannon?"

"He was never in Missing Persons. He was a Vice guy his entire career."

"And not a very competent one at that," Dantzler stated.

"My memory of him is that he was a sorry excuse for a cop," Sean added.

Dantzler said, "Jimmy Newman has been dead for, what, three, four years now, Sean?"

"More like five or six."

"Wonder why his name was included?"

Julie said, "Danny probably had no idea Jimmy Newman had died. And when he gave me the list of names, Dale Larraby and Mike Perkins were still alive."

"I'm telling you, Jack, Danny knew something no one else did," Sean said.

"*Someone* else knew about it or Danny wouldn't be lying dead up in his apartment," responded Dantzler. To Julie: "Who other than the three of us know about this list?"

"Alex Shannon and Eddie Campbell," answered Julie.

"Have you spoken with them?"

"Yes."

Sean said, "I can't imagine those two being very helpful."

"Trust me, they weren't," Julie said.

"What did they tell you?" Dantzler asked.

"Basically, that I was wasting my time, that Danny Michaels was a hustler and a con man, and that I should drop the book project and move on."

"I would venture a guess that Alex Shannon was the more forceful of the two," Dantzler stated.

"Definitely. He was kind of scary."

"Jack, Marianne Ramsey also knows about Gloria Nash, but not about the list of names," Sean said.

"How did that happen? And why?"

"Danny wanted to trade information about Gloria's murder in exchange for Marianne dropping all charges. He also said if he did give all the details he needed to be placed in the Witness Protection Program. That his life wouldn't be worth a can of beans."

"If that's the case, then only Campbell, Shannon, and the three of us know about the list," Dantzler said. "But I'm still puzzled as to why Shannon's name was included. For me that's the most intriguing aspect about this."

"Do you guys think Alex Shannon is capable of murder?" Julie asked.

Neither Dantzler nor Sean answered immediately. It was Dantzler who finally responded.

"Yes."

"But only under someone else's orders," amended Sean. "Shannon was a tough guy, but he wasn't a leader."

"Did I make a mistake by telling Shannon and Campbell about the list?" Julie said.

"It would have been better if you hadn't," Dantzler answered, adding, "but that door can't be closed now, so there's no use lamenting about what's already been done. The info you've provided, combined with events from the past week, gives me a starting point, which is more than I had fifteen minutes ago."

"Did Danny give you the name of Gloria Nash's sister?" Sean said to Julie.

"No, he didn't."

"Can Bobby get that for you, Jack?"

"Should be able to. I'll call him first thing tomorrow morning."

"Who's Bobby?" inquired Julie.

"Bobby Clark. He's head of the Missing Persons Unit."

"Can he be trusted? Can anyone in Missing Persons be trusted?"

"Bobby's rock solid," Dantzler said. "He took over the unit long after Shannon and Campbell had retired. He'll help in any way he can."

"If you say so," Julie said, sounding far from convinced.

"Where are you staying?" Dantzler asked her.

"Embassy Suites on Newtown. Why?"

"I would recommend that you leave town, at least until we get this mess sorted out."

"No way. I'm here until this is finished."

"That could be a mistake."

"Why? You don't seriously think my life is in danger, do you?"

"I don't know. But are you willing to take that risk? Mike Perkins and Danny Michaels were both murdered within the past forty-eight hours. Mike was on the list, Danny gave you the list. By your own account, you, Shannon, and Campbell are the only people in town who know about the list and the names it contains. It should be clear to you that someone is eliminating those he views as a threat. That would include you."

"I'm not leaving," Julie said, adamantly. "I'll be vigilant but I'm staying."

"Jack's got a point, Julie," Sean said. "You live in Cincinnati, right?"

"Yes."

"That's a stone's throw from Lexington. Why not commute? That would be the wise thing to do."

"Guys, you aren't listening. I'm sticking around."

"Then you should at least change hotels," Dantzler advised. "And I need to know where you go, and how I can get in touch with you at all times."

"Not a problem."

"One last question, Julie. When you spoke with Danny, did he ever mention the name Lawrence Brady?"

This question got Sean's attention. Leaning forward, he said, "Why are you asking about 'Shady' Brady?"

"His name came up during a conversation I had with Robbie Newcome."

"No, Danny never mentioned that name to me," Julie said. "Why? Does he figure into this?"

"Julie, at this stage, everybody with a pulse and a heartbeat figures into it," Dantzler said, shutting off the AC. "And believe it or not, that includes you."

Before exiting the Mercedes Dantzler gave Julie one of his cards, and she wrote down her cell phone number for him. Dantzler tried once more to persuade Julie to leave town until the murders were solved, but quickly decided that he was wasting his breath. The woman was more stubborn than a mule.

Once they excited the vehicle Sean walked Julie to her car while Dantzler went across the street to Danny's apartment. Jake was coming out just as Dantzler reached the front door.

"Find anything interesting, Jake?" Dantzler asked.

"Just this," Jake said, holding up a piece of paper. "Arnie found it in Danny's pants pocket."

"What is it?"

"A note to Danny," Jake said, handing the paper to Dantzler. "From Robbie Newcome."

Dantzler unfolded the paper and read out loud: "Can't carry you any longer, Danny-boy. You owe big dollars, yet you keep avoiding us. You're leaving us no choice but to come by and collect in person. You don't want that. Come see me soon."

"That's a major league threat," Jake said. "No other way to characterize it."

"You're right about that. And the key word is 'us'. Who else was Robbie referring to when he used the plural term?"

"Robbie worked in Missing Persons, didn't he? So did Dale Larraby and Eddie Campbell. The note was written prior to Larraby's death. Maybe Robbie was referring to one of those guys."

"Maybe's not good enough, Jake. We need to find out for certain. And that's exactly what we're going to do, starting first thing tomorrow morning."

"Roger that."

CHAPTER TWENTY-THREE

The cool evening breeze carried on its shoulders the smell of rain. Off to the inky black eastern horizon a sudden bolt of lightning split the sky, followed seconds later by a long rumbling thunder. This was nature's warning that the storm was not far away. The wind rustled the leaves. In one of the trees surrounding the lake, an owl, undaunted by the impending rain and wind, hooted to its heart's content. The sweet scent of honeysuckle was a pleasing perfume.

Dantzler came home around eight that evening, fully intending to give his mind a night off from this case. He ate a quick supper consisting of two pieces of cold chicken, some potato salad, and a Diet Pepsi. Then he turned on the tube and watched some baseball. Cubs against the Dodgers. Two quality teams. Should be fun. But only four innings into a scoreless game the detective in him got the better of his love for baseball. He clicked off the TV, went into the kitchen, fixed a Pernod and orange juice, and went out onto the deck.

Now as midnight approached (along with the storm), and well into his third drink, he sat in the chair and thought about the case. Thought about what he knew and what was still missing. There was plenty in both of those camps, but, of course, uncovering what he didn't know dominated his thoughts. This was his top priority. Unless he could do that the case wouldn't be solved.

But *what* case was he talking about? On the surface that sounded almost like a trick question. Yet it wasn't. In truth, it might very well be *the* question of questions.

Yes, he had two recent homicides that had to be solved, both of which had been committed by the same individual. He knew this with unshakeable conviction. Those bruises on Mike Perkins and Danny Michaels were not only identical, they were in virtually the same place on each man's neck. The killer could almost claim that as his signature.

But were those homicides simply evil descendants spawned by the alleged murder of Gloria Nash? If so, was there a connection between what happened to her and these recent deaths? And had that crime not been committed (if indeed it had been), would Mike Perkins and Danny Michaels still be alive? Dale Larraby? Yes, was the answer to those questions.

Okay, so what triggered these latest two homicides? What was the catalyst?

Had to be that damned list.

And yet . . .

This entire structure was built on shaky legs, on a weak foundation. Haunting everything was the most-important question of all: Was there an earlier murder? Was Gloria Nash the victim of a homicide, or was she nothing more than what she was reported to be—a missing person? Maybe she wasn't really missing. Maybe she just decided to take flight and get away from Lexington. Many young people, unhappy with their current circumstances, for a multitude of personal reasons, head off for new territory. Could be she fell into that category? She wouldn't be the first, nor would she be the last.

Adding to the shakiness of the structure was the teller of this tale —Danny Michaels. How did a petty thief and long-time con artist learn about a crime the police knew nothing about? Where did he get this information? From whom? When? Had he been sitting on it for a lengthy period of time, or had he recently learned about it? And what was his motive for sharing the information with Julie Bradley? What was his reasoning, his angle? And, finally, was any of it true?

Well, Danny Michaels was dead. That had to mean something. His killer wouldn't have felt the need to silence a voice that had nothing important or incriminating to say. That's an unnecessary risk.

Sitting on his porch, the storm growing ever closer, Dantzler tried to make sense of it all. He couldn't. Not yet, anyway. But he would, eventually. This much he knew with absolute certainty. The dead deserve justice; the evildoers deserve punishment. He would see that both sides got what they were entitled to.

Buried somewhere inside all his thoughts was a piece of crucial information that continued to elude him. It was a tidbit he'd heard or seen or read, but where, when? Closing his eyes, letting his mind wander, he dug deep into the past few days, sifting through the jumble of information he'd collected, hoping what was lost would come out of hiding. It didn't. Whatever it was remained in the shadows.

There was nothing he could do but wait and hope that it would eventually come to the surface.

Dantzler considered another drink but opted against it. Four was one too many. Instead, he shifted his focus to the cast of characters involved in this violent drama. The living ones only, since the dead had already taken their final bow.

Alex Shannon and Eddie Campbell. Two retired cops, neither of whom had remarkable or distinguished careers. Pedestrian in every sense of the word. They put on the uniform, drove to work, went through the motions, punched out at the end of their shift, and went home. Never did either man rise above the ordinary. Nor were they the kind of men you wanted to be in a foxhole with when the bullets started flying. They couldn't be trusted to have your back.

Alex was pure asshole, Eddie a little less so. Neither man bubbled with warmth or kindness, but Eddie could on occasion crack a genuine smile. Not Alex. His face was set in stone. He wanted you to know he had no desire to be your friend.

Julie had asked a very good question: Was Alex Shannon capable of committing murder? Dantzler's "yes" answer had been quickly amended by Sean, who agreed but added that it would only be done if someone else gave the order. Okay, if both answers were correct, then who handed out those orders? Couldn't have been Eddie Campbell; between the two men, his was the weaker personality. He'd be subservient to Alex. This means another individual was directing Alex's actions.

But Dantzler now had to ask himself if he was leaping to an unjustified conclusion. Just because two guys were assholes and mediocre cops didn't mean they were cold-blooded killers. Even assholes are innocent until proven guilty.

What about the two newest names added to the cast of characters? Lawrence Brady and Robbie Newcome? Are they major players, or do they only have a minor role in all this? Or any role at all? Hard to say at this point, but the two men did have a connection with both their dead and living costars. Robbie's threatening note to Danny Michaels was worthy of hard scrutiny. That part of the investigation would begin tomorrow. So would a closer look at Brady. Was he involved in these murders, or was he just an unlucky shmuck who happened to have been on a bowling team with men now under suspicion for murder?

Dantzler's gut said Brady was involved, but, again, was that yet another unjustified conclusion? Even asshole attorneys are innocent until proven guilty.

This brought Dantzler to the final cast member, the outsider, Julie Bradley. She was the only one he knew wasn't a killer, but she was also the one he worried about the most. He couldn't escape the feeling that her life was in danger. She was the messenger, the bearer of dangerous news, and those that felt threatened weren't likely to overlook the possibility she knews more than she'd already shared. That was a chance they couldn't afford to take. They didn't yet know she had spoken to the police. Right now, they have to be concerned that at some point she would go to the authorities with this information and were probably feeling a sense of panic. They will soon realize, if not already, that silencing the messenger was the only choice they had. And they would want to do it sooner rather than later.

Julie should have taken his and Sean's advice and gone back to Cincinnati until this storm, like the one that just hit Lexington, had safely passed. But that wasn't going to happen. Julie was going to stick around until this drama played out. Dangerous as her decision was, Dantzler understood it. In her own way she was a lot like him. Both followed a similar code of conduct: never leave the stage until the final curtain falls.

CHAPTER TWENTY-FOUR

"The local grapevine says you Homicide guys only work bankers' hours," joked Bobby Clark. "Yet here you are on duty at seven-thirty in the morning. What gives, Jack?"

"Bobby, you want to know how I feel about business-related grapevines?" replied Dantzler. "They produce lousy grapes."

"I suppose I shouldn't be all that surprised to see you here this early considering what's happening in your world. Two homicides so close together. That's bound to increase your work load. First, Mike Perkins, then that kid you found yesterday. Any connection between the two?"

"Not sure at this point, but if I had to toss out a wild guess, I'd say yes."

"That would make your job a little easier, wouldn't it? Especially if the same person killed both men."

Dantzler didn't immediately respond to Clark's question. He was tired, beat. Too much Pernod and a restless night's sleep had him feeling crummy. Right now he'd pay a hundred bucks for six hours of good, sound sleep. But that wasn't going to happen, not until these murders were solved and the killer—or killers—were behind bars. And no, Bobby, that won't be easy, he thought.

Plopping down in the chair across from Clark, Dantzler said, "How well did you know Mike Perkins?"

"Didn't really know him at all."

"What about Eddie Campbell and Robbie Newcome?"

"Again, I really didn't know them. You have to remember, that crowd had cleared out by the time I took over Missing Persons. Oh, over the years I've crossed paths with them at a handful of retirement parties and a few funerals, but that's the extent of it. I can't tell you anything about either of those guys. Sorry for not being more helpful."

"Don't apologize, Bobby."

"Why are you inquiring about Campbell and Newcome? They involved somehow?"

"Just following through on some things, that's all. Got one more name for you—Alex Shannon. What can you tell me about him?"

"Nothing. Like the others you asked about, he had retired before I took charge here. But he wasn't in Missing Persons, was he? I thought he was always a Vice guy."

"Yeah, he was."

"It's troubling when the lead homicide investigator currently looking into two unsolved murders starts asking questions about other cops," Clark said, shaking his head. "Is that the direction your investigation is taking you?"

Dantzler shrugged, said, "I don't know, Bobby. What I can tell you, and this is strictly between the two of us, is that a similar neck bruise was found on Mike Perkins and Danny Michaels. It's a bruise usually caused by a choke-hold."

"Cops aren't the only ones who utilize a choke-hold. Guys with a military background are trained to use it. Someone with extensive martial arts experience would know how it's done. Hell, Jack, with so many violent cop shows on TV, just about any redneck asshole with a tendency toward violence could have learned how to use it. Just saying, use of the choke-hold isn't strictly limited to law enforcement personnel."

"No one wants it to not be a cop more than I do," Dantzler said, rubbing his tired eyes. "The reason I came to see you, Bobby, is I need a favor."

"Whatever you need, just ask. I'll help in any way I can."

"It involves an old case I'm interested in."

"Which one?"

"About fifteen years ago a young woman named Gloria Nash went missing. Her older sister filed a report. The case was looked into, briefly, but nothing ever came of it. I need to know everything you can tell me about that case, beginning with who took the lead on the investigation."

Clark scribbled Gloria's name on a notepad. "You happen to know the sister's name?"

"No."

"Well, it should be in the report, but locating her might be difficult. Folks move around a lot these days. And as we know all too well, some die."

"If we're lucky she's still alive and living around here."

"And you say this happened fifteen years ago?" Clark inquired. "Wasn't Joel Howard head of Missing Persons back then?"

"He was."

"Didn't he commit suicide eight or nine years ago?"

That question hit Dantzler head-on with the force of an oncoming locomotive. He had completely forgotten that Joel Howard, the man who was supervisor over Dale Larraby, Eddie Campbell, Jimmy Newman, and Robbie Newcome, had put a pistol to his head and blown his brains out. Dantzler was pissed at himself for overlooking an incident that might be of relevance to the cases he was now working. A detail of such potential importance should not have slipped his mind.

Most likely, there was no connection. But . . . that possibility couldn't be dismissed outright.

It was inexcusable that he hadn't already thought about this.

"Am I wrong about how Joel Howard died?" Clark asked, breaking the extended silence.

"No, you're not. He died of a self-inflicted gunshot to the head." Dantzler slowly came out of his chair. "Get me what you can on the Gloria Nash case, Bobby. And as always, sooner is better than later."

"I'll try to have you something no later than noon."

"Thanks for the assistance, Bobby."

On the way back to his desk Dantzler noticed that Captain Bird was sitting alone in his office. He was leaning back in his chair, feet propped up on his desk, reading a copy of the local newspaper. When Bird saw Dantzler standing in the doorway he lowered the paper and motioned for his lead detective to come in.

"And I thought I was the early bird, no pun intended," Dantzler said, taking a seat. "Anything important in the news today?"

"Yeah. My Powerball numbers failed me once again. Looks like I'm retiring a poor man."

"You play the Lottery, Rich? Why? That's nothing more than government-sanctioned theft. It's the old numbers racket. Criminals got sent to prison for running that scam." Dantzler laughed, said, "And in case you haven't figured it out yet, it's not a very sound retirement plan."

"We all have our dreams, Jack. Mine is to be wealthy."

"And how is this Lottery thing working out for you?"

"Not all that well. But there's always the next one. You never know." Bird folded the newspaper and put it in a drawer. "I'm meeting with Eric at ten this morning. It's time to let him know what the plan is. And to gauge his reaction."

"Is that when you offer him the job? Provided he reacts the way I'm sure he will?"

"I can't offer him the job. That's above my pay grade. But if Eric says yes to me, we march on over to Chief Douglas's office, and he will officially make the offer."

"Eric will say yes. He's no dummy."

"Would you care to sit in on the meeting? Be nice to have you on hand."

"You can handle it without me, Rich," Dantzler said, standing. "Besides, I've got a pair of homicides I need to solve. That's my top priority, not personnel matters."

"One final question before you go: Do you still want Victoria Jefferson in Homicide?"

"She would be an asset, so I say yes."

"Then I'll see that it gets done."

Dantzler left Bird's office and wandered over to the War Room, where he found Jake making quick work of an onion bagel. Dantzler went into the room and closed the door behind him. After grabbing a bottle of water from the refrigerator, he said, "Got some news for you, Jake, that needs to be kept under wraps for a while. It's . . ."

"This about Eric taking over Captain Bird's position?" Jake asked.

"You already knew?"

"Everybody knows."

That damn Rawlinson. "Who told you? Bruce?"

"You want the truth?"

"Yeah."

"Eric told me. Two or three days ago."

"He's not supposed to know. Nobody is."

"Sorry, but the secret is out."

"Eric tell you how he feels about it?"

"Conflicted. On the one hand he would love to have the job. But he also feels some guilt because it's him and not you."

"He's meeting with Rich at ten o'clock. Rich will tell him in no uncertain terms that I don't have any interest in taking that job. In fact, I was the one who recommended Eric. How do you feel about Eric being your boss?"

"I'm cool with it. Eric's a winner, so I'll have no problem taking orders from him."

"I've also asked Rich to move Vee into our unit on a full-time basis. We'll probably get her within the next few days. You also cool with that?"

"Most definitely. She'll add much-needed class and beauty to our motley crew."

"Roger that," Dantzler said, stealing Jake's famous retort.

Jake was still cackling when Dantzler disappeared down the hall.

CHAPTER TWENTY-FIVE

On the previous evening Sean had followed Julie to the Embassy Suites, stood next to her when she checked out, and then helped load her luggage, what little there was, into her car. Later, she checked in at the Hyatt in downtown Lexington. This was done at Sean's insistence. He convinced her that being in a more crowded area and in close proximity to the police station was a safer option than continuing to stay alone and so far away from downtown. Julie remained unconvinced that her life was in danger, but Sean insisted on the change of location, so she agreed.

Between leaving the old hotel and checking in at the new, Julie and Sean stopped at a restaurant called Bonefish Grill on Sir Barton Way. This was also at Sean's insistence. Since Julie was famished, she offered no resistance to his suggestion. Anywhere was fine with her, she told Sean, just get us there pronto.

Once they were in the restaurant and seated at a table, they both ordered drinks. Julie chose a red zinfandel, while Sean went with a bottle of Blue Moon beer. When the waiter arrived to take their orders Julie urged Sean to go first. He ordered Sea Scallops and Shrimp, garlic whipped potatoes, and coleslaw. Julie closed her menu, handed it to the waiter, and said she would have the same.

"You've obviously eaten here on previous occasions," Julie said, after taking a sip of wine. "No hesitation about what you wanted."

"I've been here a couple of times," answered Sean. "But not enough to be considered a regular."

Julie dug her cell phone from her purse and held it up. "I need to make a phone call, Sean. Do you mind?"

"Not at all. Do I need to take a bathroom break?"

Julie shook her head as she punched in the numbers. The call was to Darvis, to fill him in on what had recently transpired. She made the call now because she knew neither he nor Nancy would answer. Tonight, the Cubs were hosting the Dodgers, which meant Darvis and Nancy were at Wrigley Field. It was doubtful they would hear the phone ringing, and even if they did, the call would be ignored. Nothing was more important to them than their beloved Cubs.

Just as she suspected, she got Darvis's answering machine. Julie didn't hesitate. She'd already rehearsed in her mind what she would say.

"Guys, this is Julie. Just wanted to let you know that I have moved from the Embassy Suites to the Hyatt in downtown Lexington. A lot is happening right now. Danny Michaels was murdered. I've shared all my information with the police. Don't worry about me, I'm safe. In fact, I'm sitting with a handsome ex-cop right now. I know you guys are at Wrigley Field, but call me when you get time. Talk to you later. And go Cubs."

Sean said, "It's probably not wise for someone living in Cincinnati to say 'go Cubs.' That could cause you some serious grief."

"They're playing the Dodgers, not the Reds, so I'm not turning into Benedict Arnold. But that was my boss, and he signs the paychecks. I'd say 'go ISIS' if that was who he supported."

"Yikes."

"Relax, Sean, I'm only joking."

"Good to know."

The back and forth stopped when the food came. Neither spoke until both had finished their meal. As the waiter picked up the empty dishes, he asked if they wanted dessert. They said no, but they would like a second round of drinks.

"A fine choice you made, Sean," Julie announced. "That was a splendid meal. So good in fact that I'll pay."

"Not a chance. This one's on me. You can pay for the next one."

"Provided there is a next one."

"Yeah, provided there is a next one." Sean took a long drink from the second bottle of Blue Moon. "What are the odds there'll be a next one?"

Julie furrowed her brow like she was deep in thought, then said, "Three to one."

"For or against?"

"For. I never bet against anything."

"Then I like my chances."

"Changing the subject, how good a detective is this Dantzler fellow?"

"There are none better, anywhere," Sean said. "He's never failed to solve a case. That's really all you need to know."

"I can tell from your voice that you care about him."

"Jack's my best friend, and I'd venture to say he considers me his best friend. We go back a long way, to before I was on the police force. We're also business partners. He and I, along with David Bloom, own the Lexington Tennis Center."

"Do you play tennis?"

"Yes."

"Can you beat Dantzler?"

"No one beats Jack. He has professional-level talent. As a kid, playing in a junior's tournament, he lost a close three-set match to John McEnroe. Jack could have gone pro if he'd chosen to go that route. So, forget about me beating him. It isn't even a remote possibility."

Julie sipped her wine, said, "Tell me, Sean. Who do you think is behind these murders?"

"Honestly, I don't know. Clearly, the same individual committed both murders. Jack's right about that. But there is one thing that has me stumped."

"What's that?"

"Danny knew about the names on the list, so I can understand the killer's motive for eliminating him. But according to you, Mike Perkins didn't know. So, why was he killed?"

"Because he had knowledge relating to Gloria Nash's murder."

"You're jumping the gun, aren't you? We don't know for certain that Gloria was murdered."

"She was, Sean. Danny knew what he was talking about."

"Look, I'm not disagreeing with you, Julie. But I'm looking at it from a cop's perspective. There needs to be evidence, because without it you have nothing but speculation. And you don't arrest people based on speculation."

"I like Alex Shannon for this," Julie said.

"That's based on your dislike for the man on a personal level and not on any real evidence. That won't cut it. Being an asshole doesn't mean he's a murderer."

"You've got a point, I suppose. Presumption of innocence still counts for something."

"Finish your wine, Julie. It's late, and I want to make sure to get you tucked in at the Hyatt."

"Excuse me?"

"Oh, my bad," Sean said, grinning sheepishly. "That's known as a 'Montgomery misrepresentation'. What I meant to say was I wanted to make sure you got 'checked in' at the Hyatt. Sorry about that."

"I may not know who the killer is, but I do know this for certain: I've got to keep an eye on you, Sean. You're a dangerous character."

"Presumption of innocence, remember? Presumption of innocence."

CHAPTER TWENTY-SIX

As Julie picked over a light breakfast the next morning her thoughts were still on the previous evening she spent with Sean. Their time together had been cozy and comfortable, much more so than most initial meetings she'd had with other men. She wasn't particularly surprised by this. Sean was, she quickly judged, one of the good guys.

And it was obvious that he had an interest in her.

Thinking about it now, she had to admit that if she allowed her imagination to take flight, she could envision having a relationship with him. Why not? He was handsome (very), kind, respectful, and successful. True, some women, especially those who fancied themselves modern feminists, would likely consider him to be somewhat overprotective. She didn't fall into that camp. To her way of thinking, that now old-fashioned virtue was endearing. It was a comfort knowing he would be there to protect her if necessary.

And with what was happening in Lexington, she just might have need for that protection.

While Julie silently acknowledged being attracted to Sean, it was Dantzler who intrigued her. There was something about the man she found compelling. Magnetic, almost. It was virtually impossible to avoid being drawn to him. He pulled you in without your even realizing that it was happening. Why? she asked herself. Was it his eyes, his confident demeanor, his voice? Maybe it was all those things, she concluded.

Like Sean, Dantzler was tall, handsome (very), successful, and physically imposing. Both men took great care to stay in shape, and not because of ego or to impress the ladies, but because it was the right thing to do. They held firm to the old adage that your body is a temple, and as such it made sense to keep the temple in good working order. Julie admired them for keeping their bodies in shape. She also promised to get back into a more disciplined workout routine once the book project was finished. Too much sitting on her ass wasn't healthy.

Julie paid the check and left the restaurant, unsure what her next course of action should be. Going back and interviewing either Alex Shannon or Eddie Campbell would undoubtedly be a waste of time. Those two were more tight-lipped than a corpse. She ran through a couple more possible options but felt neither would lead anywhere. In the end she decided to go back to her room, get on the computer, and do more research. That wasn't much, she had to admit, but it would keep her busy and give her the feeling of moving forward. If she could do that, keep advancing, eventually she would strike gold.

The gold was out there, somewhere, and sooner or later she would find it.

_^_

Bruce Rawlinson handed Dantzler a note. "Arnie Edwards left that for you," Bruce reported. "It's the results of Danny Michaels's autopsy. Arnie said there was no need to speak with you about it, but if you do have questions, give him a call."

Dantzler opened the file and went straight to the Cause of Death section. Scanning it, he muttered, "Damn" loud enough to grab Bruce's interest.

"What's it say, Ace?" asked Bruce.

"Danny died of a massive heroin overdose. Something called carfentanil was also mixed in with the heroin. That shit is used to sedate elephants and other large animals. Arnie says Danny probably died instantly."

"No doubt. I've never heard of that stuff. Have you?"

"If I'm not mistaken, it was found in some of the heroin up in Cincinnati a year or so back, when that city had a sudden spike in heroin overdose deaths."

"How would Danny's killer get hold of that stuff?"

"Don't kid yourself, Bruce. If it's in Cincinnati, it's in Lexington. Danny's killer probably got it right here in town."

"Can't help but feel sorry for that poor kid, dying that way. Had to be horrible." Bruce started to walk away, stopped, and turned back. "You gotta catch that kid's killer, Ace. And Mike's killer. The sick bastard needs to be behind bars."

"I'll catch him, Bruce. You can bet on that."

Dantzler picked up his phone and punched in the number for Victoria Jefferson. He'd made an earlier call and learned that she had the day off. She answered after several rings, sounding totally out of breath.

"You all right, Vee?" Dantzler asked. "You sound winded."

"I just finished my morning run, so, yeah, I'm sucking air."

"Want me to call back later?"

"No, no. I can talk. What's up? Are you calling about Eric's promotion?"

"So it's true. Everybody knows."

Vee chuckled. "Did you really think something like that would remain a secret? Not gonna happen, not in that place."

"Obviously."

"What was Eric's reaction when it was made official?"

"Don't know. Eric is still meeting with Captain Bird."

"Funny, but Captain Bird left me a message while I was running. Said he wants to meet with me tomorrow morning. Any idea what that's about?"

"Yeah. He's going to ask if you want to move to Homicide."

"Permanently or on a temporary basis?"

"Permanent. You'd be one of us."

"Yes, definitely, I would love to be part of your team. Are you okay with it?"

"It's not my team, Vee. It's Eric's. And yes, I'm okay with it. I'm the one who recommended you."

"Thanks, Detective Dantzler. I'm truly grateful. And I'll do everything I can to justify your faith in me."

"You can start by calling me Jack."

"How soon before this happens?" asked Vee. "I mean, when will I officially join the unit?"

"Paperwork needs to be done, along with a few other changes, so I'd say no sooner than early next week. But the reason I called, Vee, is to ask if you're up to doing some detective work this afternoon."

"Definitely."

As Dantzler told Vee what he wanted her to do, Jake came into the War Room, sat, picked up the autopsy report, and began reading. By the time Jake finished, Dantzler had ended his conversation with Vee.

"Heroin laced with something strong enough to knock an elephant on its ass?" Jake said, holding up the report. "Poor Danny Michaels."

Dantzler started to say something but didn't. What could he say? Poor Danny Michaels said it all.

Jake said, "Think Vee is ready for an assignment like that?"

"She's ready," Dantzler replied, just as Eric walked in. Dantzler looked at Jake, and said, "Hey, Jake, the boss has arrived."

"What do you always say when I call you boss?" asked Eric.

"That Springsteen is The Boss."

"Then that's my reply to you. I'm not the boss. Let Springsteen own that moniker."

"Congratulations, Eric," Jake said. "Seriously. You deserve the gig, and you can handle it."

Eric glanced at Dantzler, and said, "You sure you don't want the job, Jack?"

"Too late now, Eric. It's all yours. Embrace it. And I'll echo what Jake said. Congrats. You'll be even better at the job than Rich was, and he was pretty darn good."

"Rich is still around for another two weeks, so for now we're all still working for him," Eric said. "And you're the lead on these two murders, Jack. What do you want us to do?"

"Jake, you go back over all the evidence collected at the two crime scenes. See if we overlooked anything. Also, check back with neighbors, see if they recall something they might have initially forgotten. Take a couple of unnies with you if you think you'll need them. Eric, I want you to quietly pull the personnel records for Alex Shannon, Eddie Campbell, Robbie Newcome, Jimmy Newman, and Mike Perkins. Bring them here and thoroughly study them. I'll help when I get back. So will Jake. Any questions?"

Head shakes from both men.

"Good. Then let us go forth and solve these murders."

_^_

Julie winced when she saw the name on her caller ID. It was from Darvis. She had wondered how long it would be before he got back in touch with her. Last night's message, which included the word murder, surely got his attention. She was somewhat surprised he hadn't phoned earlier. But then or now, this wasn't a conversation she wanted to have. No doubt Darvis and Nancy were having reservations about going forward with the book. She just knew Darvis was going to unload on her. Well, she reasoned, as she readied herself for the war soon to begin: The Cubs beat the Dodgers last night, so maybe she could use that to her advantage.

"Darvis," Julie said, "I was expecting your call."

"I'm sure you were. Listen to me, Julie. Nancy and I are both in agreement that you need to go back to Cincinnati until this nasty business in Lexington has been taken care of. Don't worry about the book —we will publish it. You have my word on that. If you need more money I'll get it to you. With what has happened down there, Nancy and I are also convinced that you have stumbled upon a story that needs to be told. However, having said that, you cannot write a book from the grave. We are terribly concerned about your safety."

Darvis had practically vomited out his words, hardly taking time to breathe. But the content of his spiel took Julie by surprise. She was fully expecting him to give her an ultimatum: Go home or I'm pulling the plug on the project.

But there was no ultimatum, only concern. Hearing this, she was moved to tears.

"I know you and Nancy are worried about me, but you shouldn't be," she said, trying to sound stronger than she felt. "I'm going to be okay. I've moved to a hotel downtown, and I've told the police everything I know. They'll make sure I stay safe."

"Their job is to catch whoever is committing these murders, Julie, not to keep watch over you. Go back to Cincinnati where you'll be safe. You can continue to communicate with the police from there. Then when it's all over you return to Lexington, finish your research, and write another best-seller. That's the smart thing to do."

"I'll make a deal with you, Darvis. I'll stay here in Lexington for three more days. If the killer hasn't been caught by then I will go back home. Does that sound fair to you?"

"Fair means bubkes to me, Julie. All that counts is your safety and well-being." Darvis let out a heavy sigh. "However, if that's the best deal I can get, I'll take it. Three days and you are out of there. Do I have your word on that?"

"Yes."

⸺ˆ⸺

When Dantzler was back in the War Room after buying lunch for Eric and Jake, he got a call from Bobby Clark. "You come up with anything, Bobby?" asked Dantzler.

"Gloria Nash was reported missing by her sister, Andrea Nash, on the eighth of June, two-thousand-two. According to Andrea, Gloria had been missing for four days. Jimmy Newman was the lead investigator on the case."

"And Jimmy's dead, so I'm not learning anything from him. Do you have his case file?"

"Yeah, but it's pretty slim. It's clear Newman didn't put much effort into finding Gloria."

"Did Jimmy work it alone?"

"No. Larraby worked it with him."

"No wonder nothing came of it," Dantzler said. "What about an address for Andrea Nash? Did you find one?"

"You got lucky there. Andrea Nash lives in the same place she did back then. It's on Wilson-Downing."

Dantzler wrote down the address and thanked Bobby for the information. Before hanging up, Clark said he would send Gloria Nash's case file to him later in the day. Dantzler thanked Bobby a second time and closed his phone.

Standing, he finished off a bottle of water, tossed the empty into the recycle bucket, and headed for the door.

It was time to see an attorney.

CHAPTER TWENTY-SEVEN

Vee followed Dantzler's instructions to a T—dress casually, drive to the small bar located on Versailles Road, and engage in conversation with the owner. He also advised her to take a companion, preferably a male, the bigger the better. Vee knew the perfect person to fill that slot—Bubba Anderson. Bubba wasn't simply big; at six-seven and three-hundred-forty pounds he was truly massive. It was once said that you didn't walk with Bubba, you traveled inside his shadow.

Bubba parked his truck directly in front of the bar, which sat between a barber shop and a cash checking operation. This strip of businesses also included a bank, drug store, pool room, and gas station. Judging by the absence of vehicles in the parking area, none of the businesses were having a particularly successful afternoon.

All eyes followed Vee and Bubba as they entered the establishment and slowly wound their way to the bar. They scoped out Bubba because of his size, Vee because of her color. A quick look around the place was all it took for Vee to conclude that the bar's clientele probably didn't include many blacks. No doubt that was why Dantzler insisted that she bring along what amounted to a personal body guard.

Vee counted nine customers—two heavyset ladies sat on stools at the opposite end of the bar, six men were sitting around two tables that had been pushed together, and a lone male wearing a baseball cap sat in a booth next to the jukebox. Robbie Newcome, the man she had come to see, was perched on a stool behind the bar.

"What's your poison?" Robbie said, coming off the stool and slowly limping toward them.

"Kentucky Ale," Bubba mumbled.

"Make it two," echoed Vee.

Robbie yanked two bottles from the fridge, wiped off the sweat with a towel, opened them, and placed them on the bar. "Damn, man, you're bigger than a freakin' mountain," he said to Bubba.

"Heard that one before," Bubba said, before swiveling on his stool, effectively ending further conversation.

"Not very friendly, is he?" Robbie said to Vee.

Vee reached up and pinched Bubba's cheek. "Don't be fooled by his size. Bubba's just a very large pussycat."

"Somehow I doubt that," Robbie replied.

"How long have you worked here?" asked Vee.

"I'm the owner. Had it for about ten years now."

"A small business owner. Impressive." Vee took a drink of beer. "If you've had the place for ten years that must mean you're doing all right."

"I make a living. Tell you one thing, if more women like you came in on a regular basis, business would be a helluva lot better."

"You mean black women?"

"No, no, that's not what I meant at all. I was talking about beautiful women. And you definitely belong in that group. Shit, Halle Berry ain't got nothing on you."

"I take it that you don't have many black customers."

"I can't recall the last time a person of color came in for a drink. That is, not counting the Mexicans. Damn shame, too, 'cause I don't have a prejudiced bone in my body. I run a business. The only color that matters to me is green."

Vee turned and pointed at the wall behind the jukebox. "That Confederate flag might be a big reason why blacks don't frequent your establishment. It's not a very welcoming symbol. Kind of sends blacks a message to keep out. No black person is going to feel at home here with that damn thing hanging up there. You take it down maybe you'll get some black customers. Our money is as green as a white person's, and we spend it just as fast as they do."

"I never thought about that," Robbie said, staring at the flag as if he was seeing it for the first time. "It was up there when I bought the place. I never thought to take it down. But I'll make you a deal. I will remove it after closing time if you'll spread the word about the bar to some of your friends. What do you say? Deal?"

"Deal." Vee nudged Bubba in the ribs, said, "Need another beer, big guy?"

Bubba belched and nodded his head.

"Another one for Bubba," Vee said to Robbie. Then: "Have you always been in the bar business?"

"Nah, I used to be a cop," answered Robbie, as he handed Bubba his beer. "That was a long time ago, though."

"Why did you leave the job?"

"Automobile accident. Left me with this limp."

"Sorry to hear that."

"No big deal. It's just life. Like they say, shit happens."

"When you were still on the police force did you ever work Homicide?" asked Vee.

"Nah, first I was a patrol officer, and then I went to the Missing Persons Unit. Stayed there until I got hurt."

"Missing Persons. That sounds exciting."

"Not really. Mostly, it involved a lot of leg work. More often than not you never find the person who is missing. Truth is, most of the time they aren't missing at all. They're runaways who eventually get scared and return home. It's a pretty damn frustrating job."

"Ever go looking for a famous missing person?"

"In Lexington, Kentucky?" Robbie said, chuckling. "You gotta be kidding me."

Vee said, "Did you read about the cop who recently committed suicide?"

"Which one? There have been two."

"I think his name was Mike something."

"Mike Perkins?"

"Yeah, that's the one. Mike Perkins. Did you know him?"

"I knew Mike. We worked together in Missing Persons. He was a good guy. I also knew Dale Larraby. He's the other ex-cop who offed himself in the past week or so."

"What's going on in this city of ours? First, two former cops commit suicide, and then I read about a murder in yesterday's paper. Some kid named Danny Michaels. The article said he was found dead in his apartment. Did you know him?"

"Danny Michaels? Nah, can't say I'm familiar with him. But I thought he committed suicide. Drugs, or something, wasn't it?"

Vee realized she'd just made a huge mistake by mentioning that Danny had been murdered. That detail had not been released to the public. She needed to quickly cover her ass if she didn't want to blow this assignment.

"I think you're right about it being a suicide and not a homicide," Vee said, holding her nerves in check. "I've got them all mixed up. That Danny kid died of a heroin overdose."

"That's what was in the newspaper," Robbie said. "But I didn't know him."

Vee looked over her shoulder. Nothing had changed . . . still the same nine customers, none of whom had placed an order since she and Bubba came in. She wondered if perhaps they were stunned or enthralled by the presence of an interracial couple sitting in what was obviously a whites-only bar. Maybe they were too shocked to order the next round.

One of the women managed to get off the stool without falling. She kept her eyes on Bubba as she strolled past him. Finally, she turned her attention to the jukebox and began looking for a song to play. Vee doubted if any Motown songs were on the playlist. The odds were strong that you'd never hear Aretha Franklin or Marvin Gaye in this place.

"You ever have any trouble in here?" asked Vee.

"Trouble? What kind of trouble are you talking about?" Robbie said.

"Fights, scuffles, altercations?"

"It's a bar, so, yeah, occasionally tempers flare. But that's rare. Folks come here to drink, not fight. Why do you ask that question? You like violence?"

"No, I hate violence. I'm just being inquisitive, that's all."

"You're a lot safer in here than you are outside that door, that much I can promise you," Robbie said.

"How much do I owe you ... I never got your name?"

"Robbie. You owe me three-fifty."

Vee stood, opened her small purse, and fumbled through it until she found a five-dollar bill. Placing it on the bar, she said, "Keep the change, Robbie. Hope your bar continues to do well."

"Remember our deal. The flag comes down, you spread the word."

"Will do, Robbie." Tapping Bubba on the shoulder, she said, "Let's go, big guy."

After Vee and Bubba were gone the lone male sitting next to the jukebox called Robbie over.

"What did you and the chocolate lady talk about?" the man asked. "Looked to me like you two were having a serious conversation."

"Ah, nothing much. She recommended that I take down the Confederate flag. Said it might encourage more blacks to come in for a drink."

"And that's what you want, more black customers?"

"I want more money."

"What else did you two discuss? Thought I heard Mike Perkins's name mentioned a couple of times. What was that about?"

"She read about his death in the paper. I told her I'd been a cop, and she asked if I knew Mike. I said I did."

"Is that all you talked about?"

"Why are you making a big deal about me talking to that chick? Is it because she's black?"

"Answer my question, Robbie," the man ordered. "What else did the two of you talk about?"

"She also read in the paper that Danny Michaels had died. She said he was murdered, but I straightened her out. I reminded her that it was a suicide, not a homicide."

"You're a fuckin moron, Robbie. You know that?"

"Why the needle up your ass?"

"Here's why, Robbie. That chocolate lady happens to be a cop."

"Her? No way."

"A cop, Robbie. Her name is Vee, and she played you like a harpsi-chord. Did you tell her anything else? Think hard before answering."

"No, nothing."

"You sure about that?"

"Yes."

"You'd better be."

CHAPTER TWENTY-EIGHT

Lawrence Brady's secretary behaved as if she was guarding the U.S. president. She stood behind her desk, hands on her hips like a Nazi general, eyes sending out icy darts, her voice sounding harder than cold steel. In no uncertain terms she told Dantzler that there was no possible way he was going to speak with her boss. Not this afternoon, anyway. According to her, Brady was alone in his office preparing for a meeting in fifteen minutes with "quite possibly our most-important client."

"I'm very sorry you wasted your time, Detective, but Mr. Brady will have to see you some other time," she barked. "Let me check his schedule. Perhaps I can work you in tomorrow afternoon. That's the best I can do."

Dantzler was in no mood to hear this bullshit. Holding up his gold shield for her to see, he asked, "Do you know who I am?"

"Yes, you are Detective Dantzler. I'm quite familiar with you and your reputation. But like I said, Mr. Brady simply cannot see you today."

"Is Jesus on his way here?" Dantzler asked.

"What? Jesus? No. Why ask me that?"

"If Jesus was this most-important client you're talking about, then I might consider waiting. But since Jesus isn't coming, that makes me Mr. Brady's most-important client. Don't bother letting him know I'm here. I'll surprise him."

"But . . . that's simply sacrilegious."

When Dantzler entered the huge office Brady was sitting at his desk with his back turned, looking into a small mirror, clipping his nose hair. Nasal excavation, as Dantzler liked to call the procedure. An unopened bottle of Maker's Mark and two empty glasses sat on the desk. All this caused Dantzler to wonder who this "most-important" client might be. He doubted Brady normally made such a fuss for a typical attorney-client meeting.

"You're early, Elizabeth," Brady said, not turning around. "I'll be with you in a second."

Dantzler cringed when he heard Brady call out that name. For the past year or so a rumor had been floating around town that Mayor Anderson was having an affair with an attorney. Dantzler found it hard to believe that a classy, intelligent lady like Mayor Elizabeth Anderson would get involved with this sweaty bastard. But opposites attract, so anything was possible, including the pairing of beauty with the beast.

"Sorry, Lawrence, but you won't be seeing Elizabeth until we've had a little chat," Dantzler said, closing the door.

Brady quickly spun around, the expression on his face stuck somewhere between flabbergasted and pissed off. Had there been room for one more expression, it would have been disappointment. In any case, the man was not pleased.

"What the hell are you doing here, Dantzler?" Brady sputtered, quickly putting the bourbon and glasses into a desk drawer. "I have an important conference with Elizabeth Rayburn in a matter of minutes. She's one of my biggest clients. We can talk after I've concluded my meeting with her."

"No, Brady, you'll talk to her after you've concluded your meeting with me," Dantzler stated, relieved to learn that Mayor Anderson wasn't the client Brady was waiting for. "I'm sure Mrs. Rayburn will understand."

"I wouldn't count on it. She's not used to playing second fiddle to anyone."

"People with her kind of money usually aren't. By the way, does John Rayburn know that his wife is your 'most-important' client?"

"You have a vulgar mind, Detective Dantzler. Elizabeth is a client, nothing more."

"You serve Maker's Mark to all your clients, Brady?"

"What I do with my clients is none of your damn business."

Dantzler smiled. He'd only been in the office for five minutes and already Brady's face was bathed in sweat. "You're absolutely right, Brady," he said, grinning. "But murder is my business, and that's what I'm here to talk about."

"Murder? What the hell? I've never murdered anyone."

"That's good to hear. I'd hate to think a prestigious barrister such as you would engage in the unlawful taking of a human life."

"Then why are you here, Detective? Is it for the purpose of annoying me? Haven't you a more productive use of your time than to question me about something you know I didn't do?"

"That's a well-thought-out question, Brady. A very lawyerly response, if I may say so. I'm impressed. Perhaps those who refer to you as 'Shady' Brady have it all wrong."

"No one refers to me as 'Shady' Brady. If they did, I'd kill 'em on the spot."

"Well, that would be murder, wouldn't it?"

"I didn't mean that I would actually kill them. I was only using hyperbole to make a point."

"Maybe you were, maybe you weren't."

"I am not a killer," insisted Brady.

"But you are a bowler, aren't you?"

The question threw Brady off balance. Shrugging his shoulders, clearly perplexed, he asked, "What does bowling have to do with anything?"

"Weren't you on a bowling team with many of the guys who worked in the Missing Persons Unit?"

"No, I was never on a bowling team."

"You're telling me that you never bowled on a team called the Pin Pricks with Dale Larraby, Eddie Campbell, Robbie Newcome, Mike Perkins, and Jimmy Newman?"

"Yeah, but you're talking years ago."

"So, you did hang out with those guys, three of whom are now deceased?"

"Look, Dantzler, I was never officially on that team. Jimmy Newman and I were friends from way back. We went to school together. Jimmy hated to bowl, so he normally kept score for the guys. Whenever one of them had to be absent he'd call and ask me to fill in for him. I was a substitute, that's all. That's the extent of my involvement with that bowling team."

"You handled Larraby's will, right?" asked Dantzler, again changing directions. "Isn't that what you told me?"

"Yes, that's correct."

"What's the current status of that will?"

Brady snickered, said, "Wills don't have a status, Detective. A will is a legal document, nothing more."

Dantzler had to restrain himself from reaching across the desk and slapping the man. Holding his temper in check, he said, "Where does Carole Perkins stand vis-à-vis that particular legal document?"

"Like I told you before . . . she gets everything, including the cash found in his condo. I mean, it's legally hers once the police no longer consider it evidence, or no one else comes forward to claim it."

"How did you know about the money? That's not been made public."

"Detective, did you really think an important find like that was going to remain a secret? I heard about it the day after you found it."

"Who did you hear it from?"

"Can't remember. Sorry."

"Then let's talk about someone else's money—Mike Perkins. According to Father Steven Mulaney, you facilitated four donations to Christ the King Church totaling one-hundred grand. Is that accurate?"

"Yes." Brady looked at his wrist watch. "How much longer is this going to take, Detective? I'm sure Mrs. Rayburn is not a happy camper at the moment."

"It will take until I'm finished asking questions," Dantzler replied, sternly. "If she's not happy she can camp someplace else."

"If I lose her as a client I'll sue your ass off, Detective. Make no mistake about that."

Dantzler had finally had enough. "Threaten me again, Brady, and I will knock you on your fat ass. Then you'll have a legitimate reason to sue me. So, the safe thing to do is shut the fuck up and answer my questions. Got it?"

Stunned by Dantzler's outburst, Brady could only nod in agreement.

"How did you happen to be in charge of Mike's money?" Dantzler asked.

"Dale Larraby recommended me."

"How did Mike Perkins and Dale Larraby come into so much money?"

"Hell, man, you'd have to ask them that question."

"Hard to get answers from dead men. That's why I'm asking you."

"To begin with, I never knew Dale had that kind of money. Like everyone else, I was surprised when I heard the money had been found. He never mentioned it to me. As for Mike, well, he came to me and said he wanted to make a donation to Christ the King. Twenty-five grand. I helped him do it. That's it."

"When was this?"

"Let me think. It was about eight years ago, if memory serves."

"But that wasn't his only donation, was it?"

"No, as a matter of fact, it wasn't," Brady said, shaking his head. "There were three subsequent donations, each one twenty-five grand, made at two-year intervals, and always on the same day, June first. He was adamant about doing it on that day."

"What was the importance of June first?"

"You got me on that one, Detective. He never said."

"Did Mike give you the hundred grand all at once, then have you make the donations every two years?"

"Nope. He came to me on the last day of May, handed me twenty-five grand in cash, and ordered me to give it to Father Mulaney on June first. And that's what I did."

"And you never once questioned Mike about where he got the money?"

"Never. That was not my concern."

"It didn't trouble you that he was handing over twenty-five grand, in cash, all in hundred-dollar bills? This coming from a guy who looked like a homeless bum? That didn't cause red flags to fly?"

"I don't know what more you want me to say, Detective. Mike handed me money and gave me instructions as to what he wanted me to do, instructions I followed to the letter. The bottom line is, I haven't a clue where or how Mike accumulated that money."

Dantzler wasn't sure he was buying Brady's proclamation of ignorance, but until he could uncover incriminating evidence he had to take the man at his word. For the time being what other option did he have? None, to be precise.

Even shady, sweaty attorneys are innocent until proven guilty, he had to remind himself.

Brady seemed to sense that Dantzler had finally run out of steam. "Are we done now, Detective?" he asked, coming out of his chair. "I would really like to get on with more serious concerns. If you have questions for me in the future, please call ahead and schedule an appointment."

Dantzler didn't respond as he headed for the door, pleased for the restraint he'd showed by not punching Brady's lights out after that final snide remark he'd tossed in. The man certainly deserved to be taught a lesson or two. Another time, another place, perhaps.

Brady, however, wasn't concerned about anything but getting on with entertaining Elizabeth Rayburn. By the time Dantzler left the room, Brady had wiped perspiration from his face, put his coat on, and placed the Maker's Mark and two glasses back on his desk.

Only the best for his most-important client.

~^~

Dantzler received two text messages during his meeting with Brady, neither of which he took the time to read. Once he was in his car he opened the first message and began reading. It was from Bobby Clark.

"I put the Gloria Nash file, such as it is, on your desk. If you need anything else, give me a shout. I'll help in any way I can."

Dantzler thought about replying with a "Thanks, Bobby" but decided he would wait and see him in the morning. Instead, he opened the second message, this one from Vee.

"Meeting with Robbie went well. He denied knowing Danny Michaels. We can talk more tomorrow. Have a great evening."

He had deployed Vee to the bar for the purpose of asking Robbie one question—did he know Danny Michaels. Robbie's denial was a lie. The question now was, why would Robbie lie about that? Was it because he killed Danny? Possible, but Dantzler doubted that. He didn't see Robbie as a killer. An accomplice, maybe, but not the person who put the choke-hold on Danny, or the needle in his arm.

But Robbie did lie, and people rarely lie without a reason. What Dantzler had to do now was find out why Robbie denied knowing Danny Michaels.

Initially, Dantzler was positive that this case revolved around the money. Now, he wasn't so certain this was true. He was beginning to think the money was in some way the consequence of Gloria Nash's disappearance.

Or her murder.

Dantzler now suspected that Danny Michaels's tall tale had the ring of truth to it. And beginning tomorrow, Dantzler would open an investigation into what the Gloria Nash case really was—a homicide, not a missing person.

⌃

Julie surprised herself when she grabbed her cell phone and punched in Sean's number. Doing so was almost instinctive, as though she was acting before thinking. Maybe she was, she reasoned. But what triggered the call in the first place? Was it from her need to feel protected, or was it because she wanted to spend time with the man? Perhaps a bit of both, she concluded.

When Sean answered he seemed genuinely surprised—and pleased —to hear from her. She asked if he was interested in having dinner together. He said yes, then added that he had an important errand to run. They could either rendezvous later, he told her, or she was more than welcome to accompany him on his errand. She chose the latter of those two options. Sean said he would be at the Hyatt to pick her up in thirty minutes.

An hour later Julie stood quietly by Sean's side as he spoke with the director of a local funeral home. The purpose of Sean's visit was to iron out the details for Danny Michaels's cremation. Sean informed the man that Danny's body was still at the coroner's office, and should be released within the next few days. The coroner had been given instructions to transport the body here.

Sean inquired about the cost and was told it would be just under two-thousand dollars. Sean pulled out his checkbook, wrote the check, and handed it to the director. The two men shook hands and Sean and Julie departed.

"That was a wonderful thing you just did, Sean," Julie said, once they were in Sean's car. "Danny was fortunate to have a friend like you."

"Julie, if Danny was fortunate he'd still be alive."

"Yeah, I know. But . . . making sure he's taken care of when he's no longer alive says a lot about what kind of man you are."

"What I am is a hungry man. How about you? Ready to eat?"

"Maybe later. Right now I have somewhere else I'd rather be."

"Where?"

"Your place."

CHAPTER TWENTY-NINE

Dantzler slapped the folder labeled "Gloria M. Nash" on the War Room table, pulled back a chair, opened the file, and began reading. He was alone in the room. Eric was getting some on-the-job tutoring from Captain Bird, and Jake and Vee had yet to arrive. Dantzler had come to work early for the purpose of studying the file without distractions. He had the feeling that today was going to be an important one investigation-wise. First, he would meet with Gloria Nash's sister, then he would pay a second visit to Robbie Newcome. If all went well, some questions might find answers.

As Bobby Clark had warned, there wasn't much information or data inside the file, which consisted of three entries on two pages. This told Dantzler that the case wasn't given serious consideration by investigators Newman and Larraby, nor had they handled it in a professional manner.

The basics:

Name: Gloria Marie Nash: Born: 6/18/82; Height: 5'8"; Weight: 125; Hair: Blonde; Eyes: Hazel; No Previous Criminal Record.

The first entry was dated 6/8/2002 and written by Jimmy Newman:

"Gloria Marie Nash was reported missing by her sister, Andrea Nash, at 1430 hours this afternoon. According to Andrea Nash, Gloria had been missing since 6/4/2002. Ms. Nash stated that Gloria had disappeared several times in the past, but never stayed gone for more than three days. When my partner, Dale Larraby, asked why Gloria Nash had a habit of disappearing for extended periods of time, Ms. Nash said, 'She was with someone. My sister liked men. But then, you should know that already, shouldn't you?' I asked Ms. Nash what she meant by that last statement, but she only answered with a smile. We asked Ms. Nash to provide us with the names, addresses, and phone numbers of anyone Gloria might be in contact with. Ms. Nash did give us the information we requested. I told Ms. Nash that we would open an official Missing Persons file and immediately begin our investigation. Prior to exiting the room, Ms. Nash stated that she believed her sister was no longer living. I asked why she felt this was the case, and she said, 'just a gut feeling.' Our interview with Ms. Nash concluded at 1515 hours."

Dantzler considered a forty-five minute first interview in a missing persons case to be little more than a joke. He could think of at least fifty questions Newman and Larraby should have asked Andrea Nash but didn't. This was especially true since Andrea brought up the possibility that a murder had been committed. If he'd been conducting the interview he would have wanted to know much more about Gloria's past, her friends, her favorite places to hang out, and the names of those 'men' she liked to be with. Did she have a cell phone? Did she have a presence on social media? Most of all, though, he would have probed Andrea on her statement that "you should know that already, shouldn't you?" What, exactly, did Andrea mean by that?

The second entry, recorded two days later on 6/10/2002, was also written by Jimmy Newman:

"Andrea Nash came to my office at 0900 hours to discuss the ongoing investigation into the disappearance of her sister, Gloria Marie Nash. My partner Dale Larraby and I assured Ms. Nash that we were working the case hard. We told her a physical description of Gloria Nash, along with a photo, had been sent to all law enforcement agencies within the United States, Alaska, Hawaii, and Puerto Rico. I told Ms. Nash that if Gloria was out there, she would be found. Once again Ms. Nash stated her belief that Gloria Nash was deceased. This interview concluded at 0920 hours."

A twenty-minute interview this time. Shameful.

Working the case hard? Dantzler mumbled out loud. *They weren't working the case at all.*

The third and final entry proved this beyond any doubt. It was written by Newman on 6/15/2002:

"At 1645 hours this afternoon, Andrea Nash phoned to inquire about the status of the investigation into the disappearance of Gloria Nash. I informed Ms. Nash that we had heard nothing from any law enforcement agency. I also reassured her that we continued to pursue the case with vigor. The call lasted approximately ten minutes."

That was the extent of the 'investigation' into the disappearance of Gloria Nash—three reports consisting of two interviews that lasted a combined sixty-five minutes, and one ten-minute phone call. No mention anywhere of follow-up work performed by Newman and Larraby. No interviews with individuals who could possibly shed light on Gloria Nash's lifestyle. Not a single talk with any of those men she liked. Nor was there any evidence that Newman and Larraby had actually sent a description of Gloria Nash to other law enforcement agencies. There was nothing in this file that came close to even hinting at a legitimate investigation.

Shameful was the wrong word to describe this sad business. Disgusting was the more appropriate choice.

Dantzler picked up the small photo of Gloria Nash that was attached to the folder. She was attractive in a very unremarkable way. Pretty, but not beautiful or glamorous. In a movie she wouldn't be the female lead, she'd be the star's best friend. Her slightly crooked smile hinted at mischief. But it was her eyes that really caught Dantzler's attention. They were eyes that said, "I might be young, but I've seen and done some things in my time."

Staring into those eyes, Dantzler couldn't help but wonder if Gloria had seen and done some things that got her murdered.

Dantzler looked at his watch—it was now a little past eight. Jake should be showing up at any moment, and once he did, the two of them would meet with Andrea Nash. She deserved better than what she'd been given thus far. So did Gloria Nash, regardless of what had happened to her.

Dantzler wanted to show Andrea that not all cops were as indifferent—and incompetent—as Jimmy Newman and Dale Larraby.

Not a task that required much effort.

~^~

Julie left Sean's house a little after ten the next morning. She and Sean spent a wonderful evening together, far better than she would have imagined, and one that gave hope for a future long-term relationship. They made love with an ease and comfort rarely experienced by two people who were together for only the second time. It was bliss, she had to admit, and she wanted more.

Sean left for work at eight-thirty. After an extended kiss he told her to stay as long as she wanted, but to make sure the front door was locked if or when she left. She answered with a second kiss, promising that the house would be secure when she departed.

Julie had a glass of orange juice, took a shower, dressed, left Sean's place, and walked out to her car. Unsure what she wanted to do, but not wanting to waste another day, she decided to go see Eddie Campbell once again. It was her contention that he had more to say than he'd shared with her the first time they met. She felt even more strongly that Alex Shannon was hiding information, but visiting him would be a waste of time. That man was not going to reveal anything.

Eddie's Dodge Caravan was parked next to the house. This told Julie that in all likelihood Eddie was home. But he wasn't alone. Another vehicle, a black Audi, was parked behind the Caravan. Julie now faced a decision—to move ahead with her plan to interview Eddie while the guest was inside, or hold off until Eddie's visitor left the premises.

There was, however, a third option, and this was the one Julie chose: Write down the license plate for the vehicle behind Eddie's Caravan, then phone Dantzler and ask him to run the plates.

She took out her cell phone and punched in Dantzler's number. He answered immediately. "What's going on, Julie?' he inquired.

"I need a favor."

"Okay, tell me what you need."

"Can you run a license plate number for me?"

"Not unless you give me a legitimate reason."

"What would be a legitimate reason?"

"Well, you can begin by telling me why you need this plate number."

"Because I want to know who the vehicle belongs to."

"Not a good answer."

"Best I've got."

"Where are you, Julie?"

"Down the street from Eddie Campbell's house. There's. . ."

"Why are you anywhere near Eddie Campbell's house?" Dantzler asked.

"I came by to speak with him, but there's a car parked behind his Caravan. A black Audi. I was just wondering who was inside talking to Eddie."

"No dice, Julie. You need to drive away right now."

"Please, Detective Dantzler. Can't you at least tell me who is meeting with Eddie?"

"That's not how things work, Julie."

"Come on, help a girl out. It's the last favor I'll ask."

Dantzler turned to Jake and told him to fire up the computer. Then he asked Julie to give him the license plate numbers. When she did he repeated them to Jake. In less than thirty seconds he had the name of the vehicle owner.

"The car is registered to Alex Shannon," Dantzler told Julie. Then with force in his voice, he said, "Get the hell away from that house before Shannon or Campbell see you. That's a risk you don't want to take."

Not needing to be told twice, Julie put the car in gear and drove away.

CHAPTER THIRTY

Andrea Nash Woodson lived in small brick house on Wilson-Downing, a narrow, busy street that connected two of Lexington's most heavily traveled roads, Nicholasville and Tates Creek. Dantzler had phoned late yesterday afternoon to ensure that Andrea would be available for an interview. She told him she was an RN at Good Sam Hospital, that tomorrow was her day off, and she would be home all day. They agreed on an eleven a.m. meeting time.

Dantzler and Jake pulled into the short driveway and parked behind a late model white Hyundai Elantra. The front yard was small but well-kept. A child's overturned red tricycle glistened in the sun like a bleeding wound in the green grass. Andrea Nash stood at the front door, cup of coffee in hand, waiting to greet her visitors.

Dantzler judged Andrea to be slightly more attractive than her younger sister had been. There were obvious genetic similarities—facial bone structure, hair color, full lips—but there was one key difference—the eyes. Both women had hazel eyes, but Andrea's lacked the mischief Dantzler saw in Gloria's. Hers had a calmer, more peaceful look to them. There was nothing wild in Andrea's eyes.

Of course, Dantzler realized that his judgment was in some ways inaccurate and unfair. After all, Andrea had been alive these past fifteen years. He suspected that Gloria hadn't been alive. What she would look like now if she was still around fell into the world of conjecture.

Andrea was taller and thinner than Dantzler expected her to be. She was dressed in a pair of washed-out jeans, a black sweatshirt, and flip-flops. Once Dantzler and Jake were inside she asked them if they wanted coffee. They declined. The two detectives sat on opposite ends of the sofa, Andrea in a chair across from them.

"I'm not one of those people who has a cup of coffee in the morning and that's it for the day," Andrea said. "I drink it twenty-four/seven. That's probably not healthy, but I've been a serious coffee drinker since I was a kid. I'm afraid my mom and grand-mother got Gloria and me hooked when we were just out of diapers. I'm afraid there's not much here to drink at the moment. Some boxes of fruit juice that my son likes is about the extent of what I can offer."

"No, thanks, we're good," Dantzler said.

"I do apologize for the mess," Andrea said, pointing to floor. "My son is seven, and he loves to play with those Lego figures. Play with them, but never consider putting them back in the box when he's finished. I should have picked them up before you got here."

Andrea took a sip of coffee before continuing. "I can't begin to tell you how pleased I am that officers from Missing Persons have finally decided to speak with me concerning Gloria's disappearance. It's been years since I've heard a peep from anyone in that department."

"We're not with Missing Persons," Dantzler corrected. "We work in Homicide."

"So, I was right all along—my sister was murdered?"

"We don't have any solid evidence that Gloria was the victim of a homicide. But . . ."

"Then why are you here?"

"We've recently come across information—certain facts—that give us reason to suspect that something bad might have happened to her. Like I said, nothing solid but more than enough to justify our taking a closer look."

"That would be a first," Andrea scoffed. "Those two officers who worked Gloria's case didn't put forth *any* effort. Newman and Larraby were total jerks, if you want my honest opinion."

"Forget about those two," Dantzler said. "Jake and I are here now, and we won't let you down. We'll find out something, one way or the other. You have our promise on that. We'll talk about the case in a few minutes. But first, why don't you tell us about Gloria? Give us a snapshot of what she was all about."

Tears flooded down Andrea's cheeks. "Thank you so much for saying that. Not once did Newman or Larraby show the slightest interest in Gloria as a person, a human being." Taking a tissue from her purse she dried her eyes, and said, "What, specifically, would you like to know about her?"

Jake said, "Anything you wish to share with us. For instance, were you guys close?"

"Oh my gosh, yes, we were very close. I'm fifteen months older than Gloria, so we were practically raised like twins. Same clothes, same hair style, same toys, same everything. What one of us had, both of us had. We were twin Barbie dolls. Our father deserted us when Gloria was three months old, so neither of us had any memory of him whatsoever. We were raised by our grandmother and our mother."

Andrea went to a table, removed a frame containing two photos, and handed it to Jake. "That's the four of us," she said, smiling. "In the one on the left I was six and Gloria was five. On the right I was fifteen, she was fourteen."

Jake passed the photos to Dantzler, who looked them over, then handed them to Andrea. She placed the photos back on the table and returned to her chair. "Although my sister and I were close we were also very different," she said. "Gloria was fearless, a risk-taker, daring, willing to take chances. If there was a rule she would test it to the limits. I guess you could say she was something of a rebel. Me, I'm the exact opposite. I'm a total conformist, the girl who never took chances, never broke the rules, never caused any problems. Looking back, I have to admit that I was the family coward. Gloria certainly wasn't."

Jake said, "Did Gloria's fearlessness include the use of drugs?"

"I do know for a fact that she smoked pot. How much or how

often, I can't say. I also know that on one occasion she experimented with peyote. When I asked her what that was like, she said it made her throw up, and that the trip she had wasn't all that great. Based on that, I would also suspect that she tried LSD at some point. But Gloria was not a heavy drug user. She definitely did not use that deadly stuff like heroin, cocaine, or meth."

Dantzler opened the Gloria Nash File, looked it over for a few seconds, and then said, "In Jimmy Newman's report, when Dale Larraby asked you why Gloria had a habit of disappearing for extended periods of time, you . . ."

"I never said that," Andrea said. "All I said was that Gloria had disappeared for several days in the past. That only happened on two occasions, which I don't regard as a habit. Both times she was gone for three days. This was now day four. I was there because in my heart I knew something bad had happened to my sister."

"Why not go to the Homicide Unit?" asked Jake.

"I never thought about it, to be honest with you. I just assumed Newman and Larraby would handle it. Boy was I wrong."

"According to the file, you only had three interactions with the Newman and Larraby—two visits to their office, and a single phone call on June fifteenth, two-thousand-two." Dantzler held up the two pieces of paper and waved them. "After that, nothing. Why did you stop contacting them?"

"I cannot believe this," Andrea said, verging on tears. "I called those men three or four times a week for several years. I had to, because they never called me. In the beginning, it was, 'Ms. Nash, we're doing everything possible to locate your sister.' Then it was, 'Ms. Nash, we haven't forgotten about your sister. We're still looking into it.' Finally, it became, 'Ms. Nash, unless we catch a break, the chances of finding your sister aren't good.' Then as the years went by, Newman and Larraby retired and the new men who took over had other cases to work, so I stopped calling. I thought about hiring a private investigator, but that costs money I didn't have. By that time I was a divorced single mom attending nursing school. After a while, I had to resign myself to the fact that Gloria was dead and no one was going to help find out what happened."

Andrea shook her head and wiped away a few tears. "Gloria is dead, Detective Dantzler," she whispered. "In the last five years my granny and my mom passed away. There is no way Gloria would have missed being here for their funerals. She loved those two women as much as I did. When she didn't show up, that's when I knew beyond any doubt that Gloria was dead."

"In that initial meeting with Newman and Larraby you said something quite interesting," Dantzler said. "You said, 'My sister liked men. But then, you should know that already, shouldn't you?' What did you mean by that?"

"I was referring to the detective who was head over heels in love with Gloria."

"Which detective?"

"Mike Perkins."

"She and Mike Perkins were linked romantically?"

"That's what he wanted. The man was crazy in love with Gloria. He wanted something long-term, permanent. Gloria liked Mike but she certainly didn't love him. She was nineteen, twenty at the time. She hadn't even begun to think about settling down. Marriage, kids, the house with a two-car garage, those were not on the immediate horizon for her."

"How did Mike feel about being rejected?" Jake said.

"I don't think she rejected Mike. I mean, they were still seeing each other when she disappeared. I'm sure she made it clear to him that she wasn't ready for a long-term commitment. Since they continued to see each other, I assume he handled it okay."

"Did you speak with Mike after Gloria went missing?"

"Yes, on several occasions. But it was when he started using drugs, so he was in no shape to help me. Not long after that he was fired. I hadn't seen or heard from him since."

"Do you think Mike Perkins had anything to do with Gloria's death?"

"It's hard to believe he did, knowing how much he loved her. However, that thought has crossed my mind. Maybe they got into an argument and he hit her too hard. She fell, hit her head, and died. Or he choked her harder and longer than he meant to. He accidently kills her, gets scared, disposes of the body, and deals with the aftermath by getting heavily into drugs. But having said that, deep in my heart I don't think he had anything to do with what happened to her."

"Could be he did and you're right about why he turned to the drugs."

"I suppose anything is possible," Andrea conceded.

"You also said Gloria liked men. Is there one in particular that we should be looking at?"

"I'm sure Newman and Larraby took that to mean Gloria slept with every man in Lexington. That she was a slut, a whore. She wasn't. All I meant was that she liked to hang out with guys, to have fun with them. As to your question, no, I can't think of anyone she was having problems with."

Dantzler stood, followed by Jake. "Andrea, we are going to look into this until we have some answers for you, one way or the other. That's a promise." He handed a business card to Andrea. "If you have any questions, or if you remember something you forgot to tell us, give me a call at either of those numbers. We won't let you down a second time."

"I truly believe that, Detective Dantzler," Andrea said, shaking his hand. "You strike me as a man who lives up to his word."

_-^-_

Julie spent the next hour sitting alone in restaurant called Winchell's on Southland Drive. She nibbled at a salad and sipped at a Diet Coke, her thoughts not on food or drink but rather on what her next course of action should be. The promise she made to Darvis was also heavy on her mind. She had told him that if the case wasn't solved in the next three days she would head back to Cincinnati. She was now down to two days. Sean had said Dantzler was a great detective, but was it feasible to believe that even a great detective could solve a mystery this complex in two days? The likelihood of that happening was on par with her winning the Lottery. About a million to one.

Unable to sit and think any longer, she decided to take action. She paid her bill, got in her car, and took off. Her destination was Eddie Campbell's house, and her plan was simple: If Alex Shannon's vehicle was still there, she would keep driving. If, however, his car was gone, she would go in and try to get Campbell to speak with her. She remained convinced that he could provide many of the answers she was looking for.

That is, provided he agreed to talk, which wasn't going to happen today. When Julie got to Campbell's house, Alex Shannon's vehicle was gone. But so was Campbell's. No one was home. Julie's chat with Eddie Campbell had to be put on hold.

Silently cursing, Julie drove away from Campbell's house, unaware that she was being followed.

CHAPTER THIRTY-ONE

Dantzler and Jake were at Double H Barbeque on Versailles Road, less than a mile from the bar owned by Robbie Newcome. It was a little past noon and they were having lunch. Dantzler, a regular here, was finishing off a pork sandwich, fries, and a Pepsi, while Jake, after demolishing a full rack of baby back ribs with potato salad, baked beans, cole slaw, and a Pepsi, went back up and ordered a pulled pork sandwich.

"Where do you put all that food, Jake?" asked Dantzler.

"This is terrific barbeque," replied Jake.

"Yes, it is. But I would explode if I ate that much."

"Goes back to my time in Iraq and Afghanistan. When you're in a war you eat when you have the chance, because you never know when you'll have your next meal."

"Or if you'll ever have one."

"Well, yeah, that's always a possibility."

"I'm not sure I have the courage to do what you did, Jake."

"Of course, you do. You've been under fire, had bullets coming at you, and you handled it with courage and bravery. You'd have done just fine."

"Bullets are one thing, but mortars, RPGs, and machine gun fire are an entirely different matter."

"Not really. They can all kill you."

"What about fear? How did you handle that?"

"Funny thing, I was never scared during an actual firefight. Before and after, that's when the fear hit me. It's the wondering what *might* happen, then the realization of what *could* have happened that made me fearful."

"You have my respect, Jake. You and all the men and women who put their asses on the line for sometimes questionable reasons." Dantzler took a drink of Pepsi. "What was your impression of Andrea Nash?"

"I thought she was honest and forthcoming, especially when talking about Gloria. She loves her sister very much, yet she wasn't afraid to point out her flaws and weaknesses. She didn't paint Gloria as a saint, which, obviously, she wasn't. I also appreciated the fact that she didn't hide her disdain for Jimmy Newman and Dale Larraby. She has a legitimate right to be pissed at those guys."

"Larraby was always a lousy cop, but it's disappointing to learn that Jimmy Newman didn't put more effort into working the case. Best I recall, he had the rep for being a decent cop. The fact that he let Andrea down is puzzling."

"Maybe Larraby really ran the investigation."

"Or maybe someone higher up ordered them to shut it down."

"Who was running Missing Persons back then?" asked Jake.

"Joel Howard."

"How do you rate him as a cop?"

"Solid. He'd have expected his investigators to give an all-out effort on every case they worked. There is no way he ordered Newman and Larraby to shut down anything."

"Then we should talk to him, see what he can tell us."

"Not gonna happen, Jake. Joel Howard is dead. He committed suicide several years ago."

"Another Missing Persons cop, another suicide. What are the odds?"

Dantzler didn't answer.

Jake said, "Think there's a chance it was another staged suicide?"

"That's what we need to find out."

Dantzler picked up his phone and punched in an old, familiar number. His call was to Mac Tinsley, the long-time medical examiner who retired four years ago. Mac answered almost immediately.

"The last man on this planet that I expected to hear from on this glorious morning," Mac said, laughing. "What could an important man like you need from an old retired bum like me?"

"Don't be so hard on yourself, Mac. You're not old."

"Just a bum, right?"

"You said it, I didn't."

"But you didn't disagree."

"When did I ever disagree with you, Mac? Never."

"Enough bullshit. What do you need, Jack?"

"You remember working the Joel Howard case?"

"I remember all my cases. And yes, I remember that one. Joel committed suicide. A self-inflicted gunshot to the head. He used a .45. Why are you inquiring about Joel Howard? That was years ago."

"Do you still have access to the file on that case?"

"No. But I can get it. Once again, I have to ask—why are you suddenly interested in a case that is almost a decade old?"

"I need you to take another look at it," Dantzler answered, knowing what was coming.

"Explain to me why you want me to take another look," Mac said, angrily. "Surely you're not saying I made a mistake. Tell me that's not the reason for your request."

"No, Mac, that's not what I'm saying at all."

"From where I'm sitting, that's what it sure sounds like."

"Look, Mac, in light of what's been happening recently with Larraby, Mike Perkins, and that Michaels kid, I just need confirmation that Joel Howard did in fact kill himself. You're doing this to reassure me, that's all."

"Why can't Arnie do it? He's the medical examiner. I don't want to go behind his back."

"No, I want Arnie there with you. But it was your case, and you know it better than anyone. Both of you take a good look at it, then tell me what you find."

"We'll find that I was correct when I ruled cause of death to be suicide."

"Then I can wipe that nagging question off the slate and move on."

"You know, I'm more than a little angry with you, Jack, for questioning my professional integrity. In all the years we worked together you never once did that."

"Mac, I'm not questioning anything. I know better than anyone just how good you were at the job. You were the best. Everyone knows that."

"I will phone Arnie and get things moving," Mac said, still sounding peeved. "One of us will get back with you when we conclude the investigation."

"Thanks, Mac. I do appreciate you helping me out on this."

Dantzler ended the call, placed his phone on the table, looked at Jake, and shook his head. "That was a call I didn't want to make," he said.

"Didn't go well?"

"It went about the way I expected it to. Mac was not pleased. He's a proud man, and for me or anyone else to challenge his professionalism hits him right in the gut."

"Was he better than Arnie?" asked Jake.

"Arnie is terrific, but Mac was great."

"How will Mac respond if he discovers that he missed something while looking into Joel Howard's death?"

"He'll own up to it," answered Dantzler. "But it will break his heart."

‑‑^‑‑

The magnificent morning sunshine was now being threatened by a band of dark, ominous clouds drifting in from the west. Rain was imminent. In an hour or less Lexington was going to get soaked. High above, a single black bird flew toward those dark clouds like a dead soul on its final journey to Hades.

Alex Shannon leaned against his car while rehearsing what he was going to say when the older man showed up. He was in the parking area at Jacobson Park, not more than a few feet away from where Dale Larraby killed himself. *Smart move, Dale*, Shannon thought, *because if you hadn't pulled that trigger, I would have.*

In Shannon's view, Larraby was more of a threat than those dark clouds. Hell, Larraby *was* a dark cloud. A weak, whining, unstable pussy who eventually had to be gotten rid of. Thankfully, he did the honors himself.

Others were unstable as well, Mike Perkins most of all. Between the drugs he took for years and that damn conscience of his, that's why he had to go. The Michaels kid? He should have kept his mouth shut. Had he done that he'd still be alive. Talking to that goddamn book writer was the mistake that cost him his life.

That left only one—Eddie Campbell.

What to do with that crippled bastard?

The answer to that question was obvious: Take him out.

And that's what Shannon was going to say when the old man arrived. He wasn't going to take no for an answer, regardless of what the old man said, or how many reasons he might give for letting Eddie live. Eddie Campbell had to go, simple as that.

The old man pulled his car next to Shannon's, cut off the engine, and slowly got out. Conceding to the growing darkness, he removed his sunglasses, replacing them with his regular glasses. After a quick glance toward the lake, the old man came around the rear of his car and stood next to Shannon. He started to say something but Shannon beat him to the punch.

"Eddie has to go," Shannon proclaimed. "He's a liability neither of us can afford. You know I'm right."

"Eddie isn't the only liability. You do know that, don't you? There's the girl and two of our other friends."

"I'll worry about them later. But Eddie is the one who can bring us down. That possibility needs to be taken off the table."

"I don't disagree with your assessment. I do, however, disagree with your timing. Too many homicides, especially ones being investigated by Dantzler, that's much more of a liability than Eddie Campbell."

"Dantzler has a long road to travel before he gets to us. Eddie Campbell is his detour. Eddie is weak. If Dantzler presses him hard, Eddie will crack. I can't take that chance. We can't take that chance."

"So, you want to kill Eddie?"

"Yes."

"Then do it, Alex. You don't need my blessing. I'm not Don Corleone or Lucky Luciano. Just be damn careful that Eddie's death doesn't come back to bite us on the ass."

"It won't . . . I'll make sure of that."

"You don't know Jack Dantzler." The old man looked up just as the first drops of rain began to fall. "Why should I trust that you won't regard me as the next liability that needs to be taken care of? Answer that for me."

"We're both in the same boat, the ones with the most at stake. If either of us rats the other one out, we both go down. You could say we're each other's guardian angel."

"Make sure the Eddie thing is clean." The older man walked around his car, opened the door, and started to get in. Hesitating, he said, "It's a scary thought, Alex, being in the same boat with you. Kind of makes me feel like I'm on the Titanic."

CHAPTER THIRTY-TWO

Robbie Newcome did a quick double-take and softly groaned when he saw Dantzler and Jake come into the bar. He stopped drying beer mugs, flipped the dish rag over his left shoulder, picked up a bottle of water, and took a drink. The look on his face made it clear that he wasn't especially pleased to see Dantzler. In fact, Dantzler was about the last person he wanted to see walking through the front door.

Adding to his displeasure was the absence of Vee. If she'd been along for the ride, then Dantzler's return visit just might be tolerable. Seeing a woman as gorgeous as Vee made a lot of unpleasant things bearable.

"Where's tall, dark, and beautiful?" asked Robbie.

"Don't know who you're referring to," answered Dantzler.

"The cop lady you sent in undercover."

"Did this lady have a name?"

"Vee."

"What makes you think Vee is a cop?"

"A little bird told me."

"This bird have a name?"

Robbie shook his head. "Nah, it was a nameless bird. Sorry."

"Well, your bird was correct. Vee is a cop."

"You let Vee know that I took her advice and removed the Confederate flag. Also, tell her that it hasn't helped one damn bit. Still haven't had a single black customer."

"Robbie, I don't give a shit about the Confederate flag or the color of your clientele," Dantzler said. "What I want to know is why you lied to Vee."

"I didn't lie to her," proclaimed Robbie, more strongly than necessary.

"You sure about that?"

"Yeah, damn sure. What lie did I supposedly tell her?"

"Not knowing Danny Michaels."

"That's no lie. I didn't know him."

Dantzler opened an evidence bag and took out the note found in Danny's pants pocket. Handing the small piece of paper to Robbie, Dantzler said, "Then please explain this to me."

Robbie's face went ashen when he read the note. "Where did you get this?" he asked, his eyes glued to the paper.

"Did you write that note, Robbie?"

Nodding, Robbie again asked, "Where did you get this?"

Dantzler said, "Now that we've cleared up the lying issue, how about I ask the questions?"

"What do you want to know?"

"That note can only be interpreted as a threat, Robbie. Why were you threatening Danny Michaels?"

"It wasn't a real threat," Robbie said, shaking his head. "Here's the deal, see. About four months ago Mike Perkins loaned Danny some money. Five-hundred bucks, I think it was. Anyway, a few weeks later I ran into Mike and asked if Danny had repaid the loan. Mike just laughed and said no, that he never expected to get the money back. I was a little thin on cash at the time and could have used five-hundred dollars. So I sent the note to Danny."

"Then he's found murdered with this note in his pocket. A smart detective would see you as the number one suspect."

"Damn, I can't believe that little turd kept this," Robbie said, handing the note back to Dantzler. "I sent it months ago."

"He did, and you lied about knowing him. Why?"

"I dunno, scared more than anything. Mike died, then Danny. I knew them both. I didn't want you guys looking at me as their killer. Stupid of me, I know, but I just wanted to stay out of it. So, I lied about not knowing Danny."

"Robbie, I don't for a second suspect you of murdering either one of those guys. What I do think is that you know who did."

"I don't know anything about any murders," Robbie said, waving his arms. "And that's no lie."

"Let's take a walk down memory lane. Back a long time ago, before Mike Perkins and Danny Michaels were killed."

"Memory lane? What the hell are you talking about?"

"Did you know Gloria Nash?" Dantzler asked, pointing a finger at Robbie. "And no more lies, Robbie."

"I knew her, but not very well. That's the honest to God truth. Mike was really hung up on her, so he tended to keep her to himself. I don't know why he was so jealous. Hell, no one was going to do anything to piss him off. Mike was stronger than Hercules."

"Was Gloria hung up on Mike?"

"I never got the feeling that she was. I mean, she liked him and all, but, love him? I don't think so. Not the way Mike loved her."

"Where did Mike meet Gloria?"

"I'm not sure. Maybe in a bar, maybe the bowling alley . . . I don't know."

"Was Mike into drugs at this time?"

"Maybe smoked some pot, nothing more. This was before he went drug crazy."

"How soon after Gloria went missing did Mike get heavily into drugs?"

"Almost immediately."

"Let's talk about Gloria," Dantzler said. "What do you think happened to her?"

"How am I supposed to answer that? I barely knew the woman."

"Come on, Robbie. You were buddies with Mike, you worked Missing Persons . . . you had to know something."

"I know Mike was sad as hell. I know he soon went off the rails. I know Jimmy Newman and Dale Larraby worked the case. Beyond that, I know nothing."

"What would you say if I told you that Newman and Larraby barely worked that case at all? Their 'investigation' included two short meetings with Gloria's sister and a brief phone call. This leads me to conclude that someone had no desire to see the case get solved. Joel Howard was head of Missing Persons back then. I can't envision him ever shutting down an investigation. That means someone else gave Newman and Larraby their orders. Who was it?"

"Jesus, man, you're killing me here. I don't know. I had nothing to do with that case. Nothing at all. Only those guys can answer your questions."

"They're all dead, Robbie. Only the living can help me find those answers I'm looking for."

"Well, this living person can't help you," Robbie said.

"Okay, let's talk about the living. Tell me about Eddie Campbell."

"What do you want to know about Eddie?"

"Did he have any involvement with Gloria Nash? Or with her investigation?"

"None that I recall."

"How tight was Eddie with Newman and Larraby?"

"He wasn't tight with Newman at all. He and Larraby were close. They hung out together all the time."

"There's something missing here, Robbie. Something you aren't telling me."

"Look, Detective Dantzler, I don't know anything. That's the point I'm trying to get across to you. I haven't got a clue what happened to Gloria Nash. Go talk to Eddie Campbell. Maybe he can give you some answers."

"I plan on talking to Campbell, don't worry about that. But not until I've heard all you have to say."

"Can't this wait until later? I'm kinda busy here."

"Robbie, you have four customers. You're not exactly slammed."

"Yeah, well, those two over by the jukebox need a refill."

Jake said, "I'll take care of them, Robbie. You keep talking."

"They both want a White Russian. Know how to make one of those?"

"Yep, sure do, Robbie. I did some bartending while I was in the military."

"Great," Robbie said, half-heartedly.

"Just a few more questions, Robbie," Dantzler said. "Then I'll let you get back to running your bar."

"Ah, man, you're killing me," groaned Robbie. "What now?"

"Money."

"All I can tell you about money is I don't have any."

"Larraby had plenty, and so did Mike Perkins. How do you suppose two cops came up with all that money?"

"I can't answer that, Detective. I swear."

"Alex Shannon," said Dantzler.

Hearing the name seemed to startle Robbie. "What about him?" he asked.

"You tell me."

"I hardly know the man. He worked Vice, not Missing Persons. Why are you asking about him?"

"What was his relationship with Larraby, Mike, and Eddie?"

"You need to ask Eddie these questions. I'm not the guy who can provide the answers you're looking for. Mike and I were close, but I barely knew Larraby and Campbell. As for Alex Shannon, I didn't know him at all. They moved in a different orbit than I did. That's all I know, Detective."

Dantzler said, "Don't plan on leaving town anytime soon, Robbie. This might not be the last time we talk."

"I practically live in this dive. I'm not going anywhere."

The moment Dantzler and Jake headed for the door Robbie glanced to his right, to the booth next to the jukebox, thankful that his little bird wasn't sitting in his usual spot.

Had he been, then things could have gotten ugly in a hurry.

CHAPTER THIRTY-THREE

What Lincoln called the mystic chords of memory had yet to swell the chorus of information Dantzler was seeking to locate. Presently, those chords were playing a blank tune. He was hearing nothing but silence. A key memory existed, one that held important and valuable information, but it continued to remain out of reach, hidden in a distant cave like a long-buried biblical scroll.

He had to locate it, to dig it up like a coffin that must be exhumed in order to uncover missing or overlooked evidence on the body contained within. Right now, this case was a sick patient, and unless he could find that missing piece of the puzzle, the patient was destined to become a corpse.

But what was that memory? What had he seen, heard, or read that was buried somewhere deep in his memory bank? What was he missing? Why wouldn't his chords play a winning tune?

That lost memory was foremost on his mind as he sat alone in the Tennis Center concession area. How could it not be? Locating that memory was the key to solving four homicide cases—Gloria Nash, Joel Howard, Mike Perkins, and Danny Michaels.

And perhaps reveal the reason why Dale Larraby chose to commit suicide.

Find it and the entire house of cards came crashing down.

Although that lost memory continued to haunt him, it wasn't the only thing on his mind. A close second was his concern for Julie's safety. This was a serious matter, one she seemed to be unwilling to grasp or to acknowledge. She was headstrong to a point he considered to be nothing short of reckless. In his experience reckless behavior invariably led to a bad outcome. He never ceased to be amazed at how intelligent people could behave in such a dumb—and dangerous—way. But they chose to do so, and Julie was the perfect example of someone who did.

Julie had no business being anywhere near Alex Shannon or Eddie Campbell, yet there she was, parked on the street in front of Campbell's house. Why would she dare take such an unnecessary risk? If Shannon and Campbell were involved in these murders—and Dantzler was convinced they were—then they wouldn't hesitate for an instant to put her six feet underground. They'd see her as a problem that needed to be done away with.

Julie's desire to write another book, her unchecked ambition, was blinding her from seeing what should be her top priority—staying alive.

Dantzler's buzzing phone brought him out of his semi-trance. The call was from Arnie Edwards.

"What's new, Arnie?" he asked.

"Mac and I just finished our evaluation of Joel Howard's autopsy report," replied Arnie. "Thought you'd want to know what I—we —found."

"You're right, I do. But what's with the I/we reference?"

"This is where I need to be delicate."

"Not with me, you don't. Tell me what you found."

"You can officially add Joel Howard to your list of homicides. His death was not a suicide."

"Can you say that with a high degree of certainty?"

"I can say it with one-hundred percent certainty. Joel Howard was murdered, simple as that."

"Did Mac agree?"

"He still thinks it's a suicide," answered Arnie.

"How can that be, if he's seeing the same evidence you're seeing? Mac has a reputation for never overlooking anything."

"It's all about the bruise, Jack. Mac isn't aware of the bruises we found on our recent victims. He originally noted the bruise on Joel, but felt it played no role in cause of death. He held to that conviction."

"And you didn't tell him otherwise?"

"I didn't have the heart to tell him. It would kill Mac to learn that he overlooked evidence of such importance. I just couldn't bring myself to do it."

"You did the right thing, Arnie," Dantzler said, adding, "Tell me more about that bruise on Joel. Are you convinced that it likely resulted from a choke-hold? Is that what you're saying?"

"Yes. And I would even go so far as to say with complete confidence that the individual who killed Joel Howard is also responsible for the deaths of Mike Perkins and Danny Michaels. There's simply too much similarity for me to think otherwise."

"Believe it or not, Arnie, that's good news. Better to be looking for a single perp than having to hunt down multiple killers."

"What about Mac?" asked Arnie.

"For now, nothing. Later on he may learn the truth. Hopefully, that won't happen. If it does he'll just have to deal with it. Nobody's perfect, Arnie. We all make mistakes, and that includes Mac."

"One final thing, Jack. In case you're wondering, you might want to consider exhuming Joel's body at some point in the future. That would give you some definitive answers."

"Hadn't thought about that, Arnie. I'm hoping it won't be necessary, but if it comes to that, I'll see that it gets done."

After ending his talk with Arnie, Dantzler left the Tennis Center. His destination: Home. His goal: Have a few drinks and try to locate that missing memory.

It was the corpse he had to exhume.

‑^‑

Dantzler's feelings of despair lingered long after he returned home. Well into his third Jameson and Diet Coke, he had yet to dig up whatever it was that continued to elude him. Any hopes he may have entertained that enough alcohol would provide a Eureka moment had long since passed. This memory was proving to be a lost treasure.

Finally, after mixing another drink, he chose to move past what eluded him and to sift back through information that was at the forefront of his thinking. Rather than continue to rack his brain for something that might never turn up, he opted to follow a more familiar path, one that included important facts that required another look.

First, those three words spoken by a dying priest: "Dale Larraby knows."

Okay, Dantzler thought, let's place those words in conjunction with known facts.

Fact one: Dale Larraby committed suicide *prior* to Father Riley making his death-bed pronouncement.

What does this mean? One of two things. Either Larraby was involved in Gloria Nash's murder, or he knew about it and confessed to Father Riley. Driven by feelings of guilt, or fearful of being caught, Larraby chose to end his life.

Fact two: Mike Perkins was murdered.

What does this mean? Mike also had a hand in Gloria's death (although it's unlikely that he was the actual killer), he was consumed by guilt, turned to drugs, and thus became a liability to others involved in the murder plot. His instability and sense of guilt had to be eliminated.

Fact three: Danny Michaels was murdered.

What does this mean? Somehow, some way, Danny got wind of what happened to Gloria Nash. Most likely, Mike Perkins was his source.

Fact four: Danny was killed *after* Julie Bradley had spoken with Alex Shannon and Eddie Campbell.

What does this mean? Simple. Shannon and/or Campbell killed

Danny to silence him. Given Campbell's physical limitations, Shannon was likely the one who did the actual killing.

Fact five: Alex Shannon worked Vice and was never in the Missing Persons Unit.

What does this mean? Maybe everything, maybe nothing, but it bears further investigation. Shannon is the odd man out in this scenario. Or is he? Is he the possible link that connects Gloria to both Missing Persons and Vice? Another question that demands an answer.

Fact six: Dale Larraby and Mike Perkins were in possession of enormous amounts of cash.

What does this mean? This is the question of questions. Where did two ex-cops come up with so much money? And is the money somehow tied in to the Gloria Nash case? If so, how?

Lastly, the big question: Who's running the show? Certainly not Eddie Campbell. He has neither the toughness nor the physical capability to single-handedly murder someone. Alex Shannon does, but like Sean pointed out, Shannon isn't a leader. He's more than capable—and willing—to kill, but only on someone else's orders. Alex Shannon is a willing follower.

Thinking about it now, Dantzler realized he was still standing on square one, haunted by a single thought:

Who was giving the orders?

_^_

Eddie Campbell rolled his wheelchair into the kitchen, opened the refrigerator, grabbed the bottle of vodka, closed the door, wheeled back into the living room, and parked in front of the TV. The picture was on but the volume was turned down so low Eddie couldn't make out what was being said by one of the new late-night talk show hosts who had suddenly discovered that politics was a terrific source of comedy. What those young folks didn't know—and Eddie would be more than happy to inform them if they asked—was politics and comedy have walked arm in arm for decades. And, Eddie would tell them, comedy and politics invariably lead to drama, which tends to end in tragedy.

Just like my fuckin' life.

Eddie took a long pull from the bottle, slammed it down, and cursed out loud. Tears fell from his eyes. More cursing and another drink were followed by a new round of tears. Nights were the worst for Eddie and had been ever since the accident. Here he sat, alone, chained to a goddamned wheelchair, his thoughts always drifting back to a time when he was young and strong and independent.

Not like now, an invalid with legs of straw, a dick that no longer worked, and no hope of ever being the man he had once been. On nights like this, when self-pity ruled his thinking, he couldn't help but wonder if he should follow Dale Larraby's lead and put an end to this miserable life he was now leading. Hell, he had plenty more reason to do it than that weakling Larraby did. Larraby could stand up, walk, run, get a hard-on, make love to a woman. A man capable of doing all that shouldn't take his own life. He should enjoy every second he has on this earth.

I have no cause to enjoy anything, Eddie said to himself, just as his cell phoned buzzed.

Eddie checked the Caller ID, then the time. A call from the old man at one in the morning.

This can't be good.

"Yes," Eddie said. "What do you want?"

"Don't get snippy with me, Eddie. That's not a wise thing to do."

"Why are you calling?"

"Did you keep your service weapon?"

"Of course."

"Is it still in good working order?"

"Yes."

"You'd better hope it is."

"Why?"

"You might have need for it in the very near future."

"What are you talking about?"

"Stay alert, Eddie. You never know who might show up on your doorstep."

"Who . . .?"

But the old man ended the call before Eddie could finish his question. With trembling hands, Eddie closed his phone, placed the bottle of vodka on a table, and rolled into his bedroom. Opening a dresser drawer, he removed his Glock 21, checked to make sure it was fully loaded, and then wheeled back into the living room, this time parking a few feet away from the front door.

Okay, fucker, whoever you are, step through that door and you're a dead man.

What Eddie failed to realize was that his defensive strategy was not a sound one. Had he been smart, he would have placed himself in a position that allowed surveillance of both the front and rear entrances. Where he now sat he could only see the front door. The back door was unguarded.

And unlocked.

CHAPTER THIRTY-FOUR

Julie's time was up. Three days had passed and still no murderer had been apprehended. Three days that seemed like three hours. They had flown by faster than a supersonic jet plane cutting across a clear blue sky. Faster than a bullet fired from a high-powered rifle.

Damn, now it's time to put up or shut up, she thought. *Time to test my core beliefs.*

Three days ago she had promised Darvis that if the case wasn't solved within that time frame she would skedaddle out of town. She'd given her word to the man. And now, much as she hated to admit it, a decision had to be made. She could delay no longer. She had to make a choice. And neither one was going to make her happy.

Should she live up to the promise she made to Darvis and head back to Cincinnati, or stick around Lexington until the situation was resolved? Either choice was going to make her feel shitty. Some moments simply suck, and there's no other way to describe it. Making matters even worse, this was a test. A test pitting her character against her work ethic. Her journalistic instincts demanded that she hang with the story regardless of the danger. But to do so meant breaking a promise to someone who trusted her and believed in her.

Which was worse—being a coward or going against your own code of ethics?

Jesus may have risen after three days, but for her, if she honored her commitment, these seventy-two hours translated into an ending rather than a new beginning.

Carefully moving Sean's leg off hers, she slipped out of bed. A quick check of the alarm clock told her it was only six-fifteen a.m. Still several hours before her three-day window officially closed. This meant she still had time to do more digging—and to keep her fingers crossed that Dantzler caught the killer—before having to return to Cincinnati. In her heart she knew all along that despite her inner debate she would honor her promise to Darvis and Nancy. That damn code of ethics was stronger than she realized.

She also understood why Darvis and Nancy were so concerned about her safety. There was, after all, a killer on the loose. Maybe more than one. With so many bodies piling up it was not inconceivable that this was a conspiracy of some sort. That would mean there was more than one person involved in all these murders by suicide. Either way, given that she was the one who really got all this started, the danger level for her was extremely high. She didn't need a Ph.D to understand that.

With Sean and Dantzler watching over her it was easy to feel safe, protected. Maybe too easy. No way could they keep eyes on her twenty-four hours a day. They had lives of their own to lead. Dantzler was trying to catch a killer—maybe killers—while Sean was a busy, successful attorney. Neither man had time to babysit an out-of-town writer looking to make a few bucks on a series of tragedies.

That wasn't in their job description.

Julie went into the kitchen, sat at the table, took out her cell phone, and sent a text to Darvis. Her message informed him that she would be leaving Lexington at six p.m. and heading back to her place on Mount Adams. She did add one caveat: *unless the case is solved.*

The old man went through the den, into the kitchen, and opened a door leading to his garage. He walked a few paces straight ahead until he was standing in front of an old rocking chair. Calling it old was not doing it justice; this particular piece of furniture genuinely qualified as ancient and historic.

The chair had originally belonged to his great-grandmother, having been hand built in seventeen seventy-eight by a slave who was a family friend. As a child, she sat in the chair and watched as soldiers marched off to fight against the British. Years later, his grandmother sat in that same rocking chair and watched soldiers from both the Union and Confederate armies march down the street. Even later, his mother told him stories about sitting in the chair while listening to President Roosevelt give his famous fireside chats meant to soothe a fearful nation during World War Two.

Despite those memories handed down from generation to generation, the chair meant very little to the old man. To him, it was little more than a relic. If it caught fire and burned to ashes, or if someone came in and stole it, he wouldn't shed a tear. Who cares about the past, anyway? The past is nothing but a bunch of years that have come and gone. They can't be relived or changed, so fuck 'em. The here and now is all that matters.

And the here and now was foremost on his mind at this precise moment.

The old man lifted up the rocking chair and moved it several feet away. Slowly kneeling, his knees creaking, he picked up a dusty, tattered old rug the chair had been sitting on and tossed it off to the side. Beneath the rug there were three strips of wooden boards that were loose. He removed them one by one, revealing an opening in the floor. Reaching down into the hole, he grabbed the handle to a large steel box, brought it up, and set it next to him. Standing, he took the box and returned to the kitchen. After pouring a cup of coffee, he sat at the table and opened the box. Then he turned the box up and dumped its content onto the table.

Two-hundred-fifty thousand dollars, all in hundred-dollar bills.

Virtually all the money he had collected. Only fifty grand was missing from the original amount.

Unlike the others, he held on to his cash, knowing that the time might come when he would need it to make his escape. That time, he knew, had arrived. If he didn't leave soon—*very* soon—he would likely find himself behind bars.

Or in the morgue.

The walls were quickly closing in on him.

The hounds were about to catch the fox.

And he had no one to blame but himself.

Sipping coffee, staring at the pile of money, he cursed himself for getting involved with men who wanted to walk on the wrong side of the law, men who dreamed of living like the criminals they were sworn to hunt down and apprehend. They had taken an oath to protect and serve the public, but the only thing they protected and served was their own self-interest. Their own greed.

Why he ever joined forces with that bunch of imbeciles was a mystery he would never be able to solve.

But he had, knowing all along that doing so would likely turn out to be a huge mistake. Maybe even a fatal one. *Definitely* a fatal one, unless he acted first. Alex Shannon would most certainly try to kill him, that was a given. He'd probably do it within the next couple of days. Alex was on a killing rampage. He had fear in his heart and blood in his eyes. A lethal combination. His intent was to eliminate anyone who could incriminate him, and that included Lawrence Brady, Robbie Newcome, and the female writer.

And me.

As he put the money back into the box he regretted that he wasn't fifteen or twenty years younger. If he were, he'd handle Alex Shannon in whatever manner was necessary, either by beating him to death, or by putting a bullet in his brain. Alex was a classic bully, and like most bullies he was at heart little more than a coward. Bullies tend to back down when someone presents a serious challenge. Fifteen or twenty years ago, the old man would have been that challenge.

Can't take you now, Alex, he said to himself. *But once upon a time it would have been no contest.*

The old man returned the box to its hiding place, put the wooden boards back, placed the rug on the floor, and set the old rocking chair back in its usual spot. Back in the kitchen, he traded his cup of coffee for a cold beer, sat at the table, opened the beer, took a swig, and thought about how he had ended up in such a nightmare position.

Why did he get involved in that situation in the first place? Was it for the money? No, he didn't need money. He had more than enough to live out his final years in comfort. Was it for the thrill? No, that was most certainly not the reason. Was it the desire to live outside the law? No, he had too much respect for the law to ever fall into that trap.

Then why? Why had he done it? And why had he fallen in with a group of men who lacked his intelligence, his character, and his intestinal fortitude? Two important questions, neither of which he could answer. But he had, and that was a hard, cold fact.

Events were moving fast now, meaning he had neither the time nor the luxury to sit around pondering past mistakes. Alex Shannon would soon be heading in this direction, gun in hand, ready to kill. Two days, probably, three days, tops.

Wish I could stay and face you head-on, Alex. But I'm too damn old and weary.

The old man sipped his beer and grinned. *Don't worry, Alex. There's a guy out there who will face you head-on, and he will take you down.*

_˄_

Julie was sitting in Starbucks when her cell phone chirped. Digging it out of her purse, she looked at the Caller ID, which showed a number she didn't recognize.

"Hello," she answered.

"Julie Bradley?"

Julie instantly recognized the voice. A chill ran down her spine. "Yes, Mr. Shannon, this is Julie. What can I do for you?"

"It's what I can do for you. That's the reason for my call."

"What can you do for me?"

"Give you what you want. What you've been asking for."

"And what is that?"

"Don't play coy with me, Miss Bradley. We both know what you want. The story concerning the disappearance of Gloria Nash."

"You mean, the *murder* of Gloria Nash, don't you?"

"Sorry to disappoint you, but I don't know anything about a murder. I do, however, have some pertinent information regarding her disappearance. If you're not interested in hearing what I have to say, tell me so and we'll end this chat right now. Either way is fine with me."

"I'm interested," Julie said, following several seconds of silence.

"Fine. You know where I live, so why don't you drop by in an hour or so? We can talk here."

"I don't think so, Mr. Shannon. If we meet, it will be in a public place."

"Okay. How about Jacobson Park? In an hour?"

"Jacobson Park? You mean, the place where Dale Larraby took his own life?"

"What's that have to do with us talking?"

"Jacobson Park is out."

"Then how about we do this, Miss Bradley? You come to the O'Neill's parking lot in an hour. It's on Richmond Road. I'll pick you up and we can go anywhere you like for our little chat. Does that sound safe enough for you?"

"No, it doesn't. If we go anywhere, it will be in my car."

"Not a problem. Your car, it will be."

"Then I will see you in an hour," Julie said, ending the call before he could respond. She then punched in Sean's number, which went to his voice mail. "Sean, I am meeting with Alex Shannon in an hour to discuss the Gloria Nash disappearance. I'm picking him up in the O'Neill's Pub parking lot. It would be reassuring if you could secretly follow us. I'd feel much safer knowing you were close by. Let me know when you get this message. Bye."

Julie paid her bill, walked outside, and climbed into her car. Her hands shaking, she had trouble placing the key in the ignition. Leaning back, she closed her eyes and took several slow, deep breaths, hoping to calm her shaky nerves. It didn't work. Her insides were a battle-ground where two strong and opposing forces were involved in heavy combat, two forces she was very familiar with.

Excitement and fear.

CHAPTER THIRTY-FIVE

Robbie Newcome was nowhere in sight when Dantzler and Vee walked into the bar. A middle-aged woman Dantzler had never seen was wiping off a table, and a Roy Orbison song was coming from the jukebox. Three men sat at one of the tables, while a pair of females was ensconced in one of the booths. Noon was still more than an hour away, yet the early bird drinkers were already hard at work. After all, it was five o'clock somewhere.

Dantzler and Vee approached the woman wiping down the table. She was tall and thin, dressed in faded jeans, a sweatshirt, and sneakers. Her hair was tied in a ponytail. Thirty to thirty-five years old, Dantzler guessed. She continued with her task, not bothering to look up and acknowledge the two detectives. Satisfied with her work on that table, she quickly moved on to the next one, again without bothering to look at the visitors. Dantzler didn't know whether to be impressed with her work ethic, or pissed off because she was ignoring them. Either way, it was apparent that he was going to have to initiate the conversation. She damn sure wasn't going to.

"Pardon me, Miss, but we're looking for Robbie," Dantzler said. "Is he around?"

Without missing a swipe, and never looking up, she said, "In the back."

"Would you please inform him that Detective Jack Dantzler is here, and that I would like to speak with him?"

Finally, she stopped cleaning the table, straightened up, and gave Dantzler a thorough going-over from head to toe. "What's the matter, darling? Your legs don't work? You look healthy enough to me." She then glanced at Vee. "So does tall, dark, and beautiful."

Dantzler started to respond to her snide remark but hesitated when he noticed Robbie emerge from the back. Seeing Dantzler, Robbie threw up his arms in an I-give-up gesture and grimaced as though he was being prepped for a root canal.

"You obviously didn't get the memo, Detective," Robbie said, as Dantzler and Vee moved up to the bar. "The memo that said I don't know any more now than I did when you were in here before."

"Since you're acting all cool and above it all, Robbie, that tells me you didn't get our latest memo."

"What memo are you talking about?"

"Tell him, Vee," Dantzler said.

"Eddie Campbell is dead," she said.

Robbie's face went white. "Dead?" he muttered.

"Bullet in the back of his head," Dantzler said, adding, "No staged suicide this time. This was execution style. Just like the Russians would do it."

"Damn. Eddie wasn't a bad dude."

Dantzler said, "Let's tally up the deceased, Robbie. There's Joel Howard, Mike Perkins, Danny Michaels, and Eddie Campbell. That means the top four have been taken out of the game. Who do you suppose is in the on-deck circle now? Let me think . . . that would be you, Robbie. You're next on the hit list. We both know that."

"Who killed Eddie?" Robbie asked.

"Don't go all stupid on me, Robbie. You know who killed Eddie. The same guy who murdered Joel, Danny, and Mike. Say the name, Robbie. No reason to keep it inside any longer."

"Alex Shannon?"

"Why are you phrasing that as a question? You know as well as I do that Shannon killed those men. There's no doubt about it."

"Damn. Eddie wasn't a bad dude," Robbie repeated.

"Yeah, you said that already," Dantzler pointed out. "I'm not interested in hearing you echo what you've previously said. What I need now is for you to tell me the truth. I want you to tell me everything you know about what happened to Gloria Nash, how those cops got all that money, and who is running the show. You can give me this information now in a friendly setting, or I can read you your rights, cuff you, and take you downtown for an official interrogation. It's your call."

Robbie nodded, turned, and spoke to the woman wiping down the tables "Kelly, would you mind looking after the bar for the next few minutes? I shouldn't be away too long."

"Sure, not a problem," Kelly responded, directing an icy look toward Dantzler and Vee.

"Follow me," Robbie said to Dantzler and Vee. "I have an office in the back. We can talk there."

Robbie led the two detectives down a narrow hallway and into a room large enough to accommodate a desk, three chairs, a cooler, and an army cot. In the right corner behind the desk there was a three-tier stand that was home to socks, T-shirts, underwear, boots, sneakers, and several sweaters. Shirts, jeans, a sport coat, and a couple of jackets hung from a metal rod that ran along the right wall. It was clear to Dantzler that this was more than just an office; this was where Robbie lived.

Robbie sat in the chair behind the desk and motioned for Dantzler and Vee to take the other two chairs. Vee's chair was empty, but Dantzler had to remove a case of Budweiser before he could take his seat. Once he had done that he sat and took out his notebook.

"Okay, Robbie, it's time to tell me everything you know," Dantzler said. "No more dancing around the truth, no more bullshit. Right now, I'm your friend. But if you lie to me, or withhold information, I can promise you that I won't continue to be quite so friendly."

"Look, Detective Dantzler, I'm telling you that I don't know as much as you think I do," Robbie said. "I only know what Mike told me about what happened to Gloria Nash. That's it. I swear on my mother's grave."

"Is Gloria dead?"

Robbie nodded.

"Murdered?"

Again, Robbie only nodded his response.

Dantzler said, "When did this happen? And where?"

"I'm not sure when, exactly. Probably a few days before she was reported missing. That makes sense, doesn't it? Where? In an old barn located on property owned by Alex Shannon."

"How was she killed?" Vee asked.

"Shot in the head."

"And Mike was the one who pulled the trigger?" Dantzler asked.

"No, no, Mike didn't kill her," Robbie said, shaking his head. "He was crazy about Gloria. No way would he ever hurt her."

"Then who did pull the trigger?"

"Alex Shannon."

"Why?"

"I can't answer that, Detective. Mike never said."

"How did Gloria Nash get involved with those men?"

"Through her association with Mike would be my guess."

"Why? What did they need her for?"

"I don't know."

"You sure about that?"

"Yes, positive. I don't know."

"Okay, Gloria is dead. What happened next? What did they do with her body?"

"God, this is so sick," Robbie said, tears filling his eyes. "Thinking about it makes me want to puke."

"Tell me, Robbie. I need to know."

"They disposed of her body."

"Disposed? How?"

"They chopped her up." Robbie looked away as he continued to relate the grim details. "Shannon handed Mike a saw and told him to cut her into pieces. When Mike refused, Shannon pulled his weapon and told Mike that if he didn't do it, he would be buried alongside her. Mike had no choice, so he did as he was told."

"What did they do with the remains?" Vee asked.

"Shannon ordered Larraby and Eddie Campbell to dig a couple of holes somewhere behind the barn. That's where they buried most of her body."

"Most?" Vee said.

"They put her head in a burlap bag, tied it, and tossed it into a creek that runs behind the barn." Robbie wiped tears from his eyes, then said, "Now you can understand why Mike got so heavily involved with drugs. He didn't do it to get all beefed up like everyone thought. He was trying to erase the memories of what happened that night."

"When did Mike talk to you about this?" Dantzler said.

"A month ago. Maybe six weeks. He came in one morning right before I opened the bar. He was crying, bawling like a baby. I asked him what was wrong but he wouldn't tell me. Then, a few minutes later, he opened up and told me everything I just told you."

Robbie reached into the cooler and took out a bottle of water. After taking a long drink, he continued. "Mike told me he had shared this story with an old priest he was friendly with. He told the priest that he was going to turn himself in to the police. At some point, Mike also told Larraby that he couldn't live with the guilt any longer, and that he was going to the Homicide Unit—to you, Detective Dantzler—and confess everything. That's what he should have done. He'd still be alive if he had."

Dantzler said, "So Larraby, fearing that his world was about to come crashing down, kills himself in order to avoid what he knew would be a one-way ticket to life in prison. That makes sense. Larraby wasn't about to spend the rest of his life behind bars."

"Nah, Larraby was the weakest one in that group. He was terrified of Alex."

"But at some point Larraby must have shared his concerns with Shannon, who then had no option but to silence Mike. Same goes for Eddie Campbell. Those two knew too much. They had to be eliminated. But what about Danny Michaels? Why was he murdered?"

"Mike and Danny were buddies, so I assume that Mike told Danny what happened. Probably when he was high on drugs. Danny made the mistake of talking to that lady writer. I'd say Danny's fate was sealed the moment she came around and questioned Alex."

"There are still some pieces of the puzzle that are missing," Dantzler pointed out. "The money has always troubled me, Robbie. I keep asking myself, how did a group of cops come up with hundreds of thousands of dollars? What did Mike tell you about that?"

"Nothing, I swear. I didn't even know about the money until you told me. That's the God's truth. Judging by the way Mike looked, I really thought he had no money at all."

"That leaves me with the final piece that is missing—who is running the show? Alex Shannon is a murdering thug, but he lacks the brains or the cunning to be a leader. Someone was telling him what to do. Who do you think that might be?"

"I don't know, Detective Dantzler," Robbie answered. "I didn't run with that crowd. Me and Mike were tight, but the others were almost like strangers to me. I have no idea what they were into, or who was giving the orders."

"Is there anything else you need to tell me, Robbie?"

"No, not really." Robbie paused, then said, "Am I in trouble?"

"That remains to be seen. When this all plays out, when all the facts are known, what happens will ultimately be up to the district attorney. But I will tell you this, Robbie. You were a former cop. You should have come forward with this information the moment you found out what happened. Shame on you for your failure to step up and do what was right. Regardless of what the district attorney does or doesn't do, you've lost any respect I had for you. Gloria Nash deserved better than what she got from you and from those other assholes who investigated her case. In your heart, I'm sure you know that's true."

"I am so sorry," Robbie said, tears now rolling down his cheeks. "I . . ."

Dantzler stood, said, "Until Alex Shannon is in custody, you aren't safe. Do you have some place where you can stay until we bring him in? With a relative, maybe?"

"No, not really."

"You have two options, then. Come with us and stay at the station, or get a motel room. That's up to you."

"Motel room."

"Fine. When you get checked in, call and let me know where you are. Got it?"

"Yeah, I will."

On the way to their car, Vee said, "Do you believe him?"

Before Dantzler could respond, his cell phone buzzed. The call was from Sean Montgomery.

"What's up, Sean?" Dantzler asked.

"We've got a serious problem, Jack. Julie is with Alex Shannon."

"What? How do you know this?"

"She left me a message about an hour ago, saying she was meeting Shannon in the O'Neill's Pub parking lot. She wanted me to be there so I could keep an eye on her. Or follow them if they went somewhere. When I got here, she was gone. So was her car. But there is a car here that belongs to Shannon. That means they are together."

"Are you still at O'Neill's?"

"Yeah."

"Vee and I will be there in ten minutes."

"Make it five if you can."

"We'll try."

CHAPTER THIRTY-SIX

A band of gun-metal gray clouds had stationed themselves in front of the sun, causing a sudden and unexpected drop in temperature from what it had been earlier in the morning. Then it had been in the mid-eighties; now it was in the low-seventies. Darker clouds loomed to the east, and a soft breeze was rapidly picking up force. Based on current conditions, a gambling man wouldn't hesitate to bet a bundle of cash that rain would be arriving within the next hour.

Rain, wind, falling temperatures . . . none of that mattered to Julie Bradley. At this point they were purely irrelevant. The only thing on her mind now was this: she was about to die and there wasn't a damn thing she could do about it.

No book is worth your life.

Nancy's words.

Why didn't I listen? Julie asked herself. Why did I allow my arrogance, my enthusiasm, my excitement, my go-for-broke attitude to override my common sense? Why, for once in my life, didn't I heed the advice passed along by someone much older, wiser, and more experienced than me? How could I have been so foolish to believe that I know it all?

How did I end up here? Moments away from taking my final breath?

Julie was standing in the middle of a dilapidated barn located several miles outside of town. Somewhere out in the county. Some place unfamiliar to her. The old barn was the only structure on the property, although Julie noticed a brick chimney several yards to the left that rose from the ground like a holy shrine, the last remaining vestige of what had once been a house.

Inside, the barn smelled of hay and horse manure. The floor was dusty and oil stained. To the left there were three stalls, all of which were empty. It had probably been years since any horses had been housed here, although there was plenty of evidence that they had been in the past. Bridles, saddles, and horse collars were either lying on the ground or hanging from the walls. The right half of the barn was taken up by an old tractor, which looked like it might have been the first one to roll off the John Deere assembly line. It was ancient. All the tires were flat, and much of the tractor was covered with rust and dried mud so thick that it was impossible to guess what its original color had been. The barn's wide entrances, front and rear, were both open. If there had once been doors, they were now long gone.

At the rear of the barn, to the left of the back opening, there was an old card table surrounded by five metal chairs. Three were standing, while two were overturned and lying on the floor. A bottle of whiskey, two coffee mugs, and four paper cups rested on the table top. So did a deck of playing cards.

Julie felt a shove in her back, indicating that she needed to keep moving. Which she did, with a single thought running through her head: *I'm moving toward my own death.*

She had felt fear before but nothing like this. Nothing remotely close. This went way beyond fear; this was absolute, sheer terror. Her stomach was turning cartwheels, her nerves were crackling, and her sense of panic was at a level she had never thought possible. She felt the need to scream, to cry, but her voice was frozen and the tears wouldn't come.

I am no different than a dumb animal on its way to being slaughtered.
How fuckin' sad.

She was feeling something else as well, although it was several rungs below terror. Anger. She was angry with herself. For not taking charge of the situation like she had planned. For not waiting until she heard back from Sean. For not being smarter and more careful.

She had arrived at O'Neill's fifteen minutes before the hour was up, hoping to get there ahead of Shannon. But she hadn't; he was already there, standing next to the black Audi she had seen parked outside Eddie Campbell's house. But Shannon had his back turned, which gave her time to park out of sight, and either wait for Sean to answer her earlier message or, if he didn't call back within the next few minutes, to give him a second call. Or call Dantzler. She didn't. She allowed impatience to get the better of her. Almost without thinking about possible consequences, she drove up to where Shannon was standing.

That was her first mistake. Her second was to not park the car and insist that she and Shannon have their talk inside the pub, where there would be a crowd, where she would feel safe. Where Sean was sure to look once he saw both vehicles in the parking lot.

But Shannon was inside her car before she had time to act. He smiled and ordered her to drive. When she hesitated, but before she could offer resistance to his command, that's when the gun came out. Held low but pointed upward, directly at her head. Then a more forceful "drive," followed by "unless you're ready to die right here and now."

Other than his terse directions to the barn, not a single word was spoken during the drive. Julie stared straight ahead, trying to focus on driving even as that feeling of panic was beginning to crush her insides. Shannon had angled his body in a way that allowed him to keep the gun aimed at Julie's head. A wicked smile never left his face.

Another shove from behind and Julie was only a few feet from the table. Glancing toward the rear door, she saw that the first drops of rain had begun to fall. A crazy thought ran through her head: Maybe the angels in heaven were weeping because they knew what was about to happen.

I am going to die.

Right now, she wished she could cry. But the tears refused to come.

"Take a seat, little lady," Shannon said, motioning with his gun toward one of the metal chairs. "May as well have a drink while you're at it. Party like it's your last day on earth, because it is."

"Is this where you murdered Gloria Nash?" Julie managed to say.

"Sure is. In that first stall. Want to walk over there and see if we can spot any of her blood? I'm sure we'd find some. She bled a lot. Most head wounds usually do."

"Why? Why did you kill her?"

"Doesn't matter, little lady. You see, someone might write a book about what happened fifteen years ago, but it won't be you. So, asking questions is a waste of what little time you have left."

Shannon slowly began to ease around Julie, eventually stopping when he was positioned directly behind her. His breathing was loud, heavy. She felt the barrel of the pistol against her neck. When he stopped moving Julie closed her eyes and held her breath.

This is how it ends—a bullet to the back of my head. Please, God, make it quick and painless.

But Shannon didn't pull the trigger, didn't fire the killing shot. Instead, he continued on around to her right side, picked up the bottle of whiskey, and took a drink, still keeping the gun pointed at her. That wicked smile still firmly in place.

"Little lady, you do share some blame in all this," Shannon said, sitting in the chair next to hers. "You and that fuckin' Mike Perkins. If he had kept his mouth shut, and if you had ignored that fool Danny Michaels, then Eddie Campbell and Dale Larraby would still be alive. Michaels, too, for that matter. Even more important, you wouldn't be sitting in that chair, moments away from the big send off."

"I never killed anyone, Shannon, so don't try to hang your sins on me. It won't work."

"You're a brave little bitch, I'll give you that. So was Gloria Nash. She wasn't afraid to speak her piece. I have to admit I admire bravery."

Julie started to respond but hesitated when she saw movement at the front entrance to the barn. Or thought she saw movement. It happened so fast, really just a blur, that she couldn't be sure what, if anything, she had seen. But she could have sworn she saw the figure of a man. He was bent low and moving from right to left.

Did I really see that? Or is my fear creating hallucinations, a mirage?

No, what she saw was no hallucination, no mirage. What she had seen was no longer a blur. The man was real.

Shannon saw the man at the same time as Julie had. He sprang out of his chair, took a step back, and aimed his weapon at the party crasher. The wicked grin grew even wider.

"There's an old saying, Sean, that you should never bring a knife to a gunfight," Shannon said. "But at least bring *something*. Walking toward a man holding a gun, your hands in the air and with no back-up, ain't exactly a smart move. You were a cop once. You ought to know that?"

"Take a look behind you, Alex," Sean replied, "and you'll see that I'm neither alone nor unarmed."

When Shannon peered over his left shoulder the wicked smile vanished. He saw Dantzler and Vee standing five feet apart, in the classic shooter's position, knees bent, arms extended, their weapons aimed directly at him.

Dantzler said, "You have three seconds to put your weapon on the table, Alex, or we're gonna put you down. One . . . two . . ."

Shannon complied, placing his gun on the table, and raising his arms in the air. Vee immediately went to the table, picked up the gun, and placed it in her utility belt. Then she removed her handcuffs, yanked Shannon's arms behind him, put the cuffs on, and read him his rights.

Julie leapt out of the chair, raced toward Sean, and began hugging him with all the strength she could muster. The tears that had been locked away began to cascade down her face.

At that moment Eric and Jake arrived in Eric's car. Within seconds they were inside the barn, weapons drawn. Both men seemed disappointed at having missed out on the action.

Holstering his Glock, Dantzler moved closer to Shannon. The two men locked eyes. "Karma's a wonderful thing, ain't it, asshole?" Dantzler said, sneering. "Speaking of old sayings, how about you reap what you sow? That damn whirlwind is coming your way, Shannon. And it'll blow you into prison for the rest of your sorry life."

"Lawyer," Shannon screamed.

"Jesus himself couldn't save you from what's coming. Nor would he want to."

"Lawyer," Shannon repeated. Then: "What about you, Sean? You're a big defense attorney. Would you like to represent me?"

"What I would like is to go into a room, just the two of us, lock the door, and see who walks out," Sean replied. "It wouldn't be you, Alex. That much I can promise you. I'd beat that ugly face of yours until it was jelly. And then I'd beat it some more."

Dantzler said to Eric, "You, Jake, and Vee take this miserable piece of shit to the station and get him booked. Once that's done, let him call an attorney."

"What about you, Sean, and Julie?" Eric asked.

"Julie can ride in with Sean. I'll be in later. There's something I need to do first."

After the three detectives had escorted Shannon out of the barn, Julie turned to Sean, and said, "How did you know where I was?"

Sean smiled, looked at Dantzler, and said, "Should we tell her, Jack?"

"Might as well."

"Tell me what?" Julie asked, suspicion in her voice.

"GPS," Sean said.

"You put a GPS on my car? A tracking device?"

"In your phone?"

"What? When?"

"The night you stayed at my place. While you were sleeping."

"Why?"

"Come on, Julie. You refused to take care of yourself, so we had to."

"*We*" she said, looking from Sean to Dantzler. "You were in on it?"

Dantzler shrugged, said, "It was Sean's idea. And I agreed with him. Turns out it was the right thing to do. Otherwise, you would be dead right now."

"How do you put a GPS into a phone?" Julie asked.

"There are apps for everything, Julie. Parents program them to keep track of their kids, to pretty much know where they are at all times. I used an app called Track the Hard-Headed Female Author Who Thinks She Knows Everything. Worked to perfection."

"You're full of shit, Sean."

"And you're alive, Julie. You can now write your damn book. You're welcome."

Julie nodded, leaned up, kissed Dantzler on the cheek, and started walking toward the front entrance.

"What about me?" Sean asked. "I'm the big hero here."

"I'll reward you later, big hero," she answered.

"Gotta like the sound of that," Sean said to Dantzler.

"Damn, Sean, I'd rather have your luck than a million dollars."

"It's not luck, Jack. It's charm and panache."

"Nah, Julie nailed it, Sean. You're full of shit."

"McCarthy's in a couple of hours? Drinks are on me."

"Not sure. First, I need to go see someone."

CHAPTER THIRTY-SEVEN

"So, Alex Shannon was your man all along?" Charlie Bolton said, leaning against the kitchen cabinet. "To be honest with you, I can't say I'm all that surprised. I always felt he had the devil in him."

"The devil? Yeah, right," Dantzler said. "It would take the devil to do what he did."

"Did he say anything?"

"Lawyer."

"No confession, huh? Too bad. Your life would certainly be a lot easier if he owned up to it." Charlie pushed away from the cabinet and opened the refrigerator. "Want a beer? I'm having one."

"No."

Charlie opened the beer, took a drink, and said, "Alex is an obstinate, stubborn bastard. I doubt you'll get a confession from him. He'll take his chances at trial."

"Nah, he'll confess, Charlie. You can bet on that. The district attorney will make him an offer, some kind of a deal that will be too hard to turn down. Once that happens Shannon will talk faster than an auctioneer."

"If he does you'll have all your questions answered."

"Not all of them."

"Why not? You'll have your murderer."

"There's more to this than murder."

"You're dancing around something, Jack. What's bothering you?"

"For the past few days I've had a piece of information running around in my head, one I just couldn't locate. It was something I heard or saw or read. Something important. But hard as I tried, I could never pin it down."

"That happens to all detectives. It happened to me more times than I can count."

"Then it came to me."

"Okay."

"The money, Charlie. That's what I was missing. Something having to do with the money. But there was a reason why I was missing it—I was looking in the wrong direction. I was so focused on how two ex-cops came up with so much cash that I overlooked something I heard."

"You've lost me, Jack. I'm not following."

"It was something you said, Charlie."

"Okay. What did I say?"

"When I told you I thought a cop might have murdered Mike Perkins, you said, 'What reason would a cop have to kill a poor bastard like Mike Perkins?' My answer: Maybe one-hundred-twenty-four thousand reasons. And you said, 'the money, yeah, I heard about that.'"

"Okay, so what's the big issue?"

"How had you heard about it, Charlie?"

"Jack, how many times have I told you that I have more spies in the police department than the CIA has in the Soviet Union?"

"That won't work this time, Charlie. And here's why. Only three people on this planet knew about that money—me, Eric, and Jake. I took the money to the station. I booked it into evidence. No one knew anything about Mike having that money until the next afternoon. So . . . how did you know about it?"

"Someone told me. That's all I can tell you."

"That's not all, Charlie. You also knew the killer left the money behind. Once again I have to ask—how did you know that? There's only one way you could have known. You knew Shannon murdered

Mike. But Shannon didn't take the money—I'm guessing he has plenty of his own—so he left it behind. You knew everything, Charlie, all the details."

"This is all very interesting, Jack. But where are you going with this?"

"I need the truth. More than the truth, I need to know why you allowed yourself to get involved with scum like Alex Shannon and Dale Larraby? You're the most-revered, most-respected cop in this city. How could you hook up with them? Why?"

"The truth can be ugly, Jack."

"You need to tell it. The whole story."

"If you want the whole story I'm going to need another beer." Charlie opened the refrigerator, plucked out a bottle, and sat down across from Dantzler. Opening the beer, he said, "It wasn't supposed to be what it eventually became. No one was supposed to get hurt. Not physically, anyway. We both know that in any illegal enterprise someone always gets hurt. But murder wasn't in the plan."

"But people did get murdered, Charlie, beginning with Gloria Nash, right?"

Charlie smiled, took a drink, and said, "She was a brave kid. I liked her. She just . . . got a little greedy at the wrong time."

"Take me back to the beginning, Charlie. A straight line from then to now. No detours, no twists and turns. I want to hear everything."

"I might as well give it to you now, because like you said, sooner or later Alex will spill his guts. Eventually, the truth will come out. But in this case the truth isn't going to set me free. It's going to send this old soul to prison."

"It all began with Gloria Nash, didn't it? In some way she was at the center of all this, wasn't she?"

Charlie nodded, said, "Although Mike had already begun to hang out with Gloria, he never introduced her to those other guys. Mike was the jealous type, didn't want anyone looking at her or hitting on her. Anyway, one night Alex spotted Gloria in a bar talking it up with some older guy. That's when the idea came to Alex. To have her pose as a hooker, and then blackmail the men for money. He took the plan back to the other guys and . . . ."

"Hold it right there, Charlie. We both know none of those guys are intelligent enough to come up with a scam like that. There had to be someone with brains, and that would be you."

"Okay, you're right. Alex approached me and . . ."

"Bullshit. You had the reputation of a saint. No way does Shannon come up to you out of the blue with a plan like that. You were in it from the beginning."

"You're a bright boy, Jack. You always have been."

"Why?"

"The oldest reason of all—money."

"You didn't need money, Charlie. You had plenty."

"Sure, I was retired, had my pension, some money set aside, but a few extra dollars in the bank never hurts. And the plan seemed harmless enough."

"How did you rope Gloria in?"

"Alex knew she liked to hang out at the old Bananas Bar, the one that's now O'Neill's. She had never met Larraby, so he made a point to introduce himself to her. After a few drinks he asked if she would like to get a motel room somewhere. Being a smart girl, she refused. Larraby did finally persuade her to go outside and get in his car. Gave her some cockamamie story about a necklace he wanted to show her. Once they were in the car, Alex swooped in, flashed his badge, and told her she was being arrested for solicitation."

"Gloria had no criminal record," Dantzler said.

"It was a bogus charge, a way to threaten the poor girl. Hell, no money changed hands. The girl liked to have fun, but she certainly wasn't a hooker. But now Alex had her under his thumb. He told her that if she did as she was told, not only would he not arrest her, she would also make some money. Given those options, she had no choice but to go along."

"Where was Mike Perkins when all this was going down? If he was so crazy about Gloria, why did he allow it to happen? He could have put all of you in a room and kicked everyone's ass. Why didn't he stop it?"

"He didn't have a clue what was in the works. Later on, yes. But not in the beginning. Only Alex, Eddie, and Larraby knew."

"And you."

"And me."

"Did Robbie Newcome or Lawrence Brady have any involvement?" Dantzler asked.

"No. Why would they?"

"Just something I needed to clear up. Continue with your story, Charlie."

"The plan was for Gloria to hook up with a certain type of man, someone financially well off, prominent in the city, and, most important of all, married. I knew many men with those credentials, so that's really when I got involved. I made sure those men were properly introduced to Gloria. Once that happened, well, Gloria was a lovely, sexy lady, so you can figure out the rest."

"Where? In the hotel?"

Charlie shook his head, said, "We rented a nice apartment for Gloria, then Alex, Eddie, and Larraby wired it with a couple of microphones and a hidden camera. They wanted pictures and a soundtrack to accompany all the action. Most of the men offered to give Gloria some money, but she always refused. They walked out thinking they'd just had a great time and it hadn't cost them a penny. Little did they know. Within the next few days Alex would confront the man and show him what we had. Since it was on tape, there was no way he could deny it. Then, you know what happened next."

"The guy is told to either pay up or his wife gets a copy of the tape."

"Classic extortion."

"How much did you demand?" Dantzler said.

"Not as much as you might think. Alex, Eddie, and Larraby wanted to bleed the guy for everything he had, but I vetoed that notion. I set a limit of twenty grand. The others protested but I didn't care. Greed is not in my DNA. I also ordered them to tell the guy that if he paid he would get the one and only copy of the tape. He paid."

"How many times did you do this?"

"Five or six. We had a nice little thing going, raking in twenty grand once a week. We'd give Gloria a couple grand, then divide the rest four ways."

"I keep coming back to my earlier question: Where was Mike Perkins while all this was happening? If he was so goo-goo eyes over Gloria, how could he be in the dark?"

"He'd come in out of the dark soon enough."

"Something's not computing, Charlie. If you only pulled this off five or six times at twenty grand a pop, that adds up to maybe a hundred-twenty grand split four ways, five if you include Gloria. That's a far cry from what Larraby and Mike Perkins had. At some point there had to be a big payoff."

"Well, then we got lucky," Charlie said, after taking another sip of beer. "Gloria was in the Hyatt bar waiting to meet the next mark. He was a very successful surgeon I knew. Had a wife and three kids. The perfect victim. But he never showed. While Gloria was sitting at the bar this little fellow moves in next to her and offers to buy her a drink. She refused. He persisted. When she politely rejected him a second time, he began working extra hard to impress her. At some point he told her he was in the jewelry business, and that he was transporting some diamonds from Los Angeles to New York. He then told her the diamonds were up in his room and asked if she would like to check them out. He promised her that they would blow her mind if she saw them. She said sure. In the room this guy opens a suitcase and takes out a leather pouch. He turns it upside-down and gives it a good shake. Dozens and dozens of perfectly cut diamonds fall out onto the bed. Being an enterprising young lady, Gloria realizes we've hit the mother lode. She and the guy go back down to the bar, where Gloria promptly excuses herself, hurries to the phones, calls Alex, and tells him about the diamonds. She also gives him the room number. He orders her to wait thirty minutes, then go back up to the guy's room, and offer him sex for cash. By that time Alex and Eddie are outside the door. They knock, bust in like gangbusters, and tell the poor sap that he's under arrest for having sex with a minor. They handcuff the guy, grab the pouch, and march him out to Alex's car. The guy assumes his next stop is the police station, but he assumed wrong."

"His destination was the barn where we arrested Shannon, right?"

"Right."

"Where someone shot him, right?"

"Alex."

"Okay, so now you have a bunch of diamonds. What happens next?"

"That's when I played a major role. I happened to have an acquaintance in Manhattan who, shall we say, knows how to safely and quietly move items obtained through illegal means."

"A fence?"

"I'd prefer to call him a middle man. That doesn't sound quite so nefarious"

"How much were the diamonds worth?" Dantzler asked.

"He said three million, which I knew was a lie. That many high-quality diamonds had to be worth five times that much. But I wasn't there to haggle with him. I asked how much he would give me, he said a million-five, and I agreed. The next day I flew back to Lexington with more than a million dollars in cash inside my suitcase. When I got back in town we split the cash five ways—Mike was now in on it—which computed to three-hundred grand per person. I also suggested that each of us take twenty-five thousand and give it to Gloria. That seemed fair to me. Unfortunately, Gloria didn't agree."

"I don't blame her. She was doing all the dirty work."

"That's how she saw it. Said we weren't being fair, that she deserved a full cut. She was right—it wasn't fair. But life isn't fair. There was no way she was going to get what we got. It doesn't work that way."

Charlie tossed the empty beer bottle into the recycle basket, and continued. "She kept pleading her case, especially to Mike, but he had suddenly decided that maybe he loved the cash more than he loved her. Then Gloria uttered the magic—and fatal—words, saying that if we didn't give her a full share she would go to the cops and tell them everything. Can you believe she said that, standing there surrounded by five cops? For a smart kid that was a dumb thing to do."

"I can take it from there, Charlie. Alex shoots her in the back of the head, then orders Mike to cut up the body. While he's taking care of that gruesome task, Larraby and Campbell are digging two graves out behind the barn."

"You've done your research, Jack," Charlie said. "Who'd you hear that from?"

"Doesn't matter."

"No, I don't suppose it does."

"How long did your little enterprise last?"

"That was it. We had more money than we ever thought we'd have, so we shut it down. No need to take unnecessary risks. So, from beginning to end, my time on the wrong side of the tracks lasted about two months."

"Two months or two years, it doesn't matter, does it, Charlie?"

Charlie shrugged, said, "The mistake we made was not putting Mike Perkins in the ground next to Gloria. If we'd have done that, none of these later deaths would have been necessary. You see, I'd made each man swear an oath to not spend a dime of that money for seven years. No one did, except Mike. He developed a conscience and began spilling his guts to that priest. And he started giving money to the church, as if he could buy his way into Paradise. Poor, dumb bastard. No amount of money in the world could possibly wash away sins like the ones we committed."

"No wonder Mike turned to drugs, after what you made him do."

"Oh, he cried, blubbered like a baby, said he wouldn't do it. He shut up pretty quick when Alex pointed his weapon at him and said do it or die. Mike picked up the saw and did what he had been ordered to do."

"One last question, Charlie. What about Joel Howard?"

"Being an excellent cop, Joel was never comfortable with his guys spending so much time with Alex, whom Joel detested. He began to suspect that something unholy was going on within his department. He asked me if I had heard anything. I told him I hadn't, but why not confront Alex and ask him that question. Joel agreed. One night Alex and I drove to Joel's house. You know what happened next."

"Choke-hold, then the staged suicide."

"As the Holy Book says about Enoch, 'Joel Howard was not, for God took him.' Technically, of course, it was Alex Shannon who took him."

"Damn, Charlie, I can't believe what I'm about to say. And I say it with a broken heart. I have to take you in."

"You wearing a wire?"

"No."

"Then I'll deny everything I just told you."

"Deny all you want, Charlie. It doesn't matter. Sooner or later Alex will give his version. I'm sure it will closely match yours."

"Jack, I have two-hundred-fifty thousand dollars in my garage. It's yours if you'll wait two days before turning me in. A forty-eight hour head start. That's not too much to ask, is it?"

"Don't disgrace yourself more than you already have, Charlie. You know I can't be bought. Justice isn't for sale."

"Yes, lad, I know that." Charlie stood, said, "And I would have been greatly disappointed had you agreed to my request. Knowing that you have no interest in the money, then the least I can do is get it for you. It's hidden pretty well, might be hard for you to find."

"I'll go with you. That way you can show me where it is."

"No need. I can handle it by myself."

The two men locked eyes for a split second, then Dantzler said, "Hurry, Charlie. We need to get going."

"It won't take long," Charlie answered, before heading into the garage.

The gunshot came less than a minute later, more of a soft pop than the loud bang usually heard in movies. Dantzler closed his eyes, took a deep breath, stood, and went to the garage door, expecting to see his old friend dead on the cold floor. But Charlie wasn't on the floor; he was slumped over in an old rocking chair. Blood streamed down the right side of his body, and the gun was on the floor. Next to the gun was a large steel box. A small key lay on top of the box.

The scene was almost too fantastic for Dantzler to comprehend. The great Charlie Bolton was dead, killed by his own hand. And for what? A box filled with money he never even spent. Standing there, looking down at the body, Dantzler had a difficult time grasping the implications of what had just transpired. And there would be many. When word of this began making the rounds, dozens of cops, past and present, will be rocked to the depth of their being. One of the foundations upon which their world had been constructed will have crumbled to dust.

They would be left to wonder if anything was truly sacred.

Here was yet another murder by suicide. Another killer as victim, another victim as killer. A twisted scenario that turns logic topsy-turvy. What would Camus have to say about that? What would any rational person say about it?

When Dantzler watched Charlie walk away he knew what the end result would be. Both men knew. That's why Charlie requested to go alone, and why Dantzler agreed to let him. It was the only way this scene could have ended.

Loving the old man like he did, Dantzler felt a deep sense of sadness. But not pity. Charlie had crossed the line, become one of the bad guys, and criminals deserve punishment, not pity. If the situation was reversed, Dantzler knew, Charlie would feel the same way. Any righteous cop would.

And once upon a time Charlie Bolton had been a righteous cop. Then he wasn't. He became a dirty cop, by his own choosing, fully aware that he risked destroying his flawless reputation. Which is exactly what he had done. That's why Dantzler felt the deep sadness.

But not pity.

Taking out his cell phone, he began punching in numbers.

CHAPTER THIRTY-EIGHT

The events of the next three weeks were so surreal, so Kafkaesque, that they could well have been created by the celebrated writer himself. The normal patterns had been cracked, up was down, light and dark were interchangeable, and every act, even those usually standard in nature, seemed to be slightly off-kilter.

In short, it was a bizarre period, one in which a pall hovered above everything and everyone, its grasp tight and unrelenting. There were a handful of splendid moments, to be sure, but even they were tinged with darkness. Nothing escaped what one retired cop called the "Charlie Bolton tragedy." And he wasn't alone. Among Charlie's old colleagues, tragedy was the prevailing sentiment. His death hit them hard enough, but it was his criminal actions that shattered his halo and was the dark underside no one could avoid.

It wasn't possible for the faithful to be untouched when one of their gods had fallen.

Despite the gloomy atmosphere among the rank and file, a few good times did manage to creep through the fog. Personnel changes topped that list, starting with Captain Richard Bird ending his long and distinguished career. In a nice Friday afternoon ceremony, he handed the reins over to Eric. The torch had officially been passed. At age thirty-five, Eric was now head of the Homicide Unit. No one doubted that he would excel at the job.

Vee Jefferson was bumped up to Homicide, a move that, as Eric had predicted, pissed off about a dozen men who felt they should have received the promotion ahead of her. The predictable reasons were cited—too young, black, woman, inexperienced—none of which had any impact whatsoever. The whiners were quickly told to shut up and deal with it, or hand in their resignations. No one quit.

As stated in Dale Larraby's will, the cash that had been found in his condo, along with everything else owned by him, went to his ex-wife Carole. The money discovered in Mike Perkins's apartment was given to his aunt Dana. Those two decrees were handed down by Dantzler and no one argued against it.

It was soon learned that Alex Shannon also had close to two-hundred thousand dollars in his bank account. That money, and probably more, would end up in the hands of his defense attorney. With Charlie Bolton dead, Shannon decided to fight the charges against him to the fullest extent, a battle that Dantzler knew would eventually end in defeat. Nothing was going to keep Shannon from spending the remainder of his life behind prison bars.

Regarding Charlie Bolton's situation, that's where things got some-what more complicated for Dantzler. Charlie's will, which was found in the same box as the cash, named Dantzler as the sole beneficiary. Everything went to him—the house, a cabin on Lake Barkley, a boat, car, truck, and several stock certificates. Dantzler immediately put all of it up for sale, and cashed in the stocks, figuring that everything should bring in close to five-hundred thousand dollars, which he would donate to various local charities and youth athletic organizations around town. He did not want to personally benefit from Charlie's death.

The cash found in Charlie's garage was another matter altogether. Dantzler wanted nothing to do with it. That was blood money, dirty money, and yet Dantzler felt it could be put to good use. In the end, Dantzler knew, there was really only one destination for the cash—Andrea Nash. No amount of money could ever bring her sister back to life, but Andrea deserved it, if for no other reason than the lousy way she was treated by Larraby and Eddie Campbell during their so-called investigation into Gloria's disappearance.

Gloria's remains were found and she was given a proper funeral. That helped provide some closure for Andrea, although Dantzler knew that genuine closure in situations like this simply wasn't possible. What was closure anyway? Just a nice-sounding bullshit term that had no real meaning. But a proper burial had to bring some comfort to Andrea, knowing there was a grave she could visit, a final resting place for her beloved baby sister.

Eddie Campbell's situation was the one that came as a big shock. Dantzler was sure that Eddie, like his cohorts, had a bundle of cash stashed away somewhere in his house, or in a bank account, but that turned out to be miles from the truth. In fact, Eddie was virtually broke. According to his bank records, he was living on his pension and nothing else. Why was Eddie strapped for cash? That's what Dantzler wanted to know. And the answer proved to be quite simple. It turns out Eddie was at fault for the accident that paralyzed him from the waist down. Adding to Eddie's misery, he was hit with a huge lawsuit by the driver of the other car, an elderly gentleman whose wife suffered a serious brain injury. Whatever money Eddie had went to help pay off the judgment against him.

Making matters worse for Eddie, Robbie Newcome, a passenger in Eddie's car, also filed suit against his former partner. Robbie alleged that Eddie was drunk at the time of the accident, which a blood-alcohol test proved was true. Robbie ended up getting about two-hundred grand from Eddie, more than enough to cover his hospital bills and to purchase the bar.

Julie went to work on the book, hoping to have it ready in time for Christmas sales. Adding to her rush was the knowledge that two movie producers were in a bidding war for the rights to the book once it was published. Julie stayed over a couple of nights at Sean's place, but mostly she spent her time either interviewing those involved with the case, or holed up in her Mount Adams condo writing. Dantzler was her prime source, and he gave her everything she needed to know and then some. His information alone was more than enough to ensure that this was going to be an accurate—and successful—book. With a hit book on the horizon, and the Cubs having won the World Series, Darvis and Nancy were two of the happiest people on earth.

Julie did receive one rejection while doing her research. She made contact with Alex Shannon's attorney and asked if Alex would grant her an interview. When the attorney passed along her request, Shannon's response was, "Tell the little lady I said, go to hell."

Julie's assessment: Once an asshole, always an asshole.

As the third week eased into the fourth, the dark cloud seemed to finally be lifting. For the men in uniform, Charlie Bolton's fall from grace went through three distinct stages—shock, disbelief, acceptance. It was a hard hit for everyone, yet as time passed, most of the men appeared to be more than willing to forgive Charlie for his sins.

Most, but not Dantzler. He wasn't among those in the let's-forgive-Charlie camp, even though he was extremely close to the old man and loved him like a father. How do you forgive a man whose actions were cold, calculated, and criminal? And murderous? How was that even possible? Especially when the man had been in law enforcement his entire adult life? A man who knew right from wrong better than the best preacher knew the Bible? A man who knowingly broke his own code of righteousness?

A man who shattered the hearts of everyone who loved and revered him?

You don't. Not today, anyway.

Maybe sometime down the road.

Maybe with the passage of time.

Maybe . . .

Early on a Saturday evening, Dantzler was sitting in McCarthy's with Sean, David Bloom, and Milt Brewer. Not surprisingly, recent events, most notably Charlie's betrayal, dominated their conversation. Sean and Bloom seemed to be in a more forgiving mood, while Milt, a retired homicide detective, agreed with Dantzler, saying it was doubtful that he could ever forgive Charlie for what he had done.

"I knew Charlie Bolton longer than any of you," Milt stated. "I held that man up as a god. For him to do the things he did, hell no, I won't forgive him. I can't forgive him. I cannot believe what I'm about to say, but I'm just damn thankful that Dan isn't alive to see this. It would break his heart."

Dan Matthews, Milt's long-time partner, was killed investigating the Victor Sammael case.

"How are you handling what happened, Jack?" Bloom asked. "I know you were very close to Charlie. This has to be especially difficult for you."

"I'm handling it just fine," Dantzler answered. "Charlie made his choices. No one held a gun to his head. He wasn't blind to the fact that he was putting his reputation at risk. Or that he might end up behind bars. If you're going to dance with sinners, then sin will be your partner."

"Which begs a great question," Sean said to Dantzler. "How do you judge a man who lives an exemplary life until the very end, and then makes a wrong turn? Do you judge him based on the good he did, or do you judge him based on that one final bad act?"

"Ask Judas."

Milt said, "If you are referring to Charlie, Sean, you're assuming that he only had the one bad act. I can't travel that path. If he was dirty at the end, he was also dirty at other points along the way. Using Jack's analogy, Charlie danced with sinners on other occasions. Best thing Charlie did was put that gun to his head and pull the trigger. It saved us all a lot of grief."

"What did Camus say, Jack?" Sean asked. "That suicide is a confession? That the burden of living has become too much for an individual to bear, and that the act is his confession? For once, I have to agree with Camus."

"Be careful, Sean," Bloom said. "Hang around Jack long enough and you'll run the risk of becoming an enlightened man."

"Sean? Enlightened? Never gonna happen," Dantzler stated. "Same way he'll never buy the next four pints of Guinness."

Sean caught the bartender's attention and held up four fingers. Then taking out a credit card and laying it on the table, he said, "For the rest of the night the Guinness is on me. I may never be enlightened, but no one can accuse me of being a cheap bastard."

Bloom looked at Dantzler and Milt, and said, "I have seen with my own eyes, yet I do not believe."

"Is that some sort of Hebrew wisdom, Doc?" Sean said.

"Not quite," answered Bloom, holding up his pint glass. "But if we drink enough, I just might begin to sound like wise King Solomon himself."

"Then by all means let's keep the alcohol flowing," Milt said.

Three hours later, with midnight rapidly approaching, Dantzler sat on his deck and listened as the crickets and frogs made their standard nightly music. He was weary (and slightly drunk), but full of inner energy. Despite what had happened with Charlie—no, *because* of what happened with Charlie—he was feeling excited and enthused, not unlike he felt prior to an important tennis match. He was jacked and the reason why wasn't a mystery. For the first time since he was a young man he was staring into the future through a different set of eyes, seeing it through a new lens.

He was going to leave the police force, that much he knew with certainty. He knew it in that instant when he realized Charlie Bolton was behind the death of Gloria Nash and all the subsequent nastiness that occurred. He'd wait a few months, enough time to make sure Eric was getting settled in as head of the Homicide Unit, and then he would pull the plug.

Only Bloom and Sean knew about this, and both men had been sworn to secrecy. Neither man was particularly surprised by Dantzler's decision, nor did they completely agree with it, but neither man put up much of an argument. They both knew that to argue would be a waste of time. Dantzler had his mind made up, and nothing they could say or do would cause him to alter his decision.

Dantzler had already made the move toward changing careers. First, he rented a small office in a building owned by Sean, and then he'd begun the process required to become a licensed private investigator. Even more important, he made contact with two people who might send clients his way once he did officially begin work. Grace West, a famous defense attorney in Chicago, and Mike Brennan, a Manhattan district attorney, both promised to help in any way they could. Working with them would, Dantzler realized, present him with a weird contradiction. Helping Grace would likely mean trying to get a guilty scumbag off the hook, while aiding Mike would translate into trying to put an individual behind bars. None of that mattered to him. In either case, his task was to find the truth. The courts could decide the final outcome.

Dantzler wasn't blind to the fact that he had an advantage over many who decide to change careers in mid-stream, especially those whose new job offered no guaranteed income. He was fortunate to have plenty of money. Between his pension, his savings, the income from the Tennis Center, and tennis lessons, if he chose to give them, he had the luxury of not having to worry financially. This meant he had the option to take on only those cases that were interesting and challenging. After spending the past quarter-century hunting for murderers he wasn't about to waste precious time spying on philandering husbands or cheating wives. If it wasn't a big case, let someone else handle it.

Besides, what's the point of embarking on a new adventure if it's not going to be exciting? Why take off down an unfamiliar road unless you're hoping to find new windmills to tilt at?

Sitting there in the dark, thinking about the journey he was soon to undertake, Dantzler recalled a passage from Isaiah: "Do not be afraid; you will not be put to shame. Do not fear disgrace; you will not be humiliated."

Dantzler grinned.

Easy for you to say, Isaiah. You never stared across the net at John McEnroe.

ACKNOWLEDGMENTS

Thanks again to all those who continue to be in my (and Jack Dantzler's) corner. This loyal group includes Julie Watson, Ed Watson, Sarah Small, Wanda Underwood, Chris Boggs, Scott Boggs, Christina Young, Carol Palmer, Suzanne Slinker, Bonnie Vincent, Jim Vincent, Grant Sparks, Jimmie Nell Jenkins, Peter Kiely, Roger "Roddy" O'Byrne and the entire Gillespie clan—Joe, John and Kelsey. Thanks to Michael Palmer for giving a technology challenged guy some good insights into GPS tracking devices. As always, thanks to Frank Hall for bringing me into the Hydra family, and to Tony Acree, the force who keeps Hydra Publications rolling smoothly along. Finally, thanks to Marilyn Underwood for her superb proofreading eye and her wise insight

ABOUT THE AUTHOR

Tom Wallace is the award-winning author of six previous Jack Dant-zler mysteries, including The Poker Game, The Fire of Heaven, The List, Gnosis, The Devil's Racket and What Matters Blood. He also wrote the thriller, Heirs of Cain.

His novel, Gnosis, won the prestigious Claymore Award at the Killer Nashville Writers Conference, and The Devil's Racket captured the Mystery Writers top award.

Tom, a former sportswriter, has written several successful sports-related books, including The Kentucky Basketball Encyclopedia (now out in its fourth edition), So You Think You're a Kentucky Wildcats Basketball Fan? and Golden Glory: The History of Central City Basketball.

Tom is a Vietnam vet who currently lives in Lexington. He is a member of Mystery Writers of America. His web site is www.tomwalla-cenovels.com

www.ingramcontent.com/pod-product-compliance
Lightning Source LLC
Chambersburg PA
CBHW070729280626
47159CB00023B/2952